What
Lies
Beneath
The Tide

DAPHNE PARKER

For Tim—who jumped in and saved me when I was drowning.

CONTENT WARNING

This story contains content that might be disturbing to some readers—including, but not limited to, depictions of and references to death, suicide, domestic abuse, and sexual assault. Reader discretion is advised.

CHAPTER ONE
Alex

THE THIN LINE BENEATH the strap of her cardinal dress was barely a faint marker against her khaki-colored skin. She'd worn it on purpose. Not just for the comfort but for the ease with which it might be slipped off her later.

Too bad it was a wasted effort.

She was attractive. Her honeysuckle hair was curled loosely at the ends, settling just below her peaked breasts—the plummeting neckline forcing them together. It was meant to be an inviting distraction that hopefully persuaded Alex to take her home later.

Another wasted attempt.

He wasn't opposed to a nice dinner with a beautiful woman. After all, he'd agreed to it, though more out of obligation than for personal desire.

When Diego asked him for a favor, Alex thought it was a joke.

"You want me to go out with your ex?"

"She's not my ex," Diego insisted. "She's just some woman I used to go out with."

"That's an ex," Alex countered, his voice laced with humor.

Diego didn't find it funny. "I just need you to get her off my back."

Reluctantly, Alex agreed. And now, as he sat across from the slender woman, whose crystal eyes glazed over him in hunger, he understood *exactly* why his friend called in this favor.

A badge bunny.

He didn't judge him for it—couldn't have even if he wanted to, considering they'd all taken one home at one point or another. Even Alex wasn't innocent. It was a rite of passage, a statement throughout the force with some guys competing on how many they could tally by the end of a quarter.

Usually, they were a one-and-done deal, but some were harder to shake than others. Judging by the woman sitting across from him now, Alex realized that Diego had dug himself a hole he couldn't escape alone.

She was bouncing in her chair all night—one hop away from slipping out of her dress entirely, and Alex had no intention of being treated to a show.

"You seem a little tense," she purred. Her blue eyes, glossy from the bottle of wine she'd insisted on having. Leaning over, she twisted a strand of hair between her fingers. "What's wrong Alex? Am I making you nervous?"

He tried not to roll his eyes. Sure, it would be easy to take her home and bury himself between her legs, but then what? By morning, he would have forgotten her name—*what was it again?*

"Oh my god, Jessica! Is that you?" A woman yelped behind him, sending Jessica flying out of her seat.

Great, he thought, turning slightly in his chair and typing a quick message into his phone.

"Prick."

"You can thank me later," Diego replied quickly.

"Don't worry, I plan to."

Three dots appeared on the screen, lingering for a moment before disappearing. After a few minutes without a reply, Alex assumed the conversation was over—*for now.*

At the sound of his name, he turned to find both women staring at him.

"I was just telling her how we met," Jessica said as if they were in some whirlwind relationship.

He plastered a smile on his face and reached out to shake her friend's hand. "It's nice to meet you."

The woman blushed—her delicate fingers lingering around his a little too long before finally pulling away.

"I think it's so romantic. You know her father was a cop?"

That explained it.

"Alex is a detective," Jessica corrected, taking a step towards him. She lifted her hand, wrapping it around his arm and tightening her grip.

Internally, Alex groaned.

In a matter of minutes, he'd somehow become an unwilling participant in whatever pissing match these two were having over him. Not that it mattered since he wasn't interested in either of them anyway.

When his phone rang and Diego's name scrolled across the screen, Alex was relieved.

"I'm sorry, I've got to take this," he said, peeling himself away from Jessica's side.

Official detective business, she mouthed to her friend—who nodded as he slipped away.

Once he was out of earshot, Alex answered. "Are you calling to apologize?" He asked triumphantly.

Diego's voice came in, short and firm. Alex recognized that voice—it was his cop voice. The one he used when something terrible happened.

"Alex—" he said, his voice cracking through the phone. "There's been an accident."

Alex silently thanked whatever poor bastard had done something stupid enough that he would need to be called in—despite knowing there'd be a victim, and for that, he felt

4

selfish. But as he looked over his shoulder at the two women, still vying for his attention, Alex promised he'd make up the hail Mary's for it later.

"Send me the location," he grunted into the phone, but there was a pause. "What is it Diego? Spit it out."

A deep breath. One so heavy it sucked the air from Alex's lungs, followed by hollow words. *"I'm so sorry. . ."*

Alex stared at his phone, confused. "What the hell are you talking about? Sorry for what?"

There was a tightness in his chest, like something heavy was sitting on it, making it hard for him to breathe. He tried to swallow it, to clear his lungs by clearing his throat, but it was useless. Alex knew *exactly* what would cause his best friend of twenty years to be so elusive.

Still, the impact of it, the sudden blow that loosened the tightness in his chest, was a massive one, and it caused him to crack, right down to his core.

Tears swelled in his eyes. "Just say it!" He shouted.

His sudden outburst caused the entire restaurant to go still, but he didn't care. From their table, both Jessica and her friend gaped at him.

Finally, Diego said softly, "They're gone."

———.———

The dark, moonless night made the strobing lights of blue and red seem more haunting as he approached. They blocked the road, forcing Alex to drive alongside the narrow shoulder.

It was because of those lights, he could see menacing streaks of black on the asphalt. Evidence of where tires attempted to stop but couldn't—not in time at least. They curled down the road a few feet before disappearing.

That's where their car came to rest, on its side—both windows blown out. The entire front end was smashed in.

Alex didn't see the other vehicle right away. Instead, his attention was drawn to the yellow sheet covering the passenger side window, where the outline of a body could be seen through the shattered glass.

The driver was sprawled onto the hood, their feet dangling over the mangled steering wheel, and Alex's heart twisted in on itself. It was hard to tell them apart from here, although he could wager a guess. His mother hated driving, so that left his father behind the wheel—*slumped* over the wheel.

Alex had been to hundreds of crime scenes—had stood amongst carnage and calamity but not like this, never like this.

Never had he seen it through the eyes of the families whose loved ones were covered under the same yellow blanket.

They were victims too.

Now, as he stood there, his breathing shallow and his body rigid—unsure of what to do, unsure if there was anything he *could do,* Alex found himself a victim too.

He'd never given it much thought, other than the usual empathy he felt whenever a call came in. In law enforcement, things don't get easier—you just learn how to become more numb.

You know that at the end of every call, there's a life involved—a family who lost a loved one, someone whose life was severely impacted. But by the time Alex gets involved, they're considered cases, not people.

You can't fit someone into a file. Who they are, what they like, and the people they might have influenced. Those are the variables that make a person who they are. And yet, those are the exact details that are stripped away once they become a victim.

It's how men like Alex stop themselves from making it personal. They have to, otherwise they'd never solve anything.

Staring at the husk of twisted metal and broken glass wrapped around his parent's lifeless bodies—broken inside, it was nothing *but personal.*

He didn't realize he'd walked up to the scene—wasn't in control of his body until he was face to face with Diego.

"You can't go up there," Diego insisted, pressing his large hands against Alex's chest as if that would stop him.

"Like hell I can't," Alex argued. Diego was right in front of him, and yet Alex couldn't see him at all. All he could focus on were those bright yellow sheets.

"Alex, it's an active scene, and you even being here goes against every protocol we have set in place. I can't let you go any further."

Drinking in the world around him, Alex steadied himself against his best friend. He knew Diego was right, and he hated him for it.

Even as he stared at the crumpled metal that was once their car, now unrecognizable, part of him was still convinced there was something he could do.

"You don't want to see them like that," Diego said, his voice softening.

Again, he was right, and again, Alex hated him for it.

"Where's the other driver?" It was more of a demand than a question as Alex scanned the hellish view, his eyes tracing over the red BMW a few yards away from where the impact occurred. It was dented and beat up, but nothing compared to the pretzel his parents were in.

Diego surveyed him cautiously, no doubt assessing his mental state. Alex knew he was trying to determine what he could tell him as an officer and what he wanted to say to him as his friend.

"Paramedics just loaded him up. He's in rough shape, but he'll live."

"Good," Alex bristled, and Diego knew what he meant.

"Assaulting him won't bring them back."

"You're right, it won't, but it will make me feel a hell of a lot better. Besides, it's only assault if I leave him alive." Alex realized what he said was foolish, but he didn't care.

Diego leveled a warning look at him.

"I want the results of his blood test as soon as the lab has them," Alex conceded.

Diego nodded but didn't move, not until Alex finally took a step back. "I know this isn't easy, but I need you to walk away right now and let me do my job," he said.

Alex flinched as those words clanged through him. They were the exact words he'd found himself saying countless times to others who'd been insistent on staying. Hearing them from this side, they sounded hollow—light and weightless.

Alex turned on his heels and stalked back to his truck—midnight black and outlined against the night. His colleagues had nicknamed it "The Reaper."

The title tasted sour in his mouth now.

The short walk seemed like an eternity, yet he kept his head up and his back straight so nobody could see how heavy he felt. He didn't wait for them to move his parents into the black nylon bags, where they would be taken from the scene directly to the medical examiner. Alex knew witnessing that would be his undoing, and he wasn't ready to give in.

He drove back to his apartment in silence, ignoring the calls and texts slowly trickling in. Walking into the dark and unwelcoming quiet, he didn't turn on the light or take off his boots. Instead, he stood there, enveloped in the shadows and eerie silence that seemed so loud now, before allowing his knees to buckle.

In the moment, Alex thought he felt something. The smoothness of a hand pressed against his back as he shook and shuddered into the shadows blanketing him. But he knew better than to believe it was anything other than grief announcing its arrival.

Amongst the despair, the whirlwind of emotions he was free falling through, he turned to it and whispered, "I guess it's just you and me now."

CHAPTER TWO
Maeve

I HATED THE WAY she said my name. I hated the way it pulled off her tongue and slithered into my ears, dripping down into my bones and echoing deep into my spine.

"Maeve—"

I don't know why I hated it so much. Maybe it was because I never felt like her—*like a Maeve.* Or maybe it was because whenever I looked at myself in the mirror, I saw pieces of her staring back at me.

"For the love of god, Maeve, HELLO?!"

"What?!" I demanded.

My mother has this way of looking at me, like I've done something wrong—like I'm always doing something wrong. Her eyes, sea green and bright, were defined in the corners as she glared at me from across the room.

"Have you been listening to a single word I've said?" she asked, her face pinched together like she'd eaten something sour.

"Yes," I lied.

Clicking her tongue, she returned to her vanity, where several lipstick tubes rolled off the table. Then, with a heavy sigh, she continued talking about things I didn't care to listen to.

That's how she's always been. My mother has this insatiable thirst to stand out, to do things differently, to be a little *extra*.

We are the complete opposites.

Where she enjoys vibrant colors spilled onto the low-cut shirts and skintight pants she adores, I prefer comfort over beauty—wearing more casual clothes rather than high-end, uncomfortable style.

Where she paints glitter and lipstick the color of rose petals onto her lips, I barely wear Chapstick on my own pouted smile. To some, these are minor differences that hardly run skin deep, but to me, they're part of a much bigger picture.

Her bright, bleached hair rested in tight curls around her face and shoulders. Her tan—the one she continuously pays for at the local salon—stained her skin a rusty color, several shades darker than it should be.

I rested my elbows on the counter and leaned over as I watched her apply an eclectic array of soft blues and white hues across her eyelids. I stared at her while she swiped thick mascara over her long, full lashes—her mouth hung open as if in shock, eyes wide and hand steady so she wouldn't poke herself with the wand.

"You should let me curl your hair," she suggested—my gawking at her an open invitation.

I reached up and twisted my ponytail inside my fist, where strands of charcoal hair loosened from its bind.

"We've talked about this," I said, trying not to sound bored. "I like it this way."

"I know, but you would look so beautiful if you did something other than that," she insisted—gesturing at me with her perfectly manicured hand.

Here we go again.

It's as if I'm not beautiful without blush and lipstick. As if I desperately needed some heavy foundation to cover up my already flawless skin.

In reality, it's not about makeup at all—it's about envy.

It's about *control*.

If she can paint me into something else and cover up my natural beauty the way she hides hers, we will finally be the same. Men will drift their eyes to her instead of lingering only on me, and she will no longer see me as competition in a game I don't even want to be a part of.

When I was little, random strangers constantly praised her for what a beautiful child I was. As I got older, blossoming from adolescence into womanhood, those innocent compliments became bold comments—mostly made by men.

It's why my mother puts so much effort into her appearance. Maybe it's jealousy, perhaps it's competition. Either way, it's not speculation.

I've seen the way her crisp green eyes cut sideways glances at me every time a man's gaze lingers too long on my porcelain skin. Or the way her face drops—just minimally at the mention of my own eyes, a shade so blue, they might as well be teal. I'm a walking contrast, sticking out when I desperately want to blend in.

"You know, it wouldn't kill you to come out with me tonight," she insisted as she slipped into a pair of six-inch heels. They're gold and gaudy, and they hurt my feet just by looking at them.

"Thanks, but no thanks," I said—peeling myself away from the table. "I have plans anyway."

We go through this every week, and every week, I find myself re-explaining to her why I don't want to hang out at the local bar alongside her.

"With your cat?" She asked, raising an eyebrow.

I flinched because she wasn't wrong. Still, I didn't want to openly admit that I'd much rather trade in a night filled with cheap booze and shitty music to hang out with Charles Lickens.

Instead, I rolled my eyes and laughed. A poor attempt at convincing her—*at convincing myself* that my life was not as pathetic as it outwardly seemed.

For a moment, things were quiet, with the uncomfortable weight of our relationship stripped bare between us. It was brief—mere seconds even, but it was long enough to irritate an already infected wound—one that's been festering for years.

I'd waited well into adulthood for that moment when things would change. When our relationship would inevitably shift from that of a parent and their child to one of a mother and her daughter. The kind that carries a bond. I thought it would happen instantly. I stupidly believed that when I became an adult, I would understand her more.

Now I understand her less.

———.———

Twilight cut across the sky as I walked along the sidewalk, winding through the neighborhood on the south side of the shore.

It was warm but still barely June, and the night air still held on to a leftover chill from the wet spring season.

By now, vacationers and summer residents have already started returning to Saltridge, and at the end of the month, our quiet little town would be roaring with life again.

I decided not to head straight home but instead, headed for the beach.

The moon hung heavy and full, casting a shimmering glow onto the water as the tide swept in. The view was stunning. The reflection cast off the waves looked like it's own galaxy, spilled across the sea.

I've lived here my entire life, yet I've always been an outsider—a stranger in my own home, in my own skin, someone who openly doesn't belong, like a puzzle piece that doesn't quite fit. Yet here, where the edge of the world is stitched together on a fine seam—constantly on the brink of unraveling—I feel most at peace.

There was a spot just out of reach of the hungry water, where the sand was left dry and untouched. Sitting down, I dug my toes deep into the sift, inhaling a breath of salty air. The slight sting of it tickled the back of my throat, but I didn't mind because it left behind a familiar aftertaste—one I could never seem to hold onto for very long.

For a while, I watched as the waves rolled onto the shore, crashing and pulling away slowly, dragging pieces of the world back as they retreated. It was a beautiful and well-rehearsed dance, and I wondered how long it would take before the earth had no more of itself to give. How often would the water kiss the sand before stealing every grain, leaving nothing but disappointment and emptiness upon its return?

I've always been fascinated by the ocean—its vastness, its hunger. And although I've never been in it, I can't stay away from it either.

The open sea is a dangerous creature, unpredictable and heartless. It will swallow you whole and dissolve your bones into foam. It is a lawless, wretched thing, yet equally seductive, alluring, and elusive. I cannot think of a better thing for a monster to be.

Sitting here, I craved it. Every part of my body vibrated as I stared into the dark horizon, my skin becoming covered in gooseflesh. It happens every time I come here, and I can't tell if it's from excitement, or fear.

I've tried countless times to walk into the water but can never seem to reach it because I falter every time. All the confidence I've mustered, all the courage and self-assurance I've managed to build up, somehow spills out of me and onto the shore, where I remain rooted in apprehension.

And yet, every night, it calls to me.

Every night, I lie in bed, listening to it sing. There's this part of me, a dark and wicked thing coiled beneath my skin that rattles itself awake when I listen to it cry. As if the ocean's songs were meant for it—beckoning it home.

Maybe it's not the dark and menacing water that scares me, but this ache inside my bones, the one that wants to drive me far out into the horizon until my head is underwater and my lungs give out.

Shuddering, I drew my knees to my chest, catching a glimpse of my mark in the moonlight. It was a blended shadow of purple and crimson, and like smoke, it snarled its way from one leg onto the other. A nearly perfect line, creating an almost perfect imperfection.

It is the only blemish I own, the only stain that brandishes my skin. There are no moles or wrinkles, no sun-weathered dark spots. I've never had a pimple nor found a single freckle stamped along my skin. This is all I have—this single linear signature that cuts across my legs like some faded and forgotten path.

They say birthmarks are an imprint of a past life—evidence of how you once left the world before you came back into it as someone else. But mine are tied to a life I was supposed to live—to a life I was *doomed to survive.* Now, I don't know where I belong.

CHAPTER THREE
Alex

THE FUNERAL WAS WORSE. The small cemetery outside of town was packed with people Alex didn't know or hadn't seen in years. Yet here they were, anxious to say their final goodbyes and to pay their halfhearted respects.

Some of his department colleagues had shown up, but none of them were stupid enough to bombard him with fake sympathy and empty support.

Rain poured from thick gray clouds, and Alex secretly hoped it would be enough to keep everyone from coming.

It only gave them more of a reason to show up.

Despite his selfishness, he was grateful for Diego, who had stayed after everyone left, waiting for Alex to approach him.

"Thank you for coming," Alex said as they stood, facing the empty hole his parents would now spend eternity in.

Diego nodded. "Anything you need, you know I've got you brother."

Brother. Alex never had one of those. He'd always wanted one, and he supposed Diego fit the role. After all, they'd grown up together. Since Diego's home life had been rough, he spent most of his time at Alex's house.

Standing there, neither of them saying anything, Alex realized that this was just as much a loss for him.

They'd been through everything together. Where one of them went, the other followed. And throughout their life, they'd seen each other through their fair share of successes and failures.

When Alex's mom got sick and could hardly get out of bed, Diego helped him through it.

When Diego's father was released from prison, only to show up a few days later and beat his mother within an inch of her life, it was Alex's house he'd run to. It was Alex's house he felt safe in.

It was Diego who wanted to be a cop first. His father's awful sins were his driving force, and he was determined to keep people like that off the streets.

Now, here they were. Standing side by side as the light thud of dirt hit the top of the caskets. It was the only audible sound through the rain. A final and fitting farewell.

They didn't hug or shake hands. Diego's light brown hair had become matted to his face from the rain, and his caramel skin was waxy in the overcast light.

Quietly, Diego turned and walked away. Alex heard him cough—a throaty, jagged sound that told him why his brother had left without saying goodbye.

Grief had finally found him too.

———·———

Heat rose from the pavement, baking in the afternoon sun. It was a mirage—not the kind you'd see in cartoons with a flickering oasis in the distance. There was no oasis here—only death. Death and shards of glass the cleaning crew somehow missed amongst the wreckage.

They glittered in the sunlight, and Alex's heavy boots crunched against the pieces as he walked over them aimlessly. Bending down, he picked one up—careful not to cut himself along the serrated edge as he turned it over in his hand.

Traffic was picking up. People were heading home from work early before the weekend, all blissfully unaware of the events that occurred here a few months ago.

Cars zoomed by, heedless of the lives lost on this stretch of road—at this very spot. Alex didn't blame them. He couldn't blame them—it wasn't as if he could expect their lives to stop just because his did.

He'd been here a few times since that awful night—had stood there, surveying the area and the wooded tree line around it. It was a sad and misguided attempt to spot anything that would have made their fate avoidable—not like it mattered now. What was done was done.

There were so many people he wanted to blame—people he *did blame.*

The bartender who'd over-served a desperate man—who'd let him stumble out of the bar without so much as a suggestion to call a cab.

He blamed the officer on duty that night, who'd been posted not far from here—too wrapped up in his phone to catch the guy when he sped by.

Then there was the culprit himself. A young corporate lawyer who'd lost a major case and decided to lick his wounds by dousing them in whiskey first. He'd walked away with only a few minor injuries. A miracle claimed by those who'd responded, given the rate of speed he'd been going when he'd smashed into his parent's small sedan.

Alex went blind with rage when he heard that—unhinged when the idea that his parents didn't suffer was something he should be grateful for. As if the lasting effect wasn't a slow and painful wound he'd never recover from.

There wasn't a single skid mark to show where he'd crossed the median, which told Alex that the driver didn't attempt to

WHAT LIES BENEATH THE TIDE

stop. His car landed on its hood where tall grass sprouted near the highway—offering some minor cushion that prevented him from serious harm.

The man's blood alcohol was three times over the legal limit. And even though he remained in jail, awaiting his trial, Alex knew what would happen. After all, he was a lawyer, and his connections and pockets ran deep. He'd get off easy—manslaughter, most likely. But with a plea deal, he'd walk out under the condition of time served.

Alex snorted. The justice system *he served*—the one he'd promised to uphold was now a brutal slap in the face, both as an officer and a victim.

He couldn't do much about the bartender or the cop. They had their own guilt to live with now. His fellow officer couldn't even look him in the eye when they passed each other at work. And Alex wasn't surprised when the young rookie finally requested a transfer to a different department.

Fine by him. If it were up to Alex, he would've had him fired, his badge stripped, and his credentials shredded.

"Whether you realize it or not, this punishment is worse," Diego said one night over drinks. "Letting him go would absolve him. Forcing him to face you, to face the others knowing what he's done—his shame will eat him alive if it hasn't already."

23

Three weeks later, they found his body in the backseat of his patrol car with a bullet in his head.

Two months had passed since then. And as Alex fingered that piece of glass—a morbid reminder that it *did happen*—he realized Diego was right.

Someone left flowers next to a small wooden cross and Alex tried not to scoff at it. He appreciated the sentiment, no matter how misguided it was. But no amount of prayers would ease the pain and he doubted God cared enough to show up here.

Alex's phone vibrated in his pocket, and he hesitated before pulling it out. A part of him, albeit a small part, still expected to see their names pop up on the screen. But that expectation was starting to fade as acceptance slowly settled in.

There were voicemails, several of them he'd saved over time, and some nights, when the depression hit harder, he'd listen to them. They were simple messages, *"Hey, call me back,"* and *"Just wanted to make sure you're still coming to dinner."* Easy statements he'd once taken for granted were now the only thing he had left to hold on to.

When his phone rang this time, it was a number he didn't recognize. Ignoring the ache in his chest, he answered it.

"This is Hayworth."

She was too peppy, her voice too high-pitched and light-hearted for him to bear, and he grit his teeth together when she spoke.

"Alex, hi! Lucy from Briar Realty. Listen, just checking in to see if we're still on schedule to market. Our office has you down for next week to list, and we need to schedule an appointment for our photographer to come and take photos."

The realtor. Alex sighed—he could only put this off for so long before he was forced to confront the inevitable. It was why he'd come here today, why he'd finally mustered up the courage to challenge his self-pity so that he might find the strength to do what needed to be done.

He didn't answer her right away, perhaps because he couldn't find the right words to say, or maybe because he didn't want to say them, too afraid that if he spoke, his voice would come out harsh—rough and ugly.

Lucy from Briar Realty didn't deserve that. She didn't need to deal with his bullshit.

He thought about what she might have planned for the weekend. He wondered if she intended to go out with friends and throw back a few drinks to numb the stress of a long work week and his thoughts drifted to what she might look like—not that it mattered.

"—Mr. Hayworth?" Her birdsong voice cut in, dragging him from his thoughts. "Are you still there?"

Alex cleared his throat, "Yeah, sorry. Everything is all set. We're good to go."

"Wonderful!" She bleated, forcing Alex to move the phone away from his ear as she boasted into it. "Well, if there isn't anything else I can do—"

"Actually," he cut her off, his voice no longer his own. ". . . There is."

CHAPTER FOUR
Alex

HE DIDN'T RECOGNIZE HER at first. He'd never gotten her name that night.

Her smirk said it all—a satisfied and victorious grin painted in subtle pink lipstick.

"Well, isn't this a nice surprise?" She purred.

And it was, because had he known this was the woman who'd silently competed for his attention alongside her friend only a few months ago, he never would have asked her out—much less agreed to let her sell his parents' house.

She was still dressed in her work clothes where a slim, charcoal skirt hugged the curves of her hips generously. Usually, Alex wouldn't be so obvious, but this time, he didn't care if she noticed him staring.

His hazel eyes dragged greedily over her white blouse, particularly where the top button was freed, exposing her creamy skin. Her gray-blue eyes settled on him from across the small table, and when she leaned over, a curtain of soft blonde hair fell loosely over her shoulders.

"So, have you seen Jessica recently?"

There it was—the prodding question she'd been dying to ask.

Alex shook his head. "Work's been keeping me pretty busy," he said, taking a heavy sip of whiskey from the glass in front of him.

Lucy's face twisted into a feline grin. "Oh yeah, that's right. Jess mentioned you were a cop."

He nodded, fingering his glass while she continued. "We're not close friends or anything. Her brother used to work for my father."

It always surprised him how quickly women were willing to toss each other aside—how easily they burned bridges. He wondered how many knives were in Lucy's back and how many she'd thrown into others.

"She was my best friend's ex-girlfriend," Alex heard himself say.

He didn't know why he said it. The words just tumbled out of him. Perhaps he'd been guilty of throwing a few of his own.

"Good to know." It was all she said—all she *needed to say.*

He studied the open spot on her chest, his eyes hard on the lines curving the top of her breasts. Lucy pulled her shirt tighter, exposing her nipples pebbled underneath.

How long had it been since he'd been with a woman? Half a year at least. Alex was never the type of man to casually sleep around like other guys he knew. He didn't have time to date or maneuver between what they'd want and what he couldn't give them.

But as Lucy batted her false lashes at him, Alex found himself studying all the places he could bite, lick, and bury himself in. He was untethered now. Stumbling through what he knew he probably shouldn't do and what his body told him it wanted.

He'd let her pick the bar, and when he walked in, he was wary of the seedy place. A guy like him didn't belong in a bar like this.

Now he was thankful for it.

She must have sensed his approval, because he felt her delicate hand slide up his inner thigh and grasp him from beneath the table. Heat flushed into his legs as he adjusted himself, not bothering to move as she rubbed her fingers over him in soft, subtle strokes.

Alex felt like bursting and was convinced he might if they sat there much longer. He was throbbing now, aching to be unleashed. Opening his throat, he downed the rest of his drink and stood, keeping his hungry eyes on her.

It was a silent suggestion. A plea. One Lucy understood as she straightened her blouse and quickly followed him out the door.

———·———

When they reached her place, Lucy's clothes were practically falling off her milky skin.

She was thin, with long legs and a tiny waist, and Alex noticed that her collarbone stuck out more prominently now that she was naked. He kissed her there, and she moaned, tilting her head back, wanting more, and he happily gave in.

He wasn't drunk, but he'd had enough to justify his actions. This was easy, mind-numbing. A quick escape from the shitty reality he'd been living through these past few weeks.

Part of him felt terrible, knowing that in the morning, she'd expect some sort of reassurance—a promise that he'd call and they'd do this again. He wouldn't, but for now, he'd let her think he would.

Alex leaned against the couch, and Lucy positioned herself before him. The scent of lilacs and vermouth echoed off her, but he didn't mind as she tugged on his jeans, exposing his desire for her in full view.

Gently, she grasped him, offering Alex a subtle grin before slowly taking what he had to offer into her mouth. It was all he could do not to shudder and shake as she worshiped him on her knees.

With each flick of her tongue, each stroke from the inside of her mouth, Alex quaked. And when he couldn't stand it any longer, he pulled her up by her hair and forced his mouth to hers—the remnants of himself, still sharp on her lips.

Lucy swung her legs over him, mounting herself in his lap, And Alex quickly filled the space between them. She moaned at the length of it, at the swiftness with which he entered her.

With his hands placed firmly on her hips, he thrusted into her, rocking back and forth as she held onto his shoulders with her back arched and her breasts exposed.

Alex ran his tongue over each nipple before grazing them with his teeth and she hitched another moan.

"Don't stop," she begged, and he didn't.

Instead, he went harder, faster. Each stroke, each thrust a release of its own as groaning pleasure barreled out of him.

It felt good. It felt *so fucking good,* but, in the end, the pleasure of her body swallowing his didn't take away the pain he still felt. Alex pressed his head to hers in an attempt to distract himself from what this was—a pity fuck.

Lucy's nails etched lines across his chest as she dragged her fingers down, laying them to rest above the muscles in his abdomen. He didn't mind it. In fact, it drove him further into her, her breath becoming heavy as she started reaching her climax.

Alex turned away. He didn't want to know what she looked like as her features twisted in ecstasy. Forcing his face into her neck, his body shook—releasing all the pent-up rage, hurt, and anguish he'd been carrying around these last few months.

Pulling at his hair, Lucy cried out as they both came together—her petite frame fracturing against his broad chest before finally going limp. Still, he didn't let go, and she didn't move. Instead, the two of them sat there, still tied together with the stench of what they'd just done pooled between them.

Lucy leaned back and used her fingers to gently lift Alex's chin to hers.

"Again," she whispered into his mouth, and he obeyed. Burying himself, his secrets, and his shame into her—over and over again.

CHAPTER FIVE
Maeve

THE SMELL OF GREASE and warm coffee lingered in the air, while the bell on the counter dinged noisily. Another plate was thrown into the window, and the sound of ringing was replaced by the sound of sizzling bacon.

"Excuse me!" A gentleman shouted, holding his mug in the air.

Annoyed, I made my way to the end of the counter. The blackened bottom pot was only a quarter full and probably just as old as I refilled his coffee for the seventh time that morning.

He didn't look up at me or offer a smile, hovering over his morning paper while his companion, seated next to him, extended his cup towards me.

I tilted the empty pot, swirling the gritty bottom grounds against the stained glass, and smiled at him.

"Another boat was wrecked along the harbor," I heard the one man say as I turned away from them.

"So early in the season?" His partner asked—mouth full of food.

"Says it was a crab boat, doesn't mention the port."

But before his friend responded, I whipped around to face them.

"Was anyone hurt?" I asked, my eyes straining to scan the paper in his greasy hands.

This time, he looked up, studying me briefly before returning to the article. He didn't answer me now that his needs were met, and he no longer stared at me as he held the paper up between us.

Fine. Reaching into my apron, I pulled out a check, and tossed it on the counter.

"Whenever you're ready," I said, walking away before they could ask me for anything else.

A gust of early summer wind blew through the diner as the front door swung open and a couple sauntered in—no doubt feeling as out of place as they looked.

Tourists. Their eccentric style and aberrant demeanor were an all-too-obvious sign that they weren't from here.

Soon, there would be more of them, draped from head to toe in designer clothes and perfumed in self-satisfaction. They're all the same—selfish, unaware, pretentious.

Every year, they show up here, claiming their desperate need to escape the overstimulated environment that is the outside world while spending most of their time glued to the same lifestyle they claimed they needed a break from.

"Hello, just two?" I asked, snatching a couple of menus from the host stand and plastering a fake smile across my face.

The man gawked at me, a reaction I'm used to, but quickly recovered before the woman at his side had time to notice.

Before he could fumble over words, I turned my back on them, leading them toward the first available booth. The woman, a tall and slender brunette, hesitated, brushing invisible crumbs off the seat before finally sliding in.

I bit the inside of my cheek and flipped over the off-white mugs already on the table, filling them without asking if it was coffee they even wanted. Then, I carefully set the menus down, ensuring "THE CAPTAINS QUARTERS" faced upwards in giant capital letters.

"What's good here?" Asked the man, still trying his best not to stare while skimming through the cracked, laminated pages.

Nothing, I thought. "Depends on what you're in the mood for," I said instead.

My lips were hurting from forcing a smile, and I was afraid they would crack, revealing all the rude thoughts coiled tightly beneath them.

"Home of the seafood omelet," he muttered.

Across from him, his wife remained still. Her black sunglasses, overbearing and studded with tiny jewels, remained perched across the bridge of her perfectly sculpted nose, shielding whatever revolted look she was sure to be hiding.

"That looks good," he surmised. "What do you think?"

At his suggestion, the woman slowly lowered her glasses—revealing dark brown puddles of bitter resentment hooded under thick mascara and smokey eyeshadow.

"What do I think?" He winced at the venom in her voice, and even I managed a step back before she continued. "I thought the Cayman Islands looked good. If what I thought didn't matter then, why should it matter now?"

Feeling awkward and uncomfortable, I shifted on my feet before finally clearing my throat. "I'll just give you two a few minutes—"

"That won't be necessary," he interrupted, holding up his hand and revealing a thick gold chain attached to an expensive, oversized watch. "Go ahead Trish. Tell me, What *would you like?*"

"Well, Mitch, since you asked. . ." she replied, taking off her sunglasses and setting them neatly on the table. "I would love the last ten years of my life back."

"Here we go again!" Mitch shouted, throwing up his arms.

I *do not* make enough money here.

She scowled at him before spearing her eyes on me. "I don't suppose that's on the menu, is it?" I shook my head, my lips sealed—mouth dry. She nodded, handing me back the menus. "In that case, we'll settle for the seafood omelet."

———.———

"I bet they have wild sex," Sarah smirked, her amber eyes hard over my shoulder as she leaned against the counter. "I bet he secretly loves that she's a bitch."

Brushing past her, I threw their order into the window. "There's something seriously wrong with you," I replied.

Sarah laughed, her voice worn—a deliberate side effect from years of smoking. "I prefer the term *peculiar*."

My eyes fell over the dramatic red wig tumbling freely down her back. Yesterday, it was green, with spiraled curls that hugged against her freckled face. The day before, it was bright pink. "That's one way of putting it."

"Hey, I can't help it if I'm sensitive to these things. It's a gift."

"I'd hardly call gossiping about someone's sex life a gift."

"Maybe, but you know it's probably true." She nudged me with her shoulder. "Speaking of which, he's staring at you again."

I could feel his eyes on me, like soft fingers, stroking over the delicate curves of my body as he mentally undressed me from across the room. His gray eyes were dark and hungry, and I turned, holding his stare—hoping he would back down out of shame or embarrassment.

When he didn't pull away, my blood became an icy burn—a cold vapor pooling in my eyes and frosting in my veins.

Sarah's warm voice barreled into me, and I broke first. Heat flushed into my cheeks, and the frigid blue in my eyes receded.

"What?" I asked, aimlessly.

She cocked her head and nodded towards the window. "I said your food is up."

Sucking in a breath, I exhaled slowly, giving her a pleading, desperate look.

"No," she argued, crossing her arms over her chest.

I held my palms flat against each other, mimicking a prayer. "Please," I begged dramatically, but she was already grabbing the plates from the window.

"You owe me."

I gave her a cheeky grin, letting it settle across my face as she ambled over to their table.

My eyes followed him, watching his eager expression as it fell into disappointment. He didn't bother looking at Sarah as she hovered in front of him, but instead gave me one last hopeful glance over her shoulder, and my smile shifted into lurid temptation.

Deep down, I could feel it—that dark thing swirling inside me like black smoke. It ached and whispered horrible things, sneering and mocking and jeering. Desperate to rip its way out and fill the space between us.

His wife spoke, and at the mention of his name, he turned and that sinister voice inside me faded. With him now distracted, I continued smiling—not for my sake, but for his.

CHAPTER SIX
Alex

THE HOUSE WAS A tomb—an empty, melancholy reminder of what Alex had lost. It was strange that a place once so full of life now sat barren on the corner of an unchanging drive.

A wooden swing hung limp from a mountainous oak in the front yard. His parents left it up so their future grandkids might use it one day. Now, someone else's family would enjoy it.

Alex hadn't been here in months, even before the accident. The lawn was overgrown, with weeds and other invasive plants tangled between the hedges near the front porch. Inside, a thin layer of dust settled, coating shelves and random items.

Standing in the hallway, it took Alex a moment to move his feet now that he was surrounded by all these things—*their things* that hadn't changed—hadn't moved since that fateful night. It was like the house was expecting them to walk in the door any moment, but it got him instead.

He steadied himself against the front door, the overbearing reality of it all pressing down on him as he determined where to start. They'd left it all to him in their will. And in his desperate need to get rid of all the reminders, he immediately shed himself of it.

To Alex, this place felt like chains, binding him to memories and what-ifs. He'd like to tell himself that selling it wasn't an easy decision. He'd like to think his parents would have understood, but he knew better. These were just excuses, a sad attempt to ease the guilt that followed him wherever he went.

The dark blue wallpaper was peeling in the corners of the living room, along with the swirls of ornate yellow that faded over the years. It was the first thing he'd planned to do away with when the house became his, had he chosen to keep it under different circumstances. When the hallways were filled with laughter from his children and the bedroom was furnished with his things—with his wife's things. Except that, too, was a dream that never came to fruition. One Alex always envisioned but kept making excuses for.

Standing there in the stillness, he wondered if the next family would keep it or if they'd tear it down and paint something more modern instead. More fit for a family. That's what this house needed, what it was intended for—*a family*. And he didn't have one.

Not anymore.

His father's slippers were tucked beside the couch as if he'd just taken them off to nap in his chair. His glasses, wide-rimmed and wire cut, sat gently on top of whatever book he was reading—*had been reading.*

Alex kept doing that, forgetting that everything concerning them was past tense. Those are the little things nobody prepares you for when someone you know has died—how even your language changes.

Slipping into the kitchen, he took in the green pastel cabinets—another feature he'd planned on updating one day. Next to the stove, a half-eaten loaf of bread rested on the counter, where a thick layer of mold stretched over the top.

The last thing his mother ever baked—*now dying too.*

There were a few dishes in the sink—the stench of mildew rose into the air from the sitting water they were left in. He never understood it. They had a dishwasher, but his mom insisted on using it for storage instead.

"What do I need that for?" She'd asked him the day he'd gifted it to her. It was her birthday, and Alex wanted to help alleviate some of the added stress from their daily lives. He'd just been promoted and couldn't come around to help as much, so he thought this might help soften the blow.

"Just give it a chance," he grumbled, installing the last bolt.

Another wave of guilt washed over him.

This was too much. It was all just *too much* as he took in the place where his mother spent most of her time, the place where he'd helped her bake cookies as a child.

How many times had he sat at the counter licking the batter off wooden spoons, or chosen to do his homework at that very kitchen table while she hummed and frosted cupcakes?

What is something you carry with you but never have at all? It was a riddle he'd read once on a popsicle stick, but it was only now that the significance made sense.

Memories.

Everywhere he looked, he saw ghosts. The haunting void of their presence followed him, yet somehow, it seemed like they were still alive, still in the moment with photos and small notes clinging to the refrigerator—reminders, and to-do lists already passed by.

Alex decided this was as good a place as any to start. Swinging open the double doors, the stench of rotting food filled the air, knocking him back from its staggering potency.

With his arm over his face, he opened both kitchen windows before grabbing several garbage bags from under the kitchen sink—hauling everything into them.

He stopped just before reaching the top shelf. In the back stood a single Hamm's beer can—his father's drink of choice. Alex didn't know what it was doing in here. His dad usually kept a few cases in the garage, where he drank them alongside the memorabilia he'd collected over the years.

It was terrible. Once, when he and Diego were hardly teenagers, they'd snuck inside and stolen a few, convinced they'd both hurl as they tried to force it down their throats. They managed to get halfway through one before his father caught them, holed up in his bedroom. He wasn't mad but disappointed, which somehow seemed worse, but he didn't punish them.

Instead, he sat cross-legged on the floor beside them and said, "Mind if I join you?"

They nodded, unwilling to admit they'd made a mistake. The bitterness of it was still sour on their tongues as Alex's father cracked open his own.

Eager to prove himself, Alex took another swig—right in front of his father. The stale taste was so awful, he couldn't help but choke.

"Not good, huh?" His father laughed. Alex shook his head. "Yeah, I didn't think it would be. After all, only real men drink this stuff." He remembered his father's face as he looked at them, two stupid kids desperate to prove their virility. "If it's awful, that means you aren't man enough yet."

Determined, Alex chugged the rest of his in one fell swoop, gagging violently with Diego following close behind. His father simply smirked, knowing full well what his words intended to do and it worked.

He never stole another thing from him again.

Standing in the kitchen, staring at the white and blue aluminum can, he took it in his hands and cracked it open.

"Cheers," he said, opening his throat and swallowing half of it in one gulp. It still tasted like shit, and Alex winced. "I guess I'm still not man enough."

———·———

It took him over an hour to clean the kitchen. By the time he was finished, the sun had leaked through the open windows—showcasing all the glittering dust he'd kicked up.

There was still so much left to do that it was overwhelming. Slowly, he went from room to room, his body sore and his mind tired. The most daunting part was not the physical labor but the tediousness of deciding what to toss, and what to keep. It wasn't much, but he didn't have the space for it in his modest apartment downtown.

He could get a storage unit, but then what? Spending money on a tin room to hoard his dead parents' things seemed like an invaluable way to preserve them. Moving it from one tomb to another seemed pointless.

There were aunts, uncles, and cousins, but just short of donating everything, hauling it off to the dump and thrift stores seemed the only way to go. He could host an estate sale, but Alex didn't want to deal with the headache. Whatever would get this place out from underneath him the fastest, he'd do it.

Who would want it all anyway? In his old room, model cars and old posters with muscled engines lined the walls. Those he'd keep because it was still a passion of his, no matter how far he'd allowed himself to drift from it.

He'd planned on fixing up a '71 Ford Torino GT with his old man one day. The frame was still housed in the garage, but they never found enough time to drag it out.

They were going to restore it together so that Alex might pass it down to his own son one day. Then his mom got sick, and the faded red paint faded and peeled some more—its rusted frame deteriorating as time passed.

He'd visit the garage last because it would be the hardest for him. After all, it's where his dad spent most, if not all, of his time. It's where his father taught him the very first things he learned about cars—their history and the way they worked. Alex's dad thought they'd own a shop together someday. Now, it was just another thing he could add to the mounting list of disappointments he was responsible for.

With his back hunched against the wall, Alex's stomach rumbled. With no real food in the house, that meant going into town—an endeavor that was more work than it was worth.

Still, he needed a break. With the attic left to go, he'd need some strength to muster it. God only knew what kind of harbored and forgotten things his mother had up there.

Downstairs, through the sidelights of the front door, Alex stopped. There was someone in the front yard. His hand swiftly moved to his belt, a reflex even though he'd left his gun in his truck. It was mid-afternoon, and although the neighborhood was safe, he knew criminals scoured the obituaries, looking for houses to rob.

With nothing but his size, he swung open the heavy door, but the power he'd mustered to scare off the intruder quickly died as he realized who it was.

Her back faced him as she hammered a "For Sale" sign near the driveway. Her blonde hair was twisted into a low bun at the nape of her neck, and she turned to face him when she heard his boots behind her. Alex hadn't spoken to her since that night, leaving her naked in her bed while he slipped unseen from the sheets.

"I tried calling," Lucy said, her voice wavering. "Not to. . . well, just to let you know that I'd be stopping by to put this up." She pointed to the sign with her photo on the front.

She looked considerably different from the woman facing him now. Now, she looked unsure, hesitant, and insecure, unlike the confident woman on the sign staked in the front yard.

He'd done that to her. Had made her feel like she was worth something, only to leave her wondering why she wasn't worth enough.

Alex raked a hand through his dark hair, unsure of what to say. "Yeah," was all he could think of—one lousy word.

Lucy took a tentative step towards him, then retreated. "You never called."

He met her eyes, which were more gray than blue this time as if a dark cloud hung over them. "I think we both knew I wouldn't."

She shrugged. "Maybe, but you never know."

But Alex *had known*. And yet he followed her to her bed and fucked her anyway. Until every part of him ached inside her. Not for her, but because he had nowhere else to run or escape. He'd used her, knowing this was where it would end up—with her wanting more and him wanting far less.

"It's nothing personal," he explained, even though she didn't ask him to. It was a sorry excuse, a pathetic justification that fell flat even as he said it.

Lucy studied him—her clouded eyes becoming clear as she took in his disheveled appearance.

"Not for me it isn't, but for you—" she paused, finally resting her gaze on the heavy bags under his tired eyes. "For you, it is. And in my experience, thats worse."

Alex didn't say anything as she walked away and drove off. He didn't say anything because he knew she was right. And he hated himself for it.

CHAPTER SEVEN
Maeve

AGAINST MY BETTER JUDGMENT, I agreed to pull a double shift. Now, as I swung my powder blue car into the cracked, riddled driveway of the large home-turned-apartments, the regret of that decision seeped into my lower back.

I barely missed the curb, the bottom of my bumper resting less than an inch away from the concrete, and I grimaced as the rusted edges scraped against the cement.

When I got out, I slammed the door, and those rusted edges flaked off, landing on the blades of grass forcing their way through the pavement.

The overzealous brick building—once a beautiful and prominent home, loomed like a shadow backdropped against the brilliant moonlight. Light spilled from the windows—their shutters either missing or broken. And the small wooden porch out front was in dire need of repair.

The discolored brick, once a vibrant crimson, had chipped and faded over the years. Spiders had formed webbed homes in the cratered holes where the brickwork already disintegrated.

With a hefty tug, I yanked open the front door and was immediately greeted by the incredulous sound of a TV echoing throughout the hall.

It roared all day and all night, with no reprieve in between, and although most people would find the noise unbearable, I've gotten used to it.

Mr. Jenkins lived alone in the apartment above mine. There were rumors, whispered amongst the locals, that he was crazy and unstable, but I don't know how much of that is true because in all the time I've lived here, he's never said one word to me.

Nobody comes to visit him. No children. No friends. No siblings or family of any kind. And I couldn't help but wonder if he prefers it that way. Or if the deafening sound coming from his apartment at all hours of the night was his way of drowning out the silence brought on by loneliness.

It was an effort to drag myself across the floor of the open foyer. My feet felt like weights dipped in cement, and my body groaned in protest as I forced myself along.

As I fiddled inside my bag for the key to my apartment, behind me, the front door slowly creaked open.

Her walker made it inside before she did, followed by the shuffling of tiny feet hidden beneath an emerald nightgown. Halfway inside, the heavy door swung shut behind her, smacking her the rest of the way inside.

"Damn door," she grumbled before setting her old eyes on me. "Oh, hello Maeve." Mercy O'Dell, my neighbor—and my friend, steadily made her way over to me.

Her joints cracked against each other as she hobbled across the carpet. With each small step she took, the echo of dense bone against cartilage reverberated throughout the small foyer.

Her smoke-colored hair was swept up in long braids piled high on her head, and her petite frame was bent over her walker as she dragged it along.

Mercy was like warm honey, sweet and delightful, and I loved her dearly. With no children or family, she lived alone in the apartment upstairs across from Jenkins. Why she didn't insist on relocating to the empty unit across from mine, where the stairs weren't an obstacle, was easily attributed to her stubbornness and strong will.

"Isn't it past your bedtime?" I teased. All jokes aside, part of me worried about her failing eyesight in the dark. "What kind of trouble have you been getting into?"

Mercy smiled, revealing an almost toothless grin. "Only the good kind, of course."

"Is there a good kind?"

Digging around for her keys, her hands trembled while she pulled out the one for her mailbox. "Depends on who you ask."

Leaning over to snatch the accumulated pile of letters and envelopes in her cubby that lined the stairwell, I noticed a fresh bruise on her arm. Her complexion was dark and creamy, but the blue and purple shadows bled through her paper-like skin—snarling up her bony arm and disappearing beneath the sleeve of her gown.

Raising a brow, I asked, "Is everything alright?"

Not meeting my gaze, Mercy tugged on her sleeve to cover it. "Oh yes, I'm fine. Everything's fine," she insisted, dropping her mail into the cloth basket hanging from her walker.

She was lying.

"I feel like I haven't seen you in ages. . ." she went on, changing the subject. "Where have you been?"

Glancing down at my grease-stained shirt and splattered worn jeans, I sighed. "Prison."

But Mercy didn't laugh. "You work too much," she said.

"I kind of have to," I said. "You know, bills and adulthood and all."

"Yes, yes, I know," she chided. "But there's more to life than just work. Go out, make some friends."

"I have friends," I insisted. "You're my friend."

Mercy narrowed her eyes at me. "And what are you going to do once I'm gone?"

I flinched. I didn't want to think of what would happen once I no longer had Mercy to lean on. I've known her my entire life—since the day I was born, and I couldn't imagine a life without her in it.

"That's not going to happen," I replied.

"It is going to happen. Maybe not right now, but eventually," she said.

I glanced at her arms again. "But not right now," I argued.

Mercy sighed, "No, not right now. Still, I'm worried about you. Ever since—" she glanced up the stairwell, then thought better of it.

The creature inside me sneered.

Shaking it off, I shrugged. I knew it was in her nature, but I didn't need anyone to save me. "I'm fine, I promise," I assured.

Mercy's face softened, deepening the crevices in her cheeks. "I know you are, and I know you will be."

My eyes drifted over her shoulder to the silent apartment behind her. "Things have been. . . quiet," I said.

Her gaze followed mine, and she swallowed. "Let's hope it stays that way."

Hope is an illusion.

With the daunting task of climbing the stairs still ahead of her, Mercy turned away from me. I learned my lesson years ago not to offer her any help. She was weak but wasn't incapable, and she made sure everyone knew it.

Still, watching her struggle to lift her feet onto the first step made me wince, and as I sauntered over to my front door, I stopped. "Mercy do you—"

"Now I know you aren't about to ask me if I need help getting up these stairs," she challenged.

I didn't reply as I slipped into the shadows of my apartment, but I didn't close the door all the way—not yet.

From the narrow crack in the frame, I watched her take each step slowly. Her body trembled against the exertion, but she pushed through regardless.

It wasn't until I was sure she reached the landing that I finally closed the door—loud enough for her to hear.

CHAPTER EIGHT
Alex

ONE AWFUL GAS STATION sandwich later, Alex returned to his parents' house. Staring up at the ceiling, he thought about all the times he and Diego had hidden away there. It was their unofficial clubhouse amongst the insulation and spiders.

The stairs groaned in the empty hallway as Alex unfolded them towards the floor. Most people hated the attic. His mother certainly did, but he'd never been bothered by it. He'd been in plenty of questionable and eerie places where much scarier things were waiting for him besides dust and darkness.

He took the steps one by one since they weren't sturdy. When he reached the top, he yanked on the chain to the only light in the room and waited for his vision to adjust.

When it did, Alex found himself surrounded by boxes and cobwebs hanging loosely from the rafters. It wasn't an ample space, made even smaller by the junk left here and forgotten. Most of the boxes weren't labeled or were marked in faded ink.

Steadying himself, he began the dreadful task of sorting through it. Most of it was nothing more than old papers—tax documents and files that were decades old.

Another box was filled with old crafts and scribbled drawings from when he was a kid. His mother kept all of it—every glued noodle and finger-painted masterpiece.

One by one, Alex stacked them at the base of the stairs—walking himself up and down into the hallway until the attic was almost empty. He could feel the heat and exhaustion mounting inside him. Sweat lined his brow, and he inhaled deep breaths, not realizing how stuffy it was until now. Dust shimmered in the dim light, and he sneezed repeatedly.

His throat was dry, and a dull throb pulsed at the base of his neck. He'd spend the rest of his night nursing a headache if he didn't call it a day now. Whatever was left, he'd return for later.

Heading out of the attic, Alex stumbled—the tip of his boot catching in a small gap in the uneven floorboards. Perhaps it was a good thing he was selling this house. The amount of work he'd need to put into it wasn't worth all the trouble. Pulling himself free, Alex stared into the crevice—at the glint of something metal tucked beneath it.

Sticking his hand inside and praying he wouldn't be bitten by something, Alex saw it was some kind of box, too big to pull through the hole. With the help of his pocketknife, he loosened the board above it—shimmying it free until the entire plank came loose.

The small chest was only a foot or so wide but deep. Its top was rounded over and flanked with black slats and center bands, reminding him of an old pirate chest with an iron-style lock on the front. Although it was rusted over, the steel latches still held onto some life, which was what grabbed his attention.

Raising the lid, Alex half expected to find treasure buried inside—but it wasn't gold or rare jewels stowed away for safe-keeping. Instead, he found a stack of baseball cards bound together in frayed twine—some even signed. Confused, he pulled them out, wondering who this box belonged to. No-body in his family cared much for sports, let alone enough to harbor autographed cards.

Setting them aside, Alex noticed a small wooden anchor, intricately carved from driftwood. It rested perfectly in his palm, the smooth finish revealing the fine details of the wood grain swirling together.

Maybe it belonged to the previous owner, except that would mean it was stashed here long before Alex was born. And besides, with how much time he and Diego spent up here, one of them would have noticed it by now.

Maybe it was Diego's. Perhaps he'd hidden it here without telling him. It was a far stretch, but it was the only reasonable explanation he could come up with. Diego's father had been known to steal his things, but that still didn't explain why Diego wouldn't have told him.

Rummaging through the rest, Alex discovered a postcard shoved against the bottom. When he removed it, he found himself staring at a beach. Its sandy white shores contrasted brilliantly against an alluring red sky stretching for miles above the open water. A rocky cliffside jutted out over the coast, hugging the ocean on both sides.

He didn't know what the significance of this place was, or if it even existed at all, but he was mesmerized by it—at the red and pink colors staining the horizon and the dark sea that sung to him. Touching the tip of his fingers to it, he could almost feel the calm and abrasive water on his skin.

He blinked and pulled away, flipping the card over to read the description, and he was surprised to find a handwritten note scrawled on the back.

In case I am forgotten.

No location.

Now Alex was left with more questions than answers. He turned the postcard over again, hoping those answers might suddenly appear, but there was nothing.

Pulling the final item from the box—a worn journal—he realized it wasn't filled with written words but various drawings instead.

The first few pages were random things, simple sketches of still-life objects and tiny doodles—nothing that would give him any idea of who this person was or where any of it came from.

Flipping through each page, the drawings became more complex and detailed. One showed a vast landscape where wild sage grew in tufts along a wooden fence line and another of a great lighthouse, holding steady over harsh swells from a violent sea.

There were random things, such as a cat with a large bushy tail licking its broad paw, and a full moon misting in fog amongst a dark, star-studded sky.

Whoever drew these was talented. Most of them were so realistic, Alex thought they might leap out at him.

Every page was full, except one, where a blank piece separated one section from another. Instead of wild scenery or simple line drawings, Alex stared at a portrait of a woman. Her features were a mixture of grey and black swirls blended effortlessly onto the paper but blurred into the background as if the artist was keeping her identity a secret.

It reminded him of an ink splatter erupted from a broken pen, but the delicate structure of her curved jaw and sharp cheekbones told him she was intentional. He could make out her frame but never her face—only a shadow of what she might look like.

Each page was more of the same—an outline of a woman obscured by faded streaks of black and grey smudges intermittent with specks of vibrant color.

Fascinated, he couldn't pull himself away. As each drawing progressed, her characteristics shifted—until there was nothing left of her at all but something else.

Something dark and twisted and hideous.

The coal-colored strokes that were once obscured and shaded started taking shape, forming tight lines curving around slender bone, and her eyes bled into black, cryptic voids.

Her lips, which were originally light and simple, now melted into a grin that was drawn too wide and too thin—like a giant rip in a fine seam, and it made his skin crawl.

Each page contained more of the same, each portrait more grotesque than the last, until, finally, there was nothing left but a giant black well.

Unsettled, Alex shut the book and tossed it back into the chest, slamming the lid closed. He would have had a sound mind to return it where he'd found it—to leave it and never look for it again. But he wasn't in his right mind these days, and out of pure insanity, Alex brought it home with him instead.

He wasn't afraid of most things. He'd never been afraid of the dark or of what might lurk inside it. He didn't believe in ghosts or the boogie man, and he certainly wasn't frightened by the things he couldn't see. But ever since his parents died, something in him had changed. A small part of him had become unhinged, anxious—*scared*.

Alex had always been in control of his life until he wasn't anymore. No matter how careful he was, life happened. Accidents happened, and uncertainty became the scariest thing he'd ever faced.

Abandoning the chest on his kitchen table, Alex threw a dish towel over it so he wouldn't be tempted to look inside. It was ridiculous, but he didn't want whatever lurked between those pages to sneak out and haunt him.

That night, he was restless. Tossing and turning in the shadows of his bed, he dreamt of faraway places he'd never been and of a woman he'd never seen before.

She called to him, her voice an enchanting siren song tethering him to her. Following that sound, the breathless whispers on her tongue soothed him until he reached the edge of the earth.

Clad in a white silk gown, her hair was void of color, absorbing the sunlight peeking through heavy clouds.

"Who are you?" he heard himself ask. Part of him vibrated with fear, telling him—no, *screaming at him* to get out—but he ignored it. He was too enthralled by the woman standing in front of him.

She smiled, her cream-colored lips supple and full, and Alex desperately wanted to feel her mouth against his. But she remained elusive as she pointed to the water at his feet.

Peering over, Alex gazed into the sea—so pure and still, his reflection bounced back at him, but he didn't see his face. The eyes were the same, hazel and set deep below thick brows. The curved nose and sharp jaw were identical, but when he touched them, the reflection from below did not mimic his own. The realization that he was staring at someone else suddenly dawned on him.

Confused, Alex turned to ask who the man trapped beneath the surface was. But fear caught in his throat, and he stumbled back, catching himself before falling into the now angry sea.

Her skin was stripped from her—replaced by rotted olive flesh, and her eyes, once an enchanting shade of blue and green and silver, were now obsidian craters.

She crept towards him slowly—*unnaturally,* and Alex took a step back, submerging himself in the ocean, where the firmness of the water took hold.

With nowhere to go, he gaped in horror as the woman slithered closer. His mouth hung open in terrified shock as her slender legs melted away—revealing bright and shiny scales carved into a hefty and powerful tail.

He was frozen in place and before he could cry out, she freed the joints from her jaw, splitting her head in half and sinking her teeth into his flesh.

Alex could hear the crunching of his bones as she tore him open like a fragile shell. He tried to scream, but nothing came out. His blood stained her lips, and she licked them viciously, unwilling to afford the hungry water a minor drop before disappearing below the swell—taking what was left of him, with her.

———.———

Alex lunged from his bed, his hands cascading over himself to ensure he was still alive—relieved to find he was clammy and out of breath but in one piece.

He'd never dreamt like that before—had never been plagued by nightmares or sleepless nights despite the things he'd seen. This was the first time he'd experienced something so terrifyingly real, and it made him cold with fear.

Clicking the light beside his bed, Alex stared at his phone. It was three in the morning, and with dawn approaching fast, he fell back into bed unwillingly.

Afraid someone might steal the air from his lungs, he inhaled a deep and forceful breath before allowing his heavy eyelids to close.

He didn't turn off the light.

CHAPTER NINE
Alex

"**YOU LOOK LIKE SHIT,**" SAID Diego, leaning over Alex's desk. "Smell a bit like it too."

"Not all of us can be bright-eyed and bushy-tailed," Alex replied, throwing a plastic cup at him.

Diego laughed. "You're right—then again, I've always been better at most things than you."

A few days had passed since he stumbled upon the mystery inside his parents' attic. And every night since then, he'd fallen victim to the same restless slumber.

During the day, it laid dormant in his mind. But at night, he tossed and turned until he dragged himself from bed, not bothering to shave or run a comb through his hair.

He'd lived off little sleep before, but this time was different. Every fiber in his body was weighted, dragged along by some unseen force. It was like he was running a marathon up an inclined hill, pulling chains and stones behind him.

"Were you out digging for buried treasure?" asked Diego, his brown eyes grazing over the chest near Alex's desk.

That morning, Alex decided enough was enough. "I found it in my parents' house," he said, picking it up off the floor. "It was hidden underneath the floorboards in the attic. I thought maybe it belonged to you."

Diego rubbed his freshly shaven face. "Why would you think that?"

He reached out to touch it, but Alex pulled it away. He was still holding onto it, refusing to let go even as he saw the concern flashing in his friend's eyes.

"What's in it?"

Alex recognized that look—he understood the worry in it. He didn't want to give Diego a reason to think something was wrong. He didn't want to be questioned or interrogated about his mental health either, considering he'd refused to take any time off despite the urging of his chief and other colleagues.

What Alex needed was a distraction. He needed work. Something solid to hold onto while the rest of his life spun out of control—otherwise, he'd fall apart. Without this place, without other people's tragedies to keep him preoccupied, Alex didn't have anything else. He didn't have *anyone else*. And so, against the behest of his peers, he threw himself back into the only constant thing he had in his life—his career.

Sitting across from Diego, his mind and body running on fumes, Alex didn't want to raise any alarm that he was falling apart. Other officers had been removed from their positions for less, and Alex didn't want to risk being forced into a mental evaluation over something he was still convinced he had a handle on.

Loosening his grip on the box, Alex cleared his throat. "Nothing, just some old papers and things."

"And things?" Diego asked, raising his heavy brows.

Alex unlatched the rusted lock on the front and set the baseball cards between them.

Shuffling through each one, Diego's eyes widened. "You've got some good cards here—a few that might be worth money."

Alex balked. "You know about baseball cards? I've never seen you watch a game, let alone know the stats."

"I'm not an expert by any means, but during my stint in foster care, one of my bunk mates collected them. He kept them stuffed inside his pillowcase, afraid someone might steal them. Every night, he counted each one just to make sure they were all there. Some of the other kids thought he was weird, but I understood. Those cards were his only possession, the one thing connecting him to his old life, so they meant a great deal to him."

Alex had forgotten about Diego's time in the system. Fortunately, he was only forced to experience it for a few months before reuniting with his mother.

"I found this too," he held up the whittled anchor for Diego to see.

"That looks personal," he said, taking the item in his hand. "I wonder who it belongs to."

"I have no idea," Alex replied. "If it's not yours, do you think it might belong to someone we know?"

"Maybe," Diego said. "Where did you find it again?"

"Underneath the attic floor."

"I know I wasn't your only friend, but I can't think of anyone who'd have hung out with us enough to hide something and know *exactly* where to hide it. I'd say you should ask your parents—"

"But they're dead," Alex interjected. The words sliced through him, leaving behind a jagged, open wound.

Diego grimaced. "I'm sorry. I didn't mean to..." He paused, unable to bring his eyes to Alex's. "Sometimes it doesn't seem real."

"I keep expecting them to walk through the door," Alex confessed shamefully. It was the first time he'd mentioned them to anyone. "I keep thinking that mom's going to call or dad's going to ask me to swing by and fix something." He swallowed hard before letting out a breathy laugh. It was forced, and it scratched his throat, but he needed to feel something other than the tightness in his chest.

"I used to hate it when he did that. Most of the shit he wanted me to fix, he was able to fix himself. He just wanted to see me, that's all." Tears welled in his eyes, and Alex tilted his head back to stare at the ceiling. "Why couldn't he just tell me that? Why did he think he needed to lie to me to get me to come over?"

"You know how your dad was Alex—"

"Yeah, and I know how I am," he cut in. "I was so wrapped up in my own bullshit that my own father felt like the only way he could spend time with me was to guilt me into it. And the worst part is. . . he wasn't wrong."

For a moment, they were silent, prompting Diego to finally speak. His voice was low, forcing Alex to lean in so he could hear him. "You can take some time off you know. Nobody would blame you for it."

Alex ran a rough hand over his face. The stubble from his jaw caught in his callouses. "I'd blame me."

"You already do, even though it wasn't your fault." Alex knew he was talking about the accident. He knew because everyone in the department had been handling him with kid gloves since that night. Everyone except Diego, who was the only one not compelled to walk on eggshells around him—until now.

"Don't do that," Alex warned.

Diego's face was pleading, but he didn't argue. "So, what's your plan with all this?" He asked, nodding towards the open box.

Alex didn't show him the drawings. For some reason, he wanted to keep those to himself.

"Does this place look familiar to you?" He asked, holding up the postcard.

Diego scanned the photo. "It could be anywhere," he said, rubbing his hands together. "You said you found all this in the attic..." It was more of a statement than a question, and when Alex responded with a silent nod, Diego sighed, taking in his disheveled appearance.

"Look, man... I know this has been hard for you. But you've gotta get out of your head. You've gotta—"

"I said I don't want to talk about it!" Alex erupted, his voice suddenly full of fire—kindled from the embers of all the rage, disappointment, and hurt he'd forced himself to swallow.

Diego blinked but didn't back down. "Well, you're going to have to talk to someone," he said, throwing the card back on the desk. "Because this isn't healthy. Shit, you're not even trying to hide it anymore. When was the last time you slept? Or ate something that wasn't cooked in a microwave?"

Alex stared at the postcard, at the scribbled handwriting looped in faded ink.

In case I am forgotten.

It took everything he had in him not to laugh at the irony. That's all he wanted to do was forget. Forget himself, forget the choices he'd made. Forget that night.

"You're missing things Alex, big things. Last week, you forgot to submit evidence. You're lucky I caught it and not someone else. I understand you're going through a rough time, but if you're more interested in chasing some imaginary problem over the real ones you have going on here, then maybe you should consider taking a step back," Diego said, standing.

"You think I'm making this up?"

His friend lingered in the doorway, his fingers drumming against the frame. "I think you've been through something awful, and I feel for you, I really do. But I won't sit here and encourage whatever this is either."

He didn't have to say it—Alex understood what he meant. The way his shoulders sagged—the way his olive complexion had paled—making him appear wan. He wasn't oblivious to it, despite what Diego believed or didn't.

Maybe he was right. Maybe this was a fantasy he'd created out of the desperate need for something to cling to. He felt ashamed—ashamed that he'd fallen this far, ashamed that he'd allowed Diego to witness it.

"I'm sorry," Alex whispered, and for a second, he didn't know if the apology was for Diego. . . or for himself.

It was quiet between them. A quiet filled with so many unsaid things.

"Try running it through image search," Diego finally said after a minute.

"What?"

"The postcard. Try running it through an image search. It probably won't yield much, but it's a start."

Alex folded the card into his palm. "Yeah, I'll do that. Thanks."

Diego's eyes softened, replacing the disappointment shadowing them earlier.

"Oh, and Alex?"

"Yeah?"

"When you're done with. . . whatever this is, there's a beer with your name on it at Stanley's."

It was more than an invitation. It was a lifeline—one Alex sensed wouldn't be extended again. Waving him off, he turned back to the chest, placing the contents back inside—save for the postcard, and closed the lid.

Scanning the image onto his computer, he waited patiently for the results to load.

In case I am forgotten.

The words were a hum beneath his skin. A frayed thread, waiting to be unraveled. When the results finished loading, Alex leaned forward and started pulling.

——·——

Diego was right—almost. After wading through several results of sunny beaches and seaside resorts, Alex was about to call it quits when one photo caught his attention.

It wasn't the photo on the postcard—it wasn't even a photo of a beach at all—but of an old man whose face was weathered by the sun. There was nothing spectacular about it, but what was behind him made Alex do a double take.

He was standing next to a boat docked along the harbor, and in the background, loomed against the gray horizon, was a large bluff sticking far out over the crashing waves below.

Alex clicked on the link, directing him to an archived news article that looked like it had been pulled from a tabloid magazine he had seen at the grocery store.

The kind with headings like *"Man Claims to be Bigfoot's Son"* or *"Help! My Sister Married an Alien."* This one read, *"Local Man Missing. Kidnapped by Mermaids."*

It was published over twenty years ago, and Alex didn't know if the man giving the interview was still living in the area, much less alive.

[Friday June 14th, 2001]

James Jenkins, a longtime resident of Saltridge, pleads with investigators on the whereabouts of his friend Max Wiley. A Navy Veteran, Jenkins insists that Mr. Wiley has lived in Saltridge for the last four decades. Mr. Jenkins attempted to file a missing person's report. However, Sheriff Mike Thompson insists that no records show Mr. Wiley has ever existed. "Without proof or record of this individual, we can only suspect these allegations to be a fabricated delusion. Though we take every case seriously, Mr. Jenkins's wild claims are nothing more than just that." Mr. Jenkins provided the following statement regarding his beliefs about where his alleged missing friend might be. "Sirens. Demons from the depths lured him from his bed in the night and walked him into the sea!"

Mr. Jenkins insists that Max Wiley isn't the only victim to be kidnapped by these creatures. James states that every year, someone goes missing without follow-up regarding their sudden disappearance. Family members who initially become concerned seem to forget them soon after. Sheriff Thompson promises that there are no open reports regarding any missing persons besides Mr. Wiley. Assuring the town's safety.

Saltridge sees an annual increase in population during its summer months and is best known for its various off-sea fishing appeal. Perhaps now they might add mermaid sightings to its short list of attractions.

Scanning the article, Alex noticed something. Enlarging the photo, he held the postcard to the screen, positioning it against the rough hillside looming in the background.

The angle was different as if it was taken from somewhere closer. Still, the rocks position against the sky remained the same. Evidence of erosion and the undercut from where the water receded was identical to the ones hovering behind Mr. Jenkins. Alex wasn't positive it was the same place, but he was nearly certain, and that was good enough for him.

He didn't believe in signs—had been trained not to—yet here he sat, surrounded by so many. Staring at the postcard, the ink jumped out at him again—bold and vibrant, and haunting.

In case I am forgotten.

Alex didn't think that mermaids were to blame, but he was well versed enough to trust his instincts, and right now, they were screaming at him.

Printing the article, Alex folded it in half and slipped it into his pocket. Then he powered off his computer before lifting the box off his desk and heading out the door.

It seemed like he'd be taking some time off after all. And who knows. . . maybe he'd get the chance to see a mermaid.

CHAPTER TEN
Alex

THE WOMAN BEHIND THE counter looked annoyed as her beady eyes peered out at Alex over her computer.

"We book out months in advance," she stated. "And I doubt you'll find anything else in town."

The next town was over an hour away, with only trees and long stretches of highway in between.

Alex pinched the bridge of his nose and sighed. "What about camping? Are there any grounds I can pitch a tent on?" He'd sleep in the cab of his truck if he had to.

She didn't respond, and Alex figured she'd had enough of his bullshit.

Taking the hint, he turned away, but her voice crept up behind him. "Saltridge doesn't have a campground, but we do have cabins. They're old and outdated, but they're usable. If you don't mind camping, I doubt you'll mind these."

"I'll take what I can get," he assured her.

She chuckled, the first time he'd seen her crack even the slightest smile since arriving twenty minutes ago. "I can't guarantee they're available, but you can certainly try," she said, scribbling the information on a scrap of paper and handing it to him. "Good luck."

When he got there, Alex understood what the concierge had found so funny. The cabins she suggested were not cabins at all but tiny storage sheds converted into makeshift lodgings.

The couple who owned them seemed nice. Transforming part of their small lot into weekend rentals for tourists to offset some of their retirement funds.

Three cabins were lined up in a neat row near the main house. Due to a last-minute cancellation—no doubt made *after* seeing the place—Alex secured his stay for now.

He didn't give work a dedicated timeline for his return, and they didn't ask. It was the first time he'd requested vacation, and nobody would question him, especially not now.

Inside, the musty aroma mixed with the salty air outside gave off an unpleasant, almost sour odor. It was a small, single room with no bathroom or kitchen, which was perfectly fine with him considering the furry guests it was sure to be housing. Evidence of their nightly rendezvous was obvious, but Alex had stayed in worse and didn't mind the company—so long as they remained hidden.

A single bathhouse was erected behind the sheds, forcing those renting to take turns using it. It was fitted with one stall and a shower and equipped with a push lock as the only security measure to keep someone out. He didn't know who occupied the remaining cabins and he hoped it would remain that way.

He was thankful—and surprised to see the place offered Wi-Fi. The signal wasn't great since it was shared from the couple's main house, but it was better than nothing.

After checking the bed for mites and critters, Alex sat and stretched out his legs—the ache from the twelve-hour drive settling in.

There were emails he needed to catch up on, mostly from work and a few from the realtor. To say Lucy was unhappy about his decision to postpone the listing was an understatement.

Since their relationship ended the way it did, she took the deferral personally. Alex didn't blame her—he knew how it looked, but he didn't owe her anything either—at least that's what he told himself anyway.

Running a hand through his unruly hair, it looked like he'd have to brave the shower sooner than he'd hoped. The dark strands hung loosely over his hazel eyes and were greasy from the long trip.

There was an email from Diego with questions regarding a case Alex forfeited and a short mention of enjoying his "vacation." Looking around at the rundown shack, he laughed. It was his first attempt at time off, and here he was, sleeping in a shed.

Alex had spent some time researching Saltridge the night before and was surprised that there wasn't much to learn.

Initially established in the 1700s as an English port, Saltridge was later used as a trading center after the revolution. That was. . . until ground and air travel became more efficient where it now served as a vacation destination—one with a mermaid problem, apparently.

Which brought him to Jenkins. Besides the tabloid, he found little information on the old man. He joined the Navy shortly after turning eighteen and served as an officer for over twenty years.

When he retired nearly forty years ago, he settled in Saltridge—no doubt to be close to the ocean he'd come to know and love. However, there were no records of a family, none that were still alive anyway, which made Alex question his connection to Max Wiley, the man he'd reported missing.

That's where things got strange. In the article, James insisted Max lived in Saltridge, but there were no records of him anywhere.

Even Alex's connections through the department failed to yield any evidence that this man ever existed. There was no birth certificate, which meant no death record either. His name didn't appear on any census records for Saltridge or in any other town, for that matter.

In the article, Jenkins claimed that Max wasn't the only person to have disappeared. And yet, the sheriff actively denied any open reports of missing persons.

Alex planned on speaking to Sheriff Thompson, but he wanted to gauge the seriousness of the claims first. If this was nothing more than the ramblings of an old man—perhaps the early onset of dementia—he didn't want to waste the officer's time—*or his.*

Given the size of the department Alex worked for and his rank, he was hesitant to step on anyone's toes. Small towns were notorious for harboring power-hungry officers whose big dreams of becoming the next Elliot Ness were usually crushed before they started.

If Alex barged in there, badge in hand, demanding answers based on a ridiculous theory with no proof, they'd be unwilling to help, if he wasn't laughed out of the building first.

Senile or not, James Jenkins was the best place to start. If what he claimed was true, maybe he could offer some proof—hard evidence Alex couldn't find on the internet, given James's connection with Mr. Wiley.

It took some time, but Alex finally found James's phone number. Right away, he was greeted by a familiar tone—followed by, "We're sorry. The number you are trying to reach—" He didn't wait for the automatic system to finish.

Landlines were nonexistent these days, and he doubted an almost ninety-year-old man who had lived most of his life secluded here would be open to having a cell phone.

Unable to find an address, Alex was starting to wonder if Jenkins was alive at all. Disappointment settled into his stomach, replacing the mounting ache of hunger. He should have investigated this before driving half a day and pissing away two hundred dollars on a one room shack.

Frustrated by his stupidity, he put his head in his hands. The stress of these last few months was eating away at him—causing him to miss things he usually wouldn't. He wasn't perfect, but he held himself to a higher standard, which meant that disappointment hit harder when he failed.

The delicious aroma of barbecue drifted in through the window, and outside, Alex saw the man who'd rented him the shed bending over the flames of a charcoal grill. He was starving. The savoriness of it made his mouth water, and he followed it.

"Do you need any help?" Alex asked, walking over to the wrap-around deck stretching over their backyard.

The man's wife stood, eyeing her husband warily. By the looks of it, they didn't seem to entertain the guests they housed—assuming those who stayed were most likely questionable. Crime didn't seem like it ran rampant here, but nowadays, even the safest towns held sinister secrets.

"Is there something you need?" Asked the man, closing the lid to the grill. "There're extra towels in the cabinets. The sheets on the bed should be clean, but if you don't find them to your liking, my wife can fetch you some new ones."

Alex shook his head. "No, everything's great, thank you." He needed to approach this from a practical standpoint. One where they'd offer him to stay and not by his asking. "It's not often I come across such open hospitality. Especially in my line of work."

The man cocked his head. "And what kind of work might that be?"

Alex had him hooked—all he needed to do was reel him in. "Law enforcement." His voice was smooth and welcoming. It was a tone he used when he wanted to put people at ease. Primarily those he found himself arresting, but Alex discovered it worked on just about anyone. "Detective, actually."

The man's wife stiffened. "Did something happen? Are we being arrested?"

Alex laughed, "No, ma'am. I'm here on pleasure, not business."

"I was an MP in the army myself," said her husband, opening the grill again. The smoke from the flames billowed into the air, and Alex's stomach groaned again. "Are you hungry?"

CHAPTER ELEVEN
Alex

AFTER REGALING ALEX WITH tales of his old army days, Frank—whose name he'd only learned at the behest of his wife—leaned back in his chair.

Not wanting to drag things out further, Alex cleared his throat. "Are either of you familiar with a man named James Jenkins?"

A sudden glance between them confirmed that they did. However, the unease of that glance made Alex nervous.

"Yeah, we know James," said Frank warily. "Is he a friend of yours?"

Alex wondered if the mention of James's name had Frank regretting his dinner invitation.

"My fathers, and not really, no." Alex looked Frank in the eyes when he spoke so he wouldn't catch the lies laced within his words. The best lies are the ones crafted closest to the truth. "My father passed away unexpectedly a few months ago." *The truth.* "He served in the Navy, and when I went through his things, I found some items that might have belonged to Mr. Jenkins. I thought he might want them back." *The lie.*

Frank surveyed him, and Alex was worried he sensed his deception. He'd just broken bread with these people when it was obvious they didn't do so very often. The last thing he wanted was to abuse their hospitality, and their trust.

"Sorry about your old man. Losing one of our own is always tough, no matter the branch. As far as Jenkins goes, he's still around. But I don't know if you want to pay him a visit—considering him going crazy and all."

"Frank!" His wife scolded, smacking his arm.

"What? What I say?"

She narrowed her eyes at him. "What if people went around saying that about you, huh?"

Frank rubbed his chin before shrugging his shoulders. "I suppose I'd be too crazy to care."

Alex grinned. Watching them together reminded him of his parents. "Is he dangerous?" he asked, sitting up in his chair.

"Who, Jenkins?" Frank threw his head back and laughed, causing his enormous belly to roll. "No, not at all. He's just old and. . ." Frank twirled his fingers near the side of his bald head and whistled. Earning him another smack from his wife.

"Do you mind if I ask what happened?" Alex waited for Frank to reply, but his wife spoke up instead.

"He's a nice man, or at least he used to be. Then, one night, we had a terrible storm. Do you remember that storm Frankie?" She glanced at her husband. "We don't get big ones very often, but that one was a doozy. Knocked out all the power for weeks, flooded half of Port St—"

"Get on with it Wendy. The man doesn't want to hear about the weather." Again, she cut him a sharp look and again, Alex grinned.

"Anyway," she continued. "A few days later, they found James sprawled on the beach. His clothes were all torn up, and he was soaked down to the bone. Some kids who'd come out to hunt for seashells found him after the tide receded. He didn't. . . he didn't have—"

"He was missing an eye," Frank cut in, finishing what she couldn't.

"He was missing an eye?" Alex repeated, confused.

Frank nodded. "Scared the hell out of those kids. When the police showed up to question him, Jenkins kept insisting they took his friend."

"Who?"

"The sirens," Frank replied. His wife went still, and Alex swore he saw slight fear shadowed in her eyes. "Claims he was lured down to the ocean. Some guy named Mark or Matt or—"

"Max?"

"Yeah, that's it. Jenkins was hysterical. He demanded that the Coast Guard go out and search for his friend, and they did too. For an entire week, they went out looking for this man only to find out he didn't even exist. They wasted all those resources and the good people of Saltridge's time, and for what? A bad dream?" Frank gave a dismissive wave. "It's nice to know where my tax dollars are being spent."

"What about his eye?" Alex blinked, suddenly aware of his own. "Something must have attacked him if his clothes were torn, and he was missing an eye."

Shifting in his chair, Frank said, "A shark, a sea lion. . . hell, even a dolphin could have done that kind of damage. Who knows? The ocean is a dangerous place filled with many things that can and *will kill you.*"

"Afterwards, he started warning anyone who would listen about what he saw that night," said Wendy. "Showing up at people's houses, claiming that others were going missing too. That poor woman. . ."

"What woman?" Alex asked.

She bit her lip. The conversation was becoming uncomfortable for all of them, but Alex wanted to know—*needed to know.*

"There was a woman who used to live here a long time ago. I can't remember her name. She moved here shortly after her husband died. Nice lady, still young enough to start over and was trying to do just that when Jenkins started sniffing around," said Wendy.

Frank shook his head. "They should've locked him up after that."

His wife ignored him. "He harassed her for weeks—stalked her, really. Insisting that the sirens took her son. That they drowned him in the sea."

"What happened to her son?" Alex asked, not sure if he really wanted to know.

Wendy looked at him, her face haunted. "She didn't have one."

"He cornered her in a parking lot one day. Threatening her and causing a scene," Frank spoke up. "She moved out of Saltridge after that. Crazy asshole ran her out of town."

"Frank! Language!"

"Well, he is! And I'm not sorry about it!"

Alex considered this. Between the article and the couple's dealings with James, he had no choice but to acknowledge that Jenkins might be nothing more than a crazy old man with wild ideas.

There was disappointment—slight frustration—for his decision to come out here packed with nothing more than desperation. Still, the discovery in the attic said otherwise, and it nagged at him, pricking something below his skin. Crazy or not, Alex couldn't help but feel the need to see this through.

"Where's he at now?" Alex asked.

Frank hesitated. "He lives in an apartment nearby. As far as I know, he lives alone, but two other women live in the same building. I'll never understand how they put up with him." He jotted down the address on a napkin and handed it to Alex, who stood to shake his hand. "I doubt he'll be open to a visit, but I wish you luck all the same."

Alex gave him a tentative smile. "Thanks for dinner."

Frank's warm hand gripped his, and he gave Alex a heartfelt tug. "It was a pleasure having you," he said, the smile beneath his whiskered face, an honest one. "It's not often we're blessed with good company. All our children are grown and gone. Too busy with their own lives, I guess. I swear, you spend so much of your life raising these kids, only for them to abandon you the first chance they get."

It took everything Alex had in him not to vomit up the guilt rotting in his stomach. "I'm sure they'll visit soon," he replied simply.

Frank draped his arm over Wendy. "We'll see. They only call us when they want something, but that's kids for you. It's a nice thing you're doing for your dad. He was a lucky man, and I'm willing to bet he'd be proud."

Another blow. Another wound ripped open. Alex could hardly breathe.

"I appreciate that, sir," he admitted, trying to hide his unease. Steadying himself against the porch rail, he gave Frank an honest look. "But you're wrong. I was the lucky one."

CHAPTER TWELVE
Maeve

I'VE ALWAYS LIKED THE ocean best at night. During the day, it was welcoming—warm, polite, and beautiful. But at night, it was a different being—mysterious and full of unrelenting danger.

Shifting oneself like that is a powerful thing—the ultimate camouflage for all the dangerous creatures lurking underneath it.

I could see it from my bedroom window—not too far, but close enough, and it was as close as I could get. I could hear it singing—like light whispers on the breeze blowing off each swell as it crashed onto the shore. The words were faint and hollow, but I knew they were meant for me.

Down the hall, Charley groaned—a guttural sound as he hissed and growled at the soft and alluring voices laced within the wind. Despite his efforts to sound harsh, I knew the voices scared him. They scared me too.

The sun escaped an hour ago, but the richness of the moon and stars lit up the horizon, mirroring daylight. And from wherever he was hiding, it wasn't the cats hissing or moaning that dragged me from my window, but the unexpected vibration of my buzzing phone.

"Hey Maeve." The music and laughter barreling through the receiver muffled his voice, but I knew who it was and why he was calling.

For a split second, I wondered what would happen if I hung up. What would happen if I turned it off and, for once, allowed myself the luxury of not having to burden myself with my mother's problems.

But it wasn't about her. It was about what she might do, if I didn't step in.

Empathy is a double-edged sword I sometimes wanted to gut myself with.

"I'm on my way," I confirmed without him asking.

Grabbing my keys, I shuffled past Charley, still howling like a banshee in the night.

———•———

The thundering sound of bass rattled my dashboard the moment my tires kissed the parking lot. Outside the bar, a handful of people milled about, hidden behind plumes of cigarette smoke.

The Shell Shack, also known as the Hell Shack, illuminated the corner of the dead-end street in glowing neon lights. All the letters from its iconic sign except for the "S" shone vividly. It was unclear if Jim, the owner, was too broke to replace it or if he was using the latter as a cheap marketing ploy. Either way, it wasn't a far stretch from what lies beyond the heavy iron door and worn-out steel frame building.

During the winter, the shack was home to the most loyal locals—my mother included. During the summer, it managed to somehow cram both tourists, and residents into its questionably small space.

I passed through the crowded parking lot, groaning when I realized I needed to park in the overflow lot behind the abandoned mechanic shop across the street. It wasn't a far walk, but it was at the very end of the dead-end road, and the streetlight that used to flood the gravel clearing was burned out.

Two cars were parked on the far side of the street, and I made a point to park away from them. My own car might be a pile of rusted shit, but I still didn't want some drunk asshole hitting it on their way out.

Crossing the street, I slipped through the standing wall of people outside and pushed my way in through the crowd, catching sight of Jim behind the bar. A bachelorette party was swarmed around the front of it while the bride-to-be stumbled over her ridiculously high heels and shouted slurred demands at him for another round of shots.

From here, I could see Jim's tolerance wearing thin as he quickly poured tequila into seven shot glasses shaped like seashells.

"Tough night?" I shouted, leaning over the rail.

"The start of the season always is," he replied, popping the cap off a beer and sliding it over to a man seated next to me. The man grunted, tipped the bottle at me, then walked away.

Not wanting to waste any more time, I got straight to the point. "Where is she?"

Jim pointed at the stage where my mother stood, leaning half hazardously against a table. Her bright blonde hair shone like a beacon, bobbing up and down as her flamboyant and flirtatious advances toward the man beside her became increasingly aggressive.

"Thanks," I said, embarrassed. Jim nodded before moving on to the next group of people fighting for his attention.

We've been here before, and it won't be the last time I'll need to rescue my mother from his bar. At this point, it was expected, and he knew the drill. Call me—because nobody else will.

Focused on the stage, I wasn't paying attention to everyone around me when I suddenly felt strong hands grip my shoulder. I whirled around to see gray eyes staring back at me. I recognized those eyes—had taunted them a few days ago.

"There you are!" He shouted over the harsh noise.

"Here I am," I said, confused. I looked around for his wife but didn't see her. I wondered if she even knew he was here.

Mitch smiled, and I could see the reflection of myself in his glossy eyes. "I've been looking for you."

"You have?"

His lips twisted into a sly smirk. "Of course. You're the most beautiful woman in the room."

"Does that always work for you?" I asked, tilting my head. I shouldn't have engaged, but the words slipped out before I could suck them back in.

"I don't know. Does it?" He laughed, running a nervous hand through his dirty blonde hair, unruly from the humidity—a starch difference from the man who'd stumbled into Captains a few mornings ago.

"Sorry, not this time," I replied.

This is why I hated coming here. Never mind the over-priced drinks and the stench of stale sweat mixed with cheap booze. But because it was a prime hunting ground for unwanted attention.

Eager to get the hell out of there, I took a step forward, but he stepped in front of me, blocking me between himself and several other people.

"Well, in that case, let me buy you a drink to make up for it."

"What about your wife?" I asked pointedly. I was getting annoyed. I tried forcing my way around him again, but he was much larger than me, and I was quickly sucked back into the small space between us.

"Wife?" He asked. "Oh, you mean my fiancé," Mitch replied smoothly as if that made a difference. "She's back at the hotel, probably sleeping off a valium cocktail." He took a hearty sip from his glass. "Tell you what. You let me buy you a drink, have a little conversation, maybe a dance, and I promise I'll leave you alone the rest of the night."

I didn't believe him. "Thanks, but no thanks," I said. Any hint of politeness I afforded him earlier was now gone. "I'm getting ready to leave." Again, I tried to walk away, and again, he cut me off.

My head was swimming, and the heat from everyone around me was suffocating. I needed to get out of here. I needed fresh air.

"Come on," he crooned. "It's just one drink. You've got time for one, don't you?" He was on top of me now, and the pungent stench of body odor mixed with whatever cologne he'd doused himself in was overwhelming.

I closed my eyes. It was all I could do to keep myself from throwing up, and I begged that thing inside me to stir.

Dead silence.

There were no moans, no aches, or sinister whispers. My stomach churned, and the atmosphere around me swayed like a ship bouncing on a violent sea.

"Actually, I don't," I growled. I was doing my best to ease my breathing and, if anything, keep myself from passing out. God, it was so hot in here. . .

Mitch opened his mouth to argue, but a colorful string of curse words came flooding out instead when someone stumbled into him, causing him to spill his drink. This was my chance. Distracted, I shot past him.

The only thing I wanted to do was grab my mother and get the fuck out of here.

When I finally reached her, she was pressed against someone, and I was out of breath from fighting the crowd. My raven hair was sticky and matted against my flushed skin.

Her face lit up when she saw me, and the blotchy patches on her cheeks told me that she'd far surpassed her limit.

"Maeve!" She squealed—her voice slurred. Using the man as a crutch, she tried sitting up but lost her balance and fell over instead.

"Is she alright?" Someone asked as I struggled to pull her off the floor. My mother was howling with laughter as if this was a big joke.

"She's fine," I grumbled, still holding onto her. Getting her into my car was going to be a pain in the ass.

I'd barely got her standing when she flung her arms around my neck.

"It's time to go," I said, pulling her away. I didn't want to go down with her if she toppled over again.

With my hands secured around her arms, she looked at me. Her deep emerald eyes were distant and dilated. "No," she said.

No? It was hard to hear anything between the thumping of my heart pounding in my ears and the roar of the music blasting through the speakers. "What do you mean no?"

Her friend, whom she was holding onto earlier, invited himself into the conversation. "I think what she means is, she doesn't want to leave."

"I know what she meant!" I snapped. "Can we talk?" I asked her, my eyes flickering to him. "Alone?"

Ignoring me, she collapsed into his lap and for a second I contemplated kicking the chair out from underneath them.

"Whatever you have to say, you can say in front of Greg," she hiccuped.

Greg?

With his overly round face, receding hairline, and beady dark eyes, Greg looked like the kind of guy who sold used cars for a living. Not gently used either, but the kind where the mileage was high, and the undercarriage was rusting out.

"Mom. . ." I started slowly.

"Maeve, honey—what have I said about calling me that in public?"

My heart became a heavy rock in my chest as she let out a nervous laugh, waiting for me to correct myself.

With his sausage-like fingers around her waist, Greg laughed along with her—blissfully unaware of the tension between us.

"*Anna*—" I spit through clenched teeth, but she cut me off.

"Look around you Maevey. We're trying to have a good time. Come, sit, have a drink, and try not to be a buzzkill."

All around us, people were dancing and grinding into each other. One man had his tongue shoved so far down a girl's throat, I was sure she was choking on it. I pulled at my shirt. The airless room smelled sour, and the noise was so loud I couldn't hear myself think.

Blinking through the sweat dripping into my eyes, I forced a smile. Then, without warning, I snatched a shot glass off a cocktail waitress's tray, tilted my head back, and swallowed. It burned the back of my throat, taking all the effort I had not to gag it back up.

Vodka—I hated vodka.

Shaking the disgust from my face, I slammed the glass back on the table in front of her. "There. Can we go now?"

The music hummed in the background as we stared daringly at each other. Neither of us moved. And I knew she was trying to figure out what this was, why I had come here, into her space, to take what was hers.

"Please let me take you home," I begged one more time.

She opened her mouth to answer, but it was Greg who spoke. "She doesn't want to leave. Now take a hint and go away."

I shot him a withering stare. Anger stacked itself like bricks inside my throat, and my face went red as pure outrage filled my mouth. Glancing between them, I focused on my mother, waiting for her to respond—to defend me, to tell him that I was her daughter and that he wasn't allowed to speak to me like that.

But she didn't. Instead, she shrugged and fell back into his chest.

"Fine!" My voice was sharp and full of fire. "You know what? Stay here. Go home with him. I don't care anymore."

Even if she didn't care, I wanted her to feel it. I wanted her to feel the rage that was boiling in my gut like acid. I wanted her to know that what I had to say next, I meant.

"I don't care what happens to you anymore."

Then I stormed out.

CHAPTER THIRTEEN
Maeve

IT WAS RAINING—A SOFT drizzle that misted in the wind as I stalked back to my car. The overcast sky darkened the dismal night, making it harder to see. Both vehicles parked earlier were gone, leaving mine the only one in the empty lot.

Slamming the door, I shoved the key into the ignition, cursing when the engine whined but didn't turn over.

"Shit!" I yelled, slamming my hands against the steering wheel. I tried again. "Please, please, please," I begged, but it refused.

Stepping into the rain, I popped the hood and leaned in to see if I could find the problem. Not that it would have mattered—I wouldn't have known how to fix it anyway. I'd hardly managed to keep it running on a good day, and I didn't know how to change a tire.

Growing up without a father really weighs on you in moments like this.

Fidgeting with the fluid caps, my shirt became soaked as I huddled half underneath the hood. Behind me, footsteps crunched against the gravel, and I was relieved that someone bothered to help.

"Car trouble?" His voice sent a cool shiver down my spine. The rain on my back felt like ice, and the hair on the back of my neck stood up straight. I whirled around to see Mitch ambling towards me.

The faint glow across the street uncurled like a dark shadow alongside him—adding a nefarious undertone to the feline grin slowly spreading across his face.

My heart thumped rapidly, and I wondered if he could hear it too as he quickly closed the space between us.

"Want me to take a look?" His eyes traveled from my face down over my chest, where my wet shirt had become translucent. His eyes turned dark, and I swallowed.

"No thanks, I've got it handled."

Mitch rubbed his chin and leaned over me with one hand on the hood and the other at his side.

"Doesn't look like you do." His voice was smooth, filled with predatory confidence. It coiled around me, settling over my skin and seeping into my pores, making me shiver.

"I can fix it," he said, sucking his teeth. "But it'll cost you."

The overbearing weight of the situation hit me then, and I willed my feet to move. But he was fast, and his fingers gripped my wrist so tight I thought it would snap in half.

Mitch whipped me towards him and shoved me against the car—the warmth of his mouth on mine before I could cry out.

His tongue grazed the roof of my mouth and then edged along my teeth. I tried biting down, but he held me by the throat, forcing my mouth open while he used his other free hand to walk his fingers beneath my shirt.

I could feel the roughness of them as he rubbed his palms over the front of my breasts, and I groaned. Not from pleasure but from the weight of him against me. A sound he mistook for wanting, and it caused him to push harder into me—forcing the thickness of his bulging cock into my thighs.

I flattened my hands against the car for leverage, but the metal was slick from the rain, and they slipped, so I hit him instead. I clawed desperately at his chest—at his face. I tried pulling his hair, but that only made things worse.

With his hand wrapped around my throat, he removed his other hand from my shirt and shoved it into my shorts. I tried crossing my legs, but he slipped his own between my knees, forcing them apart. The tips of his fingers edged along my entrance and there was nothing I could do as he slowly inserted them.

"Someone wants to play," he grinned against my mouth.

The wetness of me puddled between my legs as he worked his way inside me—my body's way of preparing itself for the brutal reality of what I was about to face.

Working to unfasten the button on his jeans, his mouth pulled away from mine, and I let out a blood-curdling scream before he clamped a hand back over it. Nobody would hear me anyway. Not over the loud music pulsing and echoing from across the street. Not in this empty parking lot where we were hidden—two shadows camouflaged in the night.

I went limp, focusing on the gold watch wrapped around his wrist while I waited for the inevitable. I wanted to disappear, wanted to evaporate into thin air, but all I could do was let this man take me—let him do what he wanted while I silently begged for it to be over.

If I didn't fight it, maybe it would go quickly. Maybe I wouldn't feel it if I drifted somewhere else. So I started counting the links on his watch.

One . . . Two . . . Three . . .

My body was shutting down. I figured I had about five seconds before he claimed me.

Four . . . Five . . . Six . . .

It was taking longer than I thought, or maybe it just felt that way. Risking a glance, I saw he was still fumbling with his zipper. It was stuck on the cloth of his jeans.

I didn't wait. Lifting my leg and using all the force I could muster, I forced my knee into him—hard. I expected him to stumble back, to stagger in incredible pain, but I missed my target and hit him in the thigh instead.

"You bitch!" He roared.

His knuckles cracked against my face, and I spun around—away from him, the force of the blow propelling me into the side of the car. My knees buckled, and I crumpled to the ground. My vision blurred, and the warm trickle of blood dripped from my nose and into my mouth. I swayed, my vision vignetting as I struggled to keep myself upright. The vodka I'd shot back earlier burned in my gut like fire, and I could feel it making its way back up.

Bracing myself, I waited for him to finish what he started, but he never did. Instead, I heard a loud thud, followed by shouting. I couldn't see—those tiny stars were now a giant cloud. My head was pounding, my stomach—sour, and I could no longer hold myself up. My shoulders softened the fall, but my head hitting the ground made a loud "pop."

Then everything went black.

Chapter Fourteen
Alex

ALEX WANTED TO WAIT until the next day to meet with Jenkins. If he was as crazy as everyone said, confronting him in the middle of the night might not have been a good idea.

Still, he felt restless.

Allowing his forlorn thoughts to drift away, Alex decided to walk through the quiet streets of Saltridge.

He hadn't visited the ocean yet, but that didn't matter—the whole town seemed blessed with a seaside view. The tide was in, and even though Alex wasn't afraid of the water, his nightmares were enough to make him feel uneasy as he ignored the sound of crashing waves in the distance.

With his eyes adjusting quickly, he walked down the empty streets, where manicured lawns and quaint little houses quickly blended into buildings and storefronts. Staring into the dark windows of each store, Alex laughed as he passed by. This place reeked of charm, of innocence, and purity—none of which was real, despite how convincing it seemed. Behind the showcased appeal, he knew better. Places like this were always hiding something, but he wasn't here to uncover whatever sinister secrets Saltridge may, or may not be harboring.

"Not my pasture, not my bullshit," his father used to say. The words rang hollow in his ears as he made his way out of downtown and towards the western side of the city with the ocean at his back.

The buildings tapered off here, and a more squalid side of town took shape. Empty lots with abandoned buildings where rusted tin roofs stood silhouetted in the night—the side of town Saltridge didn't want you to see. The side where all the misfits most likely gathered. Alex stalked silently in the shadows with his hands shoved deep inside his pockets. He wasn't worried about wandering through here, considering he'd spent most of his career wading through the underbelly of society.

At some point, it started raining—a drizzle that dampened his skin through his shirt, and Alex shook away the biting cold it left in it's wake. He loved this kind of weather. Most people tended to avoid it, but not him. He embraced it—it gave him more time to think.

While he wandered, so did his thoughts, meandering between nonsense and other more intrusive things.

Diego, Lucy, his parents—all people he'd disappointed out of selfishness. He thought his loss would have been enough to force him to do better. But here he was, the same old Alex—the same man who couldn't see past his own gratification. He didn't need to prove anything to anyone—no one was left to prove anything to, but he couldn't let the disappointment go. The one that crept in every night and stripped him bare, revealing all the wounds he'd left open to rot and fester.

There were no sidewalks here, forcing him to walk in the middle of the road. The streetlights were few and far between, but up ahead, Alex could make out the glow of neon lights bouncing off a building.

As he approached, he recognized the sound of music spilling out onto the street, hardly contained by the small structure it emanated from. Alex wasn't surprised to find that out of all the things Saltridge lacked, a sleazy bar wasn't one of them.

His need for a drink was vicious, but his body groaned in exhausted protest. Besides, the last time he'd been out at the bar, it ended with him between the legs of a woman whose intentions went much farther than his own. He didn't want to risk another encounter like that again. Not tonight, anyway.

Keeping out of sight, he turned to walk back the same way he came, but a shout into the night stopped him. It might have come from the bar, from a drunk woman having fun, but Alex wasn't sure.

Peering over his shoulder, he caught sight of a man sucking on the end of a cigarette near the bar, but the pitch of that scream definitely came from a woman.

With bated breath, he waited. If she cried out again, Alex needed to know which direction it had come from. There was nothing wrong with someone shouting into the night, but in Alex's experience, it usually meant something was wrong.

Sticking to the shadows, he wandered over to the empty lot across from the bar. From what he could tell, it was an auto shop—though the gaping hole in the front glass window hinted it had been out of business for quite some time.

Inching closer, Alex hoped he'd just been hearing things. But optimism is a fickle thing, and as he reared the building's side, he realized the empty lot wasn't empty after all.

There was one car parked in the gravel, a rusted light blue sedan on the opposite end of a burnt-out streetlight. From his hiding place, he crouched down, surveying the two shadows pressed up against the vehicle.

Assuming this was nothing more than a consensual tryst fueled by intoxication, he started walking away—until she cried out again, this time in pain, and Alex whirled around just in time to see the guy's fist cut across her face.

He didn't hesitate, he broke into a silent run, tackling the asshole who didn't see him until Alex was already on top of him.

Dust and dirt rose into the air, forcing Alex to inhale the gritty sift as they struggled against one another. The man was scrawny but fast, and it took Alex several minutes to subdue him.

"Get the—fuck off—me," he grunted with his face pressed into the dirt as Alex twisted the man's arms, pinning his wrists behind his back.

Ignoring him, Alex struggled to free his phone from his pocket. He was careful to keep his fingers secured around the man's wrists, but the band from the guys watch kept sliding between his hands, and Alex yanked it down to get a better grip.

"Hey, watch it!" The man struggled—his voice strained with the weight of Alex pressing down on him. "That's a Rolex—a link costs more than your life."

"Shut up," Alex said, suppressing the urge to knock him out.

He hated guys like this—rich assholes who felt entitled to do whatever they wanted at the expense of someone else. Anger surged through him. If Alex wasn't already racked with personal guilt, he'd have half a mind to take the damn thing from him. It wouldn't matter—he probably had a dozen more lying around.

Once Alex secured him, he called it in. After a brief conversation with dispatch, he was surprised when a white pickup truck pulled in minutes later. He lifted the suspect off the ground, forcing him to move his feet. The man's blonde hair was caked in dirt and matted to his reddened face.

"You Hayworth?" Asked the deputy who'd stepped out of the cab. He was dressed in street clothes and had nothing more than a "Saltridge Police" hat to identify him.

"Yes sir," Alex said, handing him over. Once the cuffs were on, he flashed his badge.

"Detective huh?" Alex nodded. This *was not* how he wanted to be introduced to the local department.

The officer looked around, eyeing the scene. "And I'm supposed to believe that you just happened to be out here when all this occurred?" Alex knew what he was implying.

"Right place, right time officer—"

"*Sheriff Thompson*," he corrected immediately.

"Sheriff Thompson," Alex repeated. "I assure you that my presence here is nothing more than a coincidence. I was out for a walk when I heard someone scream. When I went to check it out, I witnessed this asshole trying to force himself on her." Alex pointed toward the woman still slumped over a few yards away. By now, a crowd had formed, and someone ran over to help her.

Thompson looked at the suspect, who glared menacingly at Alex. Blood trickled down his nose, and his eyebrow was swollen. "This how you do things where you're from?" He asked.

Alex shook his head. "I didn't have cuffs, and he was fighting me pretty good."

Thompson looped his fingers in his belt and nodded. "Alright, I'll take him and book him. Try not to make this a habit while you're here, you understand?"

The condescending tone in his voice made Alex cringe. He couldn't pull rank, but that didn't mean he needed to stand here and listen to this idiot lecture him on how to behave. By the looks of him, the sheriff didn't seem to take his title seriously—his overinflated ego was much larger than his expanding waistline seemed to suggest.

"I'll need a quick statement before you go," said Thompson.

"What about her?" Alex asked.

At some point, the woman managed to pull herself up.

The sheriff followed his gaze. "She looks alright to me."

"She looks *alright* to you? With all due respect officer—"

"Sheriff."

"*Sheriff*," Alex bit out reluctantly. "She was just assaulted in a parking lot. I'd think her statement would weigh a little heavier than mine, don't you think?"

The rain was heavier now, and the chill in the air nipped his skin, but it wasn't the cold that made Alex shake. Anger swelled inside him like a balloon, ready to pop.

"And with all due respect to you, Mr. Hayworth—"

"*Detective*," Alex smirked. He couldn't help but be a little petty.

Thompson stared down his reddened nose. "Which department did you say you were out of again?"

"I didn't," Alex said, his fists clenched at his sides.

"That's right. Well detective, I don't know how you do things where you're from, but around here, we do them a little differently. Maeve knows where the stations at. If she wants to come in and make a statement, she's more than welcome to do so."

Maeve. Her name pulsed on Alex's tongue. He opened his mouth to object but thought better of it. As much as he hated to admit it, the sheriff was right. This wasn't his town—it wasn't his jurisdiction. And even though all of this felt very wrong, Alex wasn't in a position to argue.

Across the lot, an engine roared to life, and the small car started making its way through the crowd. Behind the shadows of the dark windshield, Alex strained to make out her face but couldn't. All he could see were her bright blue eyes, moving like two glaciers in the night.

Thompson followed behind her, and the crowd finally dispersed.

Alex sighed. *So much for a fucking vacation.*

Chapter Fifteen
Maeve

I could taste the gritty texture of gravel in my mouth. I could feel the damp puddle of rain, or maybe it was blood—soaked into my hair and crusted over my skin.

"Are you ok?"

The silhouette of someone hovering over me made me flinch. My vision was blurry, and it hurt to blink. My entire face was hot and tender.

"He gave you one hell of a blow," said the silhouette.

I couldn't make out his features. My brain was a mess of fog and confusion.

I tried sitting up but couldn't, when suddenly, the pressure of strong hands wrapped around my arms, and I recoiled—my voice a hoarse cry as I yelped into the night. Backing against the cool metal of my car, the horrific memory of what happened became clear.

Flashes of his hands against my throat, under my shirt.

His hands between my legs...

Whatever confusion I'd felt earlier was now replaced by fear.

"Whoa," said the stranger, pulling away. "Take it easy. You're ok."

I blinked several times—trying to clear away the rain and dirt and the disorientation as the defined edges of the man who knelt before me started taking shape. I recognized him as one of the Shell Shacks bouncers. His name was Victor, but everyone called him Vegas.

Sliding my hands over my legs, I prayed for the hopeful comfort of knowing my jeans were still around my waist.

Understanding what I was searching for, Vegas caught my gaze. "He didn't have the chance," he assured me.

I nodded. Tears swelled in my eyes, and I blinked them back against the pain.

"Thank you," I said—my voice cracked and broken.

He smiled painfully. "As much as I'd like to take credit for kicking that guy's ass, I'm not the one who found you." He gestured towards the opposite end of the parking lot where another stranger stood, chatting with the sheriff. "Thank him, he's the one who stepped in before. . ." the rest fell away, and Vegas swallowed. "He's the one who saved you."

My head started aching, a dull throb that would become a raging headache by morning. Through the commotion, a crowd gathered, people from the bar who'd come to gawk.

"Is there someone I can call for you?" Vegas asked. I shook my head, knowing my mother was too drunk to give a shit. "If you want, I can take you home," he tried again. I knew he meant well, but I declined anyway.

"I can drive," I assured him, hoisting myself up slowly. A sudden rush of blood to my head made me dizzy, and I staggered.

Vegas stared at me, concern rippling across his face. "Are you sure? Maybe you should get checked out, just to be safe."

"I'm fine," I insisted, forcing myself away from him and into the car. I offered him a smile, but it came out painful and halfhearted.

He said something, but whatever it was became lost over the roar of the engine.

Of-fucking-course.

I couldn't help it—I made a crude gesture at the universe for its dark and insidious humor. Everyone's heads turned at the sound, and as I crept along, I caught a glimpse of the man who'd stepped in.

What had he seen? Did he think I deserved it?

Maybe I did.

He was facing me now, cloaked within the night, but I managed to catch his eyes. I didn't know if he could see me, but I held mine there anyway—a silent thank you before finally driving away.

Heading home—towards safety—I cracked my windows so the night air would drift in and soothe me. Outside, the ocean screamed, and the creature inside me whispered painful thoughts.

You're only a victim if you allow yourself to be.

———·———

That night, I dreamt of dark places tinted with iridescent light shining through the crags of dark trenches. They cratered into the sea like giant pillars disappearing into the endless hollow below. Pure obscurity. That's what waited for me down there. A place devoid of light and life that sent an icy shiver down my spine within the tepid water.

It called to me—that void—and I couldn't help but allow its weight to pull me in. Its claws wrapped around my ankles as I fell into its depths.

Like prey to a predator, willing to be devoured.

Light rippled above the water, slowly fading away as the trenches surrounding me thickened, the darkness becoming heavier. When the light disappeared, there was nothing. Only me and the seeping blackness suspended in nihility.

There was a pureness to it—something free and exhilarating. I could spread out and feel my limbs moving through the syrupy water, thick from the pressure of being so deep, yet I was weightless.

I don't know how long I drifted there, a speck in the void of nothingness. I didn't care. I felt free, felt at ease amongst the obscurity as I floated more profoundly into the hungry mouth of the ocean. Soon, specks of light glowed beneath me. Like city lights, they twinkled, shining through the seaweed and unseen things lurking there.

Silted dust shimmered as my feet met the smoothness of the sea floor, and I realized those lights were not lights at all—but bioluminescence radiating from the creatures dwelling here. In my presence, they swarmed, tucking themselves within the floating strands of my hair that swirled around me like black ink. Reaching out to touch them, they glowed like fireflies on a moonless night before drifting away and out of sight.

Once again, I was alone, enveloped in the dark as one by one, those lights vanished, and there was nothing left but me—me and the sea and the soft sound of that same melody calling to that dark thing inside me.

It burned my skin, hot and acidic and bitter. I could feel it slither and twist between my bones, forcing its way into my throat—filling my mouth with a cloud of heavy, endless smoke. I tried to swallow it away and root my feet against its will, but it compelled me forward. I was no longer my own. This harbored entity and I were one.

It dragged me across the ocean floor into the open mouth of a cavern hidden below the trenches, where the soft and endless melody increased. Like an army of voices, it echoed off coral-encrusted walls. The harmonious inflections sung by soft feminine voices—alluring and serene.

Come with me, oh dreamer, to a land below the sea, past the depths of darkness where light and water meet.

I panicked. The foot of the cave, where that unseen force beckoned us, vanished. I begged it, that thing inside me, as I desperately clawed at the cavern walls before being tossed over the ledge. I tried screaming, but no sound came out. No taste of salty sea burned my tongue. Only air filled my lungs. A breeze in a windless place.

Lie down, oh weary traveler in sugared sand and shimmering gold. Abate yourself with haste and release the demons that you hold.

The lyrics carried us, cradling us with their harmonious sound as we danced along the airy current before finally being set free. The monster in me groaned, throbbing at each lilt, begging to be untethered, as if it too, remembered the words and wished to sing along.

Sit with me, oh lover, and hear me while I sing. A song for many men, not a single one a king.

Thousands of glow worms dripped from the rocky ceiling. It was a separate room, a dug-out hole where a pocket of air was separated from the murky water. A magnificent waterfall sat at the entrance, where the ocean floor disappeared, so blue and clear it looked like crushed diamonds.

Come with me, oh dreamer, back up to the shore. For what you saw today was nothing more than lore.

I hummed along with it, my voice—*its voice* matching with theirs as peace settled over me. It was unleashed now, that wicked monster inside my soul, and now it was home.

In the center of the hollow cavern sat a glistening chasm, a separate lake carved in between the rocky white ledges where those beautiful voices radiated. Gliding over to it, I couldn't take my eyes off the shimmering water spilling into this pool of endless beauty. It was intoxicating, and I was desperate to be in it.

It was like bathing in pure ecstasy.

My head bobbed freely while the rest of my body disappeared underneath—too calm to care as it rippled with movement. Their presence welcomed me. As if they'd been waiting.

Around me, the song grew louder—higher pitched, shifting from a beautiful symphony to a desperate scream.

We were separate now, me and my bounded demon. It disappeared, blending into the voices that screeched and cried and begged. Moving my body, I scrambled to get out. Every part of me knew I was in danger, but it was too late.

Their hands wrapped around my feet—the roughness of them, rubbing raw against my skin as they pulled me beneath the surface. I thrashed against them, opening my mouth to scream, but nothing filled my lungs. Not air, not anything except the stale taste of something I couldn't place right away.

I thought it was the bitterness of salt, but quickly understood the coppery tang and thick texture. Once clear and crystal blue, the water was now syrupy and sinful red. *Blood.*

Through its denseness, I was able to make out sudden movements—swift and calculated as they cut through the murky claret like sharp steel. I stopped fighting, forcing myself to still as I strained to see, and what I saw sent an icy shiver down my spine.

Several pairs of almond-shaped black eyes, the color of onyx and devoid of light—peered back at me. Two small slits, where their noses should have been, were centered above gaping mouths filled with hundreds of needle-like teeth. They were serrated along the edges that jutted out over loose lips. And when they smiled, those lips stretched menacingly across their faces, touching where their ears should have been—but weren't.

Their bodies, moss green and slicked in scales, were thin but powerful as they propelled themselves with mighty tails the size of boulders. Some of them had hair the color of ebony—as sunless as their eyes, they left inky black trails behind them. Others bore the color of spun silk, and the rest—the same hue as the crimson blood they swam in. All bore spindly fingers tightly webbed together.

Abruptly, the singing stopped. And only the eerie sound of silence lingered between us.

Then, one by one, they halted, forming a narrow circle around me. Slowly, they tightened, pressing their scaled bodies against mine as if to crush me. Hundreds were now compacted into a tight death circle, gaping mouths opened wide as if to swallow me whole. Their stout aroma was overwhelming as they pushed themselves against me—like rotting fish and briny sea. I wasn't sure if I was melting into them or they were melting into me.

The edges of my vision darkened, and I began to lose consciousness. The sound of their song started again—a vociferous chant breaking my eardrums and slithering into my skull.

I was called down here to free my darkness—the one I'd lived with for as long as I've known life. As it stared back at me, its own separate being, it laughed as it watched its brethren split me open. One by one, they poured themselves into me, ripping me apart with their serrated teeth and webbed claws.

Slicing through my flesh with their sharp scales, they tore my limbs apart and snapped my bones in half. As I thrashed, and kicked and screamed, the one that lived inside of me placed its mouth over mine—inhaling the very soul from what was left of my mortal body.

Everything went dark, and I woke up screaming with my monster still cradled inside me.

CHAPTER SIXTEEN
Maeve

A PAIR OF YELLOW eyes glinted at me from across the room, followed by a threatening moan as I rose onto my elbows.

A nightmare. Another one. Under me, the bed was soaked, and the tips of my fingers felt numb as I searched for something to cover myself with. I'd kicked the blankets off the bed, and they rested on the floor in a tangled mess—a reminder that I wasn't safe, even at night, in my own bed.

Then it all came flooding back—the bar, the rain, Mitch's fingers wedged greedily between my legs, hungry for something that wasn't his.

Steadying myself against the sudden flow of blood rushing to my head, I lifted a finger to my face and winced. I didn't need to look at it to know it was a swollen mess. My head throbbed, aching like it was split open, and I whimpered as I pushed myself off the bed.

"Whoa," I mumbled, stumbling back. The air around me felt constricting, knocking the very breath from my lungs.

Everything hurt. My face, my hair, even my throat burned. I could still feel his fingers inside me—stroking me with his mouth pressed against mine. It made me feel dirty, used, and broken.

Stepping over the blankets, I made a beeline for the bathroom. I didn't want to look at myself, at the reminder of what happened to me, but I needed a shower.

I *needed* to feel clean.

The ceiling fan hummed when I turned on the light, and I immediately shut it off—its simple thrumming reminded me too much of the buzz of neon lights. The same kind at the bar last night. The same kind that drifted into the parking lot as he walked his fingers beneath my shirt.

Not wanting to shower in the dark, I removed the lamp from my nightstand and plugged it into the outlet by the sink. The light bounced off the mirror, casting a haunting glow over the sudden trauma taking shape across my face.

My once unsullied skin was now inked in black and blue, and purple hues. It spiderwebbed across my face, and every time I blinked, pain consumed me like a vice.

Fuck.

Distinct red outlines stretched across my neck where his fingers had gripped me—bright and vibrant and angry against my pale throat.

Fuck. Fuck. Fuck.

I wanted to cry. I wanted to scream and shout and sob, but I was afraid it would hurt, so I traded it in for anger instead. Anger at myself. Anger at the piece of shit who did this to me.

Anger at my mother.

In the end, it was his choice to follow me out of the bar. It was his choice to try and take what was mine, to try and force himself inside me. But she was the one who was truly responsible. If it wasn't for her, I wouldn't have been there to begin with. If she had just listened and had agreed to come home with me, he wouldn't have attacked me in the first place.

I shook my head to clear it, ignoring the pain pulsing against my temples. It might have been over, but now I had this branded reminder to haunt me for as long as it chose to stay.

My skin itched, and I pulled myself away from the mirror, away from the ghost staring back at me.

Stepping into the shower, I cranked the handle over, hoping the scalding heat would melt away my shame. I rubbed my skin until it was raw. I tried to get clean, but it was no use. It didn't matter how much I scrubbed—the filth I felt was on the inside. I scoured myself until I was bleeding—until my flesh was red and angry, and even then, I still felt dirty.

So, I gave up. Despite the rising heat outside, I dressed in loose-fitting pants tied tight around my waist and opted for a heavy sweater. I didn't want to afford anyone a glimpse of what was hidden underneath because then they too, would steal away a piece of me.

As I entered the kitchen, Charley was sitting on the couch by the window. In all the years I've owned him, he's never come near me. A few feet—maybe, but that's as close as he's ever come.

I didn't like cats, but my empathetic shortcomings have bound us together.

Empathy, and *something else.*

Licking his large paw, Charley glowered at me before abandoning his post. It was a silent threat, an implied warning that if he wasn't fed soon, there would be consequences.

I rolled my eyes at him. "I should let you starve."

He huffed what I could only describe as a sigh.

I read somewhere once that cats will eat their owners if faced with starvation. And as I watched Charley slowly rage with hunger, his plump body resting against the floor, I did not doubt that he'd already considered this—if he wasn't plotting it already.

We have an unspoken agreement. A boundary we both don't cross and have successfully managed to maintain the last few years. I feed him, and he doesn't kill me in my sleep. It's a straightforward arrangement, or at least I think so. Still, there have been plenty of nights where I've woken up and found him waiting in the shadows. His golden eyes fixed on me in pure hatred.

With a look of defiance, he jumped onto the counter—his face smug and challenging.

"You know you're not supposed to be up there," I scolded. But he ignored me anyway, stiffening his legs and flattening his paws just to make a point.

Rummaging through the cabinets, I snatched the last remaining can of food from the shelf and peeled away the tin lid. Gagging, I slopped the milky mixture into Charley's dish, and he whined. I didn't blame him—I wouldn't want to eat it either. He glared at the bowl, snarled, and flexed his claws.

"Eat it or starve," I said, setting it down in front of from him.

Giving up, he forced his face into the bowl, noisily licking away the food he deemed himself too worthy of—his grey tufted fur quickly tangling in his meal.

While he ate, I took stock of the kitchen, realizing the cabinets were filled with more dust than food. I couldn't remember the last time I went shopping since I usually ate at work. I wasn't much of a cook, so keeping a full pantry seemed like a waste. Still, standing in the middle of the meager kitchen, something about the bare-boned cupboards felt depressing, and I realized I should at least make it look like I lived here.

Leaving Charley to his vices, I returned to the bedroom. Early rays of morning sun splashed through the open curtains. I'd never slept with them closed, never slept with the door shut tight. I hated the dark—was terrified of it. It made me feel hopeless and confined—tethered to that thing lurking inside me.

Light pooled onto the beryl sheets still entwined in a heap on the floor. I didn't have the energy to move them. I didn't have the energy to do anything right now.

Falling back onto the bed, I stared at the ceiling, counting each line and notch in the plaster as I inhaled slowly. When I released it, a tear slid down my cheek, then another, then two more until I was undone. Crossing my hands over my stomach, I shuttered against each sob, trying to keep myself from spilling out.

I'd been so careful, *so guarded*, and yet, somehow, I still ended up here. It didn't matter how terrible Mitch was or how it could have happened to anyone—it didn't matter because it happened *to me.*

Vulnerable and broken, I wiped the tears from my face and sat up. Grabbing my phone with a heavy sigh, I ignored the disappointment that washed over me as I realized I still hadn't heard from my mother.

Either she didn't know what happened, or she didn't care.

I didn't want to leave the comfort of my bed, much less be forced to face the outside world, looking like a bruised peach, but it was inevitable—either face the world now or succumb to it later.

Slipping on sandals, I pulled my hair into a loose braid before giving myself a once-over in the mirror and making my way to the front door. I looked like shit, but I didn't care. I was ready to face whatever looks, stares, and whispers that were sure to be thrown my way.

Sucking in a breath, I opened the door, and that very breath caught in my throat. Standing on the other side, staring back at me, was the man from the bar.

Chapter Seventeen
Alex

THE ADDRESS FRANK HAD given him was only a few blocks from their house. After last night, he'd contemplated leaving, but Alex couldn't stop thinking about the woman he'd rescued. Every time he closed his eyes, he saw her.

He wondered if she was ok. He wondered if she'd made it home alright, even though he'd watched her leave.

Maeve. Her name glazed over his tongue.

Stop it, he thought to himself.

He hadn't even *seen her*—not really. Yet those eyes, the ones that danced in the dark as she passed by—they lured him in like a lost boy.

Alex shook his head to clear it. It was the seventh time he'd done so that morning, and it wouldn't be the last. He needed to focus. He needed to get his mind right and his story straight before confronting Jenkins.

Frank and Wendy's allegations about the man were not surprising, and honestly, he wasn't sure what to expect as he made his way across the street toward the dismal brick building. It sat alone, flanked by nothing but road and jutted cliffs.

Armed with only rumors, Alex looked around and swallowed the ball of nerves forming in his gut. Experience warned him to be cautious. Once inside, he realized Frank hadn't specified which unit Jenkins lived in. With four to choose from, he wasn't sure which was his.

He started with the one on his left—at the very least, they could point him in the right direction. So, with a heavy knock, Alex stepped back and waited.

The air in his lungs evaporated as light from the hallway fell onto the woman standing before him. Gawking like an idiot, Alex took in her sable hair, particularly the loose strands that brushed against her pale skin like inky tendrils. Her eyes—the same ones he'd seen last night—peered out at him from beneath impossibly long lashes.

"Can I help you?" Maeve asked, her voice trembling.

He could tell she'd been crying. Her face was swollen and red against the trauma glaring back at him.

"You should eat some pineapple," he said.

Nice job, idiot—he thought.

"What?" Maeve asked, tilting her head slightly.

Alex cleared his throat. "For your. . ." He pointed to the bruise on her face, and she wilted a little. "Cayenne pepper works too, but if you get it in your eyes, you'll be in more pain than you already are. Pineapple is safer. It tastes better too."

Alex knew he was rambling, coughing up random advice she didn't ask for, but he couldn't help it—he was nervous, *she made him nervous.*

Maeve stared at him awkwardly. "I'm sorry, I'm confused. Are you asking me if I want a pineapple?"

Alex's cheeks flushed. He'd let himself get caught off guard, suddenly distracted by how her mouth moved—at the way her pillowy lips pulled up in the corners when she spoke.

"Uh, no, sorry," he chuckled nervously. "I'm actually looking for someone. A man by the name of James Jenkins. I take it you're not him."

"Not I'm not," she said, moving to tuck herself back inside.

Before he could stop himself, Alex stuck his boot out to keep her from slamming the door in his face. "I'm Alex, by the way. Alex Hayworth." He was overstepping by a lot but he couldn't seem to reel it in.

Maeve inclined her head towards the second floor. "Jenkins lives upstairs, apartment 2a."

Alex waited for her to say more, but when she didn't, he pulled away. "I appreciate it, thanks." Turning on his heels, his back to her, he headed towards the stairs—towards the resounding sound of gunfire and horses galloping through the empty hall.

"He's not expecting you, is he?"

Alex whirled around to see her still hidden between the doorway, watching him. "Is it that obvious?"

She fiddled with a loose thread on her sleeve. "Jenkins doesn't get a lot of visitors, and by a lot, I mean none."

"You know him well?" Alex asked.

"Not really," Maeve shrugged, her attention now focused on the floor between them. "Just don't look him in the eye."

A sliver of alarm crossed his face. "What happens if I do?"

"Probably nothing," she replied. Then she looked at him, and Alex swayed.

His head felt like it was full of cotton. He was so enthralled, so captivated by whatever grasped him, that he didn't realize she'd shut the door—or that he was alone in the hallway, staring after her like a fool. He blinked, clearing away the fog as he straightened. He could still feel her there, and for a moment, he thought about knocking again—just once, to see if she'd answer.

His heart raced as he wiped the sweat from his palms. He was lightheaded, but his thoughts slowly cleared, and whatever desires he'd been feeling before were fading.

Confused, he took the stairs one by one. With his body moving towards Jenkins's apartment, his thoughts remained with Maeve. He'd been around beautiful women before, but Maeve? Something was different about her—*enchanting*. There was something ethereal and unnatural in her eyes that made him burn and ache. He hated it, felt disgusted by it as he shook away the animalistic need he felt to be inside her—to taste her, to want to feel every inch of her body weighted against his.

Shame and revulsion coveted him. Maeve was a victim. Someone he'd managed to save from a man who'd entertained the same thoughts, and it made him sick to his stomach.

At the top of the stairs, Alex faltered. On his left sat Jenkins's door, vibrating against the roaring television humming on the other side. This was it—the entire reason he'd come here, and yet, he couldn't bring himself to take that final step.

What happened when this was over? He'd go back to his life, to his job, to his empty apartment filled with grief and solitude. Nothing would change—nothing would be different. He'd still be forced to face whatever ghosts he'd left behind, but that wasn't what bothered him.

Alex realized that when this was over, he wouldn't be able to run away again. He'd finally have to confront what he didn't want to admit from the very beginning—that he was scared. Not of his parent's sudden death or of the aftermath, but of something internal, something he couldn't escape from.

What Alex feared most was himself.

CHAPTER EIGHTEEN
Alex

THE ROAR THROUGH JENKINS door was deafening. How anyone managed to sleep or even think in this building was beyond him. Alex gave a confident knock against the heavy door—though he doubted Jenkins would hear it.

After his encounter downstairs, he didn't know what to expect. He knocked again, and this time, he was sure he'd heard the volume increase—as if it had been deliberately turned up.

Someone was in there, and they had no intention of answering the door.

Alex knocked again and again nobody answered. Frustrated, he inhaled a deep breath. He had no authority to be here, but that still didn't deter him from banging his fist against the heavy oak one last time.

"Mr. Jenkins, I need to ask you a few questions about your friend, Max Wiley." He might as well get right to the point.

At the mention of Max's name—the sound immediately quieted, replaced by shuffling from behind the closed door. Alex waited, and it didn't take long before he was greeted by a pair of wide eyes peeking at him warily.

Just don't look him in the eye.

Her words seized him—ones he barely remembered her saying, but Alex couldn't help it. The small scar running down James's sagging lid led directly to the rounded black marble mounted above it. It was like gazing into a black hole flecked with obsidian, and he shuddered.

Through the cracked door, the old man kept his face hidden, but Alex caught the unmistakable glint in his good eye—the one hued in grayish blue. Behind it, James looked haunted, like he was staring at a ghost.

"Mr. Jenkins, my name is Alex Hayworth. I'm a private investigator hired to investigate Max Wiley's disappearance. I understand the two of you were close."

He didn't want to lead with his title as a detective. If Jenkins was as crazy as everyone claimed, Alex didn't need him finding out which department he worked for and calling to verify his credentials.

"Did anyone see you?" Jenkins asked, his voice hushed.

Alex thought of Maeve but decided to keep that detail to himself. "No, sir. It's just me."

James threw a glance over Alex's shoulder. "Come in, hurry," he insisted, stepping aside.

The apartment was dark. The shades from the front window were pulled tight. The only viewable light was from the television set, which James quickly unmuted.

"Does it have to be so loud?" Alex shouted over it.

Jenkins nodded. "Yes, it keeps them quiet. You can't hear them over the noise."

"Who?" Alex asked, but something told him he already knew.

"The sirens."

With his eyes still adjusting, Alex tried not to let his doubt show. Following Jenkins, he was relieved when the old man finally clicked on a lamp in the corner of the room, but when he did, the doubt Alex was trying to hide quickly shifted into shock.

The entire place was littered with trash. Empty soda bottles and crushed cigarette boxes blanketed the floor. In the center of the small living room sat a worn leather recliner where chip crumbs and old wrappers collected in the middle.

Alex coughed. The smell of garbage and stale smoke hugged him tightly, and he choked. The overpowering stench stung his eyes, making them water, and he couldn't decide if it was better to inhale small breaths or breathe in from his mouth, afraid that if he did, the odor would linger on his tongue.

"Please, have a seat," Jenkins said, pointing at the kitchen table.

Eyeing the cluttered dining room, Alex did his best not to wince. Several newspapers—both old and new—were stacked in piles on the table, forcing Alex to scoot a section of it over to one side.

"Do you leave it on all night?" Alex asked, pointing at the television.

Jenkins nodded. "Oh yes, I must. Some days are louder than others, but you get used to it."

Alex couldn't imagine ever getting used to the obnoxious noise echoing off the walls. "And the neighbors, they don't mind?" He asked, thinking of Maeve.

Taking a seat across from him, Jenkins gave Alex a dismissive wave. "To hell with the neighbors," he grumbled.

"You've been in Saltridge a long time I gather?"

Jenkins stared at him with his black eye unblinking—*unmoving,* and Alex couldn't help but leer at the crisp and prominent scar running through it. What type of animal caused an injury like that? Something with claws—something with precision.

"Tell me, mister . . ."

"Hayworth. Alex Hayworth."

Jenkins nodded. "Tell me, Mr. Hayworth—do you believe in the devil?"

The question took Alex by surprise, and he wasn't sure how to respond. He did, in a way, given everything he'd witnessed throughout his career, but did he think the devil was a little red man with horns on his head who carried around a flaming staff and punished the wicked? No.

Alex had experienced evil firsthand. He'd observed many nefarious things, but attributing those sins to the devil seemed like a pathetic excuse. An easy way to explain why people did terrible things because, at the end of the day, that's all it was. It wasn't the devil or demons or some creature lurking below the water. It was simply people—and bad people did bad things.

Alex cleared his throat. "I think there's a little devil in all of us, Mr. Jenkins."

"Please, call me James," he grinned, revealing crooked yellow teeth against dry, cracked lips. "And that may be true, but there are other things out there. . . things that put the boogeyman to shame. Things that make a man, such as yourself, fear the dark."

Alex knew better than to play into whatever narrative Jenkins hoped to sell, but he couldn't help himself. "Like what?" He asked.

The old man leaned back in his chair, fixing both eyes on Alex. "There are evil things in this world Mr. Hayworth—creatures and monsters and demons prowling in the night."

His stare intensified, and Alex shifted uncomfortably in his seat. He'd sat across the table from many evil men—murderers and rapists and kingpins. And in those interviews, he never wavered, never faltered. He never showed fear. Now, as he sat across from Jenkins, his ebony eye bearing down on him—he found himself slightly intimidated.

"You're talking about the mermaids?" Alex asked, shaking off the disquiet.

"*Sirens,* Mr. Hayworth—not mermaids. Mermaids are storybook characters, lovely and sweet and full of magic. Sirens are nasty and hideous creatures, created for only one purpose—to steal the souls of men."

Alex thought about the woman in his dreams—the one who followed him down to the water and bled him dry on the sand, leaving the seagulls to feast on whatever was left. He knew it wasn't real, but the vividness of it, the cool touch of the breeze on his skin—it felt real.

"You've seen one, haven't you?" James leaned forward slightly. Even sitting, he towered over Alex. The top of his head, where only wisps of gray hair remained, touched the top of the light, hanging like a pendant above them.

"They call to you, don't they? At night. . . when you're asleep?" James taunted, the weathered skin on his face stretched over his crooked grin.

"With all due respect, Mr. Jenkins, I don't believe in monsters or any kind of make-believe, for that matter."

"Ahh, but that's where you're wrong," James insisted, waving a bony finger in Alex's face. "There's always some validity to the stories we tell, even the ones more ancient than ourselves. Mythology and lore, even bedtime stories have all been crafted from some shred of truth. Something tells me that in spite of your resistance, part of you believes that to be true."

"I came here—" Alex stopped. He'd convinced himself of a hundred different reasons why he'd shown up in Saltridge. Why he'd knocked on James Jenkins's door, regardless of the stories he'd heard. And yet, he was actively denying all the mysterious and unexplainable events that led him here.

"You came here to ask me about Max, or so you say, but I think there's something more. Something you haven't quite admitted to yourself, am I right?"

Alex tugged at the collar of his shirt. He suddenly felt hot—*too hot*—and his mouth went dry. "Could I bother you for a glass of water?"

Jenkins stood and handed Alex a glass of tepid water. It was bitter, like it had been sitting for days, but he didn't care. He inhaled each sip, closing his eyes as relief poured down his throat.

"What happened to the woman you chased out of town?" He asked when he was finished. Alex was tired of playing games. He was tired of stories and speculation. Seeing Jenkins now, he realized he needed to change his approach. If dancing around the inevitable wasn't working, he supposed being more direct would have to do.

"Which one?" Jenkins asked.

Alex sensed that the old man was toying with him, and his patience was wearing thin.

Setting the glass down in front of him, he made a point to look Jenkins in the eye. "Cut the bullshit, James. You know *exactly* who I'm talking about."

Jenkins held his unwavering stare. "Do I? And what exactly are you looking for?"

"The truth, for starters. And not this fairy tale shit you keep trying to sell, but the honest truth," he demanded.

James scoffed. "I find that rich coming from a man who's done nothing but lie to me since he walked through my door."

Alex stiffened. "I've done no such thing," he argued.

"No?" Jenkins asked, leaning over until his face was only inches away and Alex could smell his rotted breath. "What would you call it then, Mr. Hayworth? Or should I say. . . *detective?*"

CHAPTER NINETEEN
Alex

A LUMP FORMED IN Alex's throat. "Why didn't you say anything earlier?"

Jenkins shrugged, his shoulders cracking against his joints. "I was going to give you the benefit of the doubt. Since you lied to me, I figured there must be a good reason. Now I'm not so sure."

Alex felt exposed, but he remained stone-faced. "Looks like we're even now."

"Are we? The way I see it, you came here looking for something *from me*—though we both know it has nothing to do with Max and everything to do with you."

Relaxing into his seat, Alex crossed his arms over his chest. "Alright, fine. You caught me. Yes, I lied. No, I don't feel bad about it. Put yourself in my position James . . . You're asking me to believe—asking *the world* to believe in fairytales and fantasy. Now, if I didn't know any better, I'd say that perhaps you had something to do with these alleged disappearances."

Jenkins let out a throaty laugh. "Come on now Alex, we both know you're reaching. You have nothing, otherwise you wouldn't be here. Your department doesn't even know you're here, do they?"

"My being here is on a need-to-know basis."

"And by need to know, you mean your buddy Diego." Alex jolted at the mention of his friend's name. "Ahh, there it is—the truth. Too bad it was your face that gave you away and not your morality."

"How do you know about Diego?" Alex's voice was barely a whisper—a breath on the tip of his tongue through gritted teeth.

James's lips curled into a sinful grin. "Oh, I know a lot of things about you Alex. Born May 31st, 1990, to Lydia and John Hayworth—both who passed away recently—sorry for your loss. You joined the force when you were twenty and made detective soon after that. You're not married, you don't have any kids, and from what I can tell, not much of a life outside of that shiny badge of yours either."

Alex bristled. "Congratulations, you know how to use the internet." He didn't come armed—he didn't think he needed to but now he wasn't so sure. Jenkins had done his research, but even with access to Google, there were some things you couldn't find—not easily at least.

Jenkins splayed his hands out on the table. "So, do you want to start by telling me why you're *really here?*"

"I'm surprised you haven't figured it out already since you seem to know so much about me."

James laughed. "I'm flattered, but unfortunately, my abilities only extend so far. I am an old man, after all."

An old man whom Alex severely underestimated. Backed into a corner he was pissed at himself for crawling into in the first place, Alex was silent for a moment.

Perhaps it was best to come clean—not just for James's sake, but for his as well. He didn't need to tell Jenkins everything. He didn't need to reveal how disheartened he was or how empty and dark his days were. He didn't need to admit how every time he looked in the mirror, he felt nauseous and disgusted with himself.

He didn't need to confess that all of this was nothing more than a sad and desperate attempt to feel something again—anything to reassure him that he wasn't lost.

Alex drummed his fingers against the table. "As you already know, my parents passed away a few months ago," he began slowly. He hated talking about them, hated offering up that jagged piece that burned his mouth when he spoke of them. It made him feel vulnerable, and he didn't like feeling vulnerable.

"A few weeks ago, I was cleaning out their house when I found a box in the attic." Alex waited for Jenkins to say something, but he remained still. "It wasn't mine, but the things I found inside were... *unsettling*."

"What kinds of things?" Jenkins asked.

Alex fingered the empty water glass, still perched in front of him. "Some baseball cards, a wooden anchor. There was an empty postcard—of Saltridge." He'd decided to forgo the ominous message written on the back. He didn't want to give Jenkins more fuel to add to an already blazing fire of insanity. "And this..." Alex tossed the small sketchbook on the table, having stowed it away inside his jacket earlier.

He didn't know what compelled him to bring it—he almost didn't. But there was something personal about these drawings, something he couldn't quite put his finger on. Now, here it was, the faded brown cover, a sinister relic between them.

Jenkins hesitated but ultimately slid the notebook over to himself before glancing at Alex. "Oh yes, this is unsettling, isn't it?"

Alex nodded, his throat was dry and he wished he'd asked for more water.

James's face was unreadable as he flipped through the pages, but the marble lodged inside his skull darkened. When he reached the final page, Jenkins closed the book and set it back on the table.

When he didn't say anything, Alex started rambling again. "I was hoping to return it—the box, everything. When I tried tracking down the owner, I found an article about you and Mr. Wiley. The photo in the paper matched the photo on the postcard, and I thought, maybe you might know who this belongs to." He pointed to the sketchbook but made no move to touch it.

Jenkins took him in, his good eye bouncing between the haunting notebook and Alex. "You think I don't know what they say about me?" His voice was low and threatening, like a wet wick under a mighty flame. "I'm not a stupid man, and I'm no fool either. I see how they look at me, how they avoid me in the street. I hear the whispers beneath their breath and the rumors they spread—but I know the truth," he hissed. With a spotted hand, he pointed to his ebony eye. "I was there that night, and I know what I saw."

Alex pulled away, taking the notebook with him. "I'm not here to speculate," he insisted, tucking it back inside his jacket. "I just want to find who this belongs to and go home."

The sound of the TV drifted in the background. Alex hardly noticed it now. He'd been too caught up in whatever this was to give it any attention.

Realizing he wouldn't get much further, Alex stood. He was eager to leave, anxious to escape this desperate cry for help. Looking around, he understood that Jenkins wasn't any better off than he was. Hell, if he didn't get his shit together soon, this might *be him* one day.

"Thank you for your time, Mr. Jenkins," he said, heading for the door.

"I have proof," James claimed, making no move to stand up.

Alex pivoted on his heels. "Unless you have hard evidence, I'm no longer interested in entertaining this nonsense. I shouldn't have come here, and I'm sorry I did."

It was the truth, but Alex wasn't apologizing to the old man whose stories and beliefs were enough to earn him his reputation. Alex was apologizing to himself—and for the time he wasted chasing nothing.

"I have proof," Jenkins said again. This time, his voice came out harder—more desperate. Rising from his seat, Alex winced as the sound of brittle bones shifted against each other. "You came all this way. What's a few more minutes of your time going to cost you?"

My sanity, Alex thought. "You have two minutes to show me whatever you think might persuade me."

Jenkins smiled, his yellow teeth glowing in the low light. "I only need one."

While Jenkins disappeared, Alex looked around the room, and his heart sank. In addition to the filth, the place was piled high with clutter. Tall bookshelves crammed with random knickknacks guarded the hall near the entryway. The door on the front closet was missing, and Alex saw an enormous pile of shoes stacked from floor to ceiling. None of them matched. Boots, sandals, tennis shoes, and even loafers of varying sizes and colors were thrown together carelessly.

"I keep them all," James's voice crept up behind him, and Alex jumped, not realizing he was standing there.

"Why do you have so many?"

"They wash up on the shore, always one—never both and sometimes not at all. But I bring them back here, dry them out, and add them to the rest of the pile."

"What happens when you run out of room?"

Jenkins let out a deep sigh, whistling between his teeth. "I hope it never comes to that."

It was a haunting sight, coupled with an equally morbid statement.

"Here," he said, shoving a manilla envelope in Alex's direction.

"What is this?"

"Answers. Questions. Proof. The start of your undoing." At that, Alex stifled a laugh. "When you've looked through it all—and *only after* you've looked through it all, come back. I'll answer any questions you might have."

"If you had all this information, why didn't you turn it in to the police?" Alex asked.

"I tried," Jenkins insisted. "When a siren takes a soul, it takes the very memory of that person. Pictures, records, everything . . . poof, gone. Max was my best friend, and if it hadn't been for this," he pointed to his false eye. "I would have forgotten about him too."

Alex tried to ignore the weight of the folder in his hands. "What happened to your eye anyway?"

A mischievous grin spread across James's face. "Why don't we save that for another day? Best to tackle one tale at a time, don't you think?"

Alex opened the door without another word, but Jenkins called after him. "They say to walk a mile in a man's shoes is to know him. What kind of man are you, Alex?"

With his back turned, Alex's voice was hollow, "A broken one."

CHAPTER TWENTY
Maeve

"**WHY DIDN'T YOU CALL** me?" Mercy demanded, her hands shaking as she inspected my face.

I winced as her fingers curled around my jaw. "What were you going to do? Beat him to death with your walker?"

Her eyes flared, but the corners of her mouth curved up. "Maybe," she smirked. "You of all people, know better than to underestimate me."

Images of her chasing Mitch across the parking lot ignited a laugh, and I flinched against the sudden pain.

"I'm fine," I insisted. "Nothing happened."

"Nothing happened?" She scoffed with my face still clutched in her palms. "Looks like a hell of a lot of *nothing* to me."

"I mean he—he didn't—someone stopped him before he could finish," I finally managed to spit out.

The words might as well have been a physical blow as Mercy let go, and a faint cry escaped her throat.

"Where was your mother?" She asked bitterly.

I sighed. "Where do you think?"

It was rare to see her angry. Even though her brown eyes have become more opal over the years—flecks of auburn still tinted the edges.

They were full of fire now.

"You're her daughter—you think that would mean something," she muttered to herself.

You'd think so, but it doesn't.

"She probably doesn't even know," I replied. But even as I said it, the words were bitter.

Why was I defending her? She didn't fucking deserve it.

"Trust me, *she knows*," Mercy said pointedly. "If I were a betting woman, I'd say she probably encouraged it."

At that, my head snapped up. "You don't really think she would do that, do you?"

In the kitchen, I watched as Mercy put on a kettle. Her dark skin looked sickly under the fluorescent light as she moved about slowly.

"It's hard to say," she replied, averting my gaze. "Your mother isn't like us. She exists to survive—even at the pain of someone else."

Even if that someone was her own daughter.

DAPHNE PARKER

"I don't think she had anything to do with it," I admitted—though it would've been easier to blame her if she had. "Mitch's actions were his own and his alone."

Behind her, the kettle whistled, and Mercy hummed quietly as she poured us both a cup. Taking it into my hands, I inhaled the sweet and comforting scent of hibiscus and honey.

Mercy's apartment was small but cozy, and as she settled on the couch next to me, I inhaled her. She was the only person who understood me. With her, I felt safe. With her, I felt validated. With her, I felt *loved*.

Inside, her and I were the same. In more ways than one.

The steam billowing over her cup curled in the air. Mercy brought it to her lips and it made her look wicked as she whispered. "Actions have consequences, and sooner or later, he'll be forced to face his."

———•———

Ambling down the narrow aisles of the small grocery store, I spit out a string of curse words every time the wheel on the rickety cart twisted on itself. It rattled and shook with each passing step, drawing in the attention of other shoppers nearby.

Offering them a limp smile, I quickly threw random items into my basket—bread, a jar of peanut butter, a box of cheese crackers I'd probably forget about and never eat. Things that looked like I had someone else to feed besides myself.

I'd like to say I didn't care what other people thought of me, but that would be a lie. Especially now, with this generous bruise staining my face.

By now, everyone in town had heard about what happened. Sarah was the first to call, weeping into the phone and apologizing as if she'd been the one to harm me.

I still hadn't heard from my mother. Not a single word. She didn't call or send a text. I'm sure she knew—she just didn't care.

She was probably still wrapped up in between her lover's legs, trying to prolong the inevitable hangover that was sure to plague her once she stumbled out of bed.

Every morning when I was young, I'd catch random men skittering out before dawn, never to be seen again. My mother would eventually emerge from her room with her hair a coiled mess of champagne ringlets—and her cheeks flushed with color.

It never took long to compel them. By the end of the night, they were begging her to bring them home. The desire of her was hard to resist, and she gave them what they wanted every time.

What it wanted.

It used to be an obsession for me because I was a by-product of one of them—a poor and unfortunate soul lured in with the promise of a good time. I still didn't know his name, who he was, or what he looked like.

I often wondered if his mouth curved up slightly the way mine did when he smiled. Or if his cheekbones were once as sharp as my own. Whenever I looked at myself, I wondered if his hair used to be the same nightshade as mine—thick, and wild, and full of secrets.

Would I have loved him? Would he have loved me?

That part always stung the most.

The affection my mother showed those men was nothing more than biology driven by a desperate need to satiate her own internal darkness. I didn't agree with it, but I understood it.

To those men, she was a vibrant, exciting woman. But to me, she was a fragile, empty husk. And no matter how much she tried to fill herself with starched poison and meaningless sex, it would never be enough to fulfill her. Inside, she'd always want more—*it would always* demand more, and for her, giving in was easier than fighting the inevitable.

Giving in was easy. Giving in was *comfortable.*

Turning a corner, the wheel on my shopping cart curved in again. Frustrated, I shook it violently, rocking it back and forth until it suddenly gave way, launching me forward and slamming me right into Mr. Jenkins.

Several cans fell from his gaunt arms, rolling away in different directions. One cracked open on impact, splattering whatever was inside across the floor and onto his brown shoes.

"I am . . ." but my voice fell away. I tried collecting what had fallen, but he didn't move. Instead, he glowered at me with his one good eye, towering over me like a gangly statue carved from bone. His other eye, drenched in black, remained blank, permanently fixed into an empty, lifeless stare.

His lips curled back into a scowl, revealing crooked, yellow teeth. "An eye for an eye," he sneered before walking away—leaving me alone in the middle of the aisle, still holding the fallen jars.

His words were an itch beneath my skin, ringing like a haunting bell in a hollow room. Carefully, I put the cans back on the shelf and forced myself to walk away—ignoring the sinister voice slithering into my ears and clouding my vision as it leered.

An eye for an eye.

———.———

"Are you okay?" Sarah's voice swept over me as I hung a ticket in the window. I didn't answer right away—I didn't know how. "Sorry, stupid question." I could tell she was trying to look at me without *actually* having to look at me.

Like I was a fractured thing.

Like I'd fall apart right then and there.

"It could have been worse," I said.

Sarah nodded. "Yeah, it could have been." Her hair was a vivid blend of violet and blue, resting effortlessly on her shoulders. She leaned into the kitchen window, and I caught the unmistakable skunky stench of marijuana.

"Are you . . . are you high?" I asked.

Sarah peered out at me from beneath false lashes. Her copper eyes were sunken in just a bit, and I couldn't tell if it was because of the weed or because she hadn't slept in days.

"Believe it or not, you're not the only one with problems."

A wave of guilt crashed into me. In all the years I've known her, I've never bothered to ask her anything about her life outside of work. She never volunteered any information, but maybe that was because I never showed any interest.

I always assumed she was a free spirit—a hippy who loved bright colors and flamboyancy. Sarah was fun. Wild, and free in a way I never would be, in a way I never *could be*.

It dawned on me that perhaps that wasn't who she was—but a costume. A mask she put on every day to cover up whatever internal scars she didn't want the rest of us seeing.

"I'm sorry. I didn't mean to sound like I was judging you," I relented.

She shrugged. "Don't be. We all have our demons, right?"

"Right," I offered her a weak smile, but something told me our monsters weren't the same.

Tom's bald head bobbed behind the line. "I don't pay you two to stand around and talk. If you want to chat about your problems, go to therapy."

Sarah rolled her eyes. "You hardly pay us at all."

Tom looked at us. "No one's holding a gun to your head. If that's how you really feel, the two of you can bitch while you're standing in line for unemployment."

"Jokes on you, it's all done online now," Sarah shot back. Turning to me, she winked before sashaying into the dining room, swaying her hips generously and shaking her ass.

"Shit—ouch—shit," I heard Tom scramble, and I laughed.

We never talked about their relationship—though Sarah didn't try to hide it either. Once, when I thought she'd gone home for the day, I stumbled on the two of them hidden amongst the shelves in the back. Their limbs were a tangled mess of passion as he hovered over her, grunting and moaning like a wild animal. Her wig had fallen to the floor, revealing a thin mess of strawberry blonde wisps against her face. I never brought it up, and she never mentioned it, but part of me wondered if she knew I was there.

It was morning, and the breakfast rush poured in, crowding the already cramped space. Although it looked much more prominent on the outside, The Captain Quarters was relatively small for a diner.

Cleverly placed inside an old wooden hull, Tom liked to tell people that it was once an old pirate ship. He'd even claimed it belonged to Black Beard himself, but we all knew it was nothing more than an old cargo ship he'd won at auction decades ago.

There wasn't much left of the initial vessel. Tom only managed to salvage a quarter of it—along with pieces of the original wood that now served as part of the main floor and support beams. The rest either rotted away or were too damaged to repair. Still, from the outside, it looked like part of a real ship. With some paint and cheesy decor, Tom managed to create a theme that matched his tall tales, and the tourists loved it.

Because the diner was shaped to accommodate the kitchen and bathrooms, the row of booths at the end was hidden away from the main dining room, hugging the wall of the diner.

It wasn't my usual section, especially on a busy morning, so I assumed Sarah had worked her magic on Tom, convincing him to change the floor plan.

Her magic *and* her vagina.

"Heads up, table seven wants syrup. Oh, and can you drop this check off at table four? They're squatting, and I'm over it," Sarah said, passing by. "And don't forget about the gentleman in the corner. He's been waiting awhile."

I glanced up to see the silhouette of a man outlined in the early morning light. "Yeah, sorry, I didn't realize I'd been sat."

"No worries," Sarah replied before disappearing.

Armed with a fresh pot of coffee and a smile that made me flinch against the swollen flesh on my cheeks, I sauntered over to him smoothly.

His back was to me as he stared out the small porthole window above his table. His dark brown hair was a thick mess, which he'd attempted to comb back, but pieces still hung loosely over his ears.

When I approached, he didn't turn or acknowledge me. His menu was still closed, resting neatly at the end of the table, and I assumed he never even opened it.

"Hi, welcome to Captains," I began. "The specials are—"

"Coffee, black. Two eggs, over easy with dry toast and a side of bacon."

I blinked, unsure if he was talking to me or himself since he still couldn't be bothered to look at me.

Normally, I would accept this. *Normally,* I would walk away without saying another word.

But today *was not* a normal day.

I set the coffee pot on the table. "And how would you like your manners cooked?" I asked bitterly.

I didn't care if he complained or if Tom wrote me up. I was tired of this, tired of people treating me however they wanted and expecting me to accept it.

I watched as he straightened. The muscles in his back contracted as he turned to me and the light from the window pulled away, casting a dark shade over the five o'clock shadow creeping over his sharp jaw.

"Please," he said, but I wasn't listening. My pulse quickened as recognition knocked me off my feet.

He was wearing the same clothes he had the day before—a tight grey T-shirt hugging the muscles in his chest and faded jeans folded over dark work boots.

He stared at me, and his eyes reminded me of autumn—pure hazel flecked with gold, brown, and green—like a sea of trees turning at the beginning of the season.

I realized he was waiting for me to say something, but I couldn't find my voice. So, instead, I walked away. Leaving Alex . . . and the pot of coffee sitting at the table.

CHAPTER TWENTY-ONE
Alex

DURING HIS STAY, ALEX had became quite attached to the lovely old couple whose shed he was renting. Frank and Wendy invited him into their home for breakfast, but he declined their offer. Not because he didn't want to join them but because he wanted some time alone to clear his head and pour over whatever alleged "evidence" Jenkins claimed to have given him.

He also knew word traveled fast about the attack in the parking lot, and he didn't want to sit over pancakes and coffee while Frank and Wendy hailed him a hero.

He sure as hell didn't feel like one.

Then there was Maeve, the woman he knew nothing about but couldn't stop thinking of.

He needed to get her out of his head too.

With the envelope still sealed, Alex made his way over to The Captain's Quarters, not because it looked appealing but because it was the only restaurant in town open before noon.

He was surprised to see how busy they were. The outside parking lot wasn't full, but inside, there were more customers than staff, and it took a minute before someone noticed he was waiting.

"Just one?" Said a woman with lively hair. Alex nodded, following her into the crowded dining room and towards a table next to a family of five.

"Do you happen to have anything a bit more... private?" He asked, eyeing the two children flinging scrambled eggs at each other.

The waitress clicked her tongue and looked around. "This way," she said, guiding him over to a row of booths curving off near the entrance to the kitchen.

"Thanks," he said, sliding in, but she simply tossed a menu down in front of him and walked away.

Cheap food and cheap service—fine by him. Granted, he wasn't expecting a five-star experience.

Alex stared at the fishing nets hanging from the wooden beams and laughed. Whoever the "Captain" was, he took the name seriously. Everywhere he looked, there was pirate-themed decor. Pictures of mermaids adorned the walls alongside a scaled mast, complete with a crow's nest near the front.

Even the menus were themed—designed to mimic a treasure map, with a tiny red "x" marking favorites and specials.

It made Alex think of his mother, who would have loved it. She appreciated things like that, and she often went all out over the holidays. Alex always hated it because he thought it was embarrassing.

On Christmas, their house was the brightest on the block, decked out from head to toe in lights and other holiday decor. His father always complained because he had to put everything up and take everything down once the season was over.

"One of these days, the house is going to catch on fire, and I'll be glad to see it all go," he said one day after Thanksgiving.

"If you hate it, why do you do it?" Alex asked, annoyed that he, too, was suckered into his mom's lunacy.

"Because it makes your mother happy," his father grunted, as he handed Alex box after box of Christmas lights.

"Even though it makes you miserable?"

His father wiped the sweat from his brow. "What's one month of being miserable over a lifetime of happiness?"

That was the last time they were forced to dress up the house. A few months later, his mom got sick, and the following Christmas was celebrated in a cramped hospital room. After that, she was too tired to decorate, and Alex's father was too busy taking care of her to take care of himself—or anything else for that matter.

Tears swelled in his eyes, and he blinked them away, staring out the window so nobody would notice.

When his server finally showed up, Alex rattled off his order. He wasn't trying to be rude—he just wanted to be alone—a hint she couldn't seem to take.

At the sound of her voice, Alex stiffened. Turning to face her, he forced himself to remain apathetic. When their eyes met, he watched as recognition, then panic settled over Maeve's face.

"Please," he murmured, feeling like a total dick now. But she ignored him.

Instead, she bolted from the table, nearly running into someone as she scurried away, leaving her coffee pot next to Alex's empty mug.

He stared after her, watching her disappear around a corner and out of sight. Then he picked up the coffee and poured himself a cup.

———·———

"What did you say to her?" The woman with rainbow hair was back, carrying his plate of food.

"Excuse me?" Alex asked, staring up at her. He was trying to catch her name, printed on the name tag attached to her chest, which took up a good portion of her petite frame.

"Maeve, what did you say to Maeve?" She demanded, slamming his plate down in front of him.

Sarah, her name was Sarah.

"I didn't say anything," he replied, trying to figure out why this woman was interrogating him.

Sarah eyed him warily, with her hands firmly rooted on her hips.

"Was there something else?" He asked, unwrapping the silverware from his napkin.

She leaned forward. "Let me give you a piece of advice," she said, the front of her wig shifting slightly, and Alex wondered if anything on this woman was real.

"Does it come with the meal, or do I have to pay extra?" he smirked, putting a piece of bacon in his mouth.

Sarah's face went flat. "She's not going to go out with you."

Alex choked. "What?"

"Maeve's been through a lot in the last 24 hours, and the last thing she needs is some rando coming in here and eye fucking her while she's working."

Alex sat up in his seat, suddenly conscious of his movements. Had he made Maeve feel uncomfortable? He didn't think so, but in today's world, you couldn't even breathe next to a woman without them accusing you of doing something deviant.

In Maeve's case, he understood. "I wasn't—"

"I'm sure you weren't," Sarah broke in, but the tone in her voice suggested she didn't believe him. "You're not the first guy to come in here and hit on her, and you won't be the last. They all do it. Every single one of them, and they all leave here disappointed."

"Are you finished?" Alex asked. Sarah nodded triumphantly as if she'd been planning this speech for months. "Good. I wasn't, as you put it, *eye fucking* anyone. And as far as Maeve goes, I know exactly what she's been through because I'm the one who pulled the asshole off her."

Her honeyed eyes widened, the color draining from her face. "*You're* the guy?" She gasped.

"That would be me," he said, wondering if it was too late to take it back now.

It took a second for it to register, but when it did, the fire in her eyes died down. "I'm sorry I didn't mean to—"

"Assume I wanted to fuck your friend? No, it's fine. I get it all the time."

"Cute and funny," Sarah said as if she hadn't just been grilling him moments ago. "Listen, Maeve's a good person. A little weird sometimes, but aren't we all?" It was a rhetorical question, but Alex bit the inside of his cheek anyway. "I appreciate what you've done for her, but let's not make it any more than that."

"Don't worry, I have no intentions of pursuing your friend," he assured her.

"Good," she stated, the matter now settled. "Now, I know you didn't ask, but I'm off at four," Sarah said, pulling out a pen and scribbling her number down on his napkin. "If you get thirsty later, give me a call."

She didn't give him a chance to deny her, and he didn't stare after her as she walked away, either. God forbid he'd be accused of eye fucking someone else, let alone her. Although something told him, she'd probably enjoy it.

Alex ate slowly—he wanted to savor it. Thankfully, Maeve hadn't returned, and neither did Sarah. And so he took the opportunity to investigate what was inside the mysterious envelope Jenkins had given him. Pulling up on the metal prongs, he lifted the flap and reached inside.

It took him a minute to understand what he was looking at. There were letters, dozens of them—random messages written in familiar print that Alex recognized but couldn't place.

Shuffling through the mess, he saw they weren't letters but notes—reminders and essential dates jotted down on random pieces of paper over several years. None of this struck him as proof of anything other than simple evidence of someone's personal life sprawled out on the table.

They were simple reminders, things like. *Vet appt. April 22nd—rescheduled for 26th* and *Drop off donations to Goodwill on Friday.*

Alex frowned. He felt stupid—stupid for coming here, stupid for giving that crazy old man any benefit of the doubt, stupid for running after something that wasn't his to chase in the first place rather than focusing on the responsibilities he had piling up back home.

There was more left in the envelope, things he didn't see the point in entertaining. He'd wasted enough of his time—he didn't care to waste anymore.

Stacking the papers together, Alex slid them back inside when one escaped from the bottom. He picked it up, intending to shove it in with the rest, but stopped.

Mom's first day of chemo—August 5th, St. Benedict's Hospital 2 pm.

It could have been anyone, or a different hospital blessed with the same name, but Alex knew the chances of that were slim to none. With shaky hands, he reached back into the envelope, and this time, he emptied it.

More letters, more reminders that no longer seemed irrelevant to him. *Dad's birthday—Saturday, October 30th.*

Alex's graduation—6 pm, dinner at Stanley's. His graduation from the academy.

This one was old, nearly a decade at least, and *they had gone* to Stanley's to celebrate—Alex, his mom, and dad. . . Diego. He remembered that night vividly and even recalled some of the conversations and jokes they laughed over. Diego insisted on referring to Alex as "The Rookie" all night, simply because he'd graduated the year before.

His body trembled. One by one, he picked through photos of him and his family. Some were duplicates of ones he had at home, tucked away in drawers, or displayed on the mantle in his living room.

A mixture of confusion and panic swelled inside him—where the hell did Jenkins get these, and how? Alex ran his finger over one of his parents, celebrating on the night of their 30th wedding anniversary.

That was four years ago.

These were fake. They had to be. It was the only reasonable explanation. After all, Jenkins knew all about Alex before he arrived. Perhaps he'd been following him, stalking him for months the way he had that poor woman.

A fire ignited in his belly, flooding his cheeks and burning his face as he huffed everything back into the envelope.

He didn't finish his food. Reaching into his pocket, Alex pulled out his wallet and threw a fistful of cash on the table. He didn't look for Maeve or wait for her to return as he stalked out the door.

He was going to pay Jenkins another visit. And this time, he wasn't leaving without the truth.

CHAPTER TWENTY-TWO
Maeve

THE SUN PEAKED OUT from behind puffed clouds, causing the intense heat to feel more brutal. The humidity was unbearable, a parting gift left behind by last night's rain. A thin layer of sweat settled over my skin as I heaved a large trash bag into the dumpster.

Sarah sat on the concrete steps, watching me while she huffed on a cigarette. "He's cute," she said.

"Who?" I asked, waiving away the plume of smoke as I sat down beside her.

She rolled her eyes. "Don't do that."

"Don't do what?"

"That thing you do where you pretend not to know what I'm talking about."

"I *don't* know what you're talking about," I insisted, giving her a playful grin. "I guess I didn't notice."

"Well, I did." She took another long drag from her cigarette, causing the ashy end to fall between us. "I asked him out."

A flash of green envy rushed through me. "What did he say?"

Sarah scraped the butt across the cement, then tossed it into an empty tin bucket at the bottom of the stairs. "He turned me down. Something tells me he has his eye on someone else."

"Who?"

She flashed me another knowing look. "Don't worry, I took care of it for you."

"What do you mean you *took care of it?*" I asked, my voice wavering. The last time Sarah took care of something, it ended with her screaming at a man whose intense staring was due to a seizure and had nothing to do with me at all.

"I let him know you weren't interested."

I frowned. "I didn't ask you to do that."

"No, you wait until after they've already hit on you. Then you send me in like some kind of bulldog to clean up the mess." She wasn't wrong. It was how things usually went. Still, part of me felt angry at her for stepping in without asking.

"This time, I took care of it before it became a problem. *Unless...*" Sarah cocked her head.

"Unless what?" I challenged, folding my arms across my chest.

"Unless this time is different, and deep down, you're dying to know what he looks like naked."

I rolled my eyes. "Um, no."

"No, you're not into him, or no, you don't want to see him naked?"

"Neither!" I insisted, turning away. "Now can we drop it? I'm not interested in him or anyone else." The tips of my ears were reddening, and I let my hair loose to cover them.

"*Exactly,* you never are. And why is that?" She pressed.

I fiddled carelessly with the hem of my apron. "I guess it's just not my thing." It was a lazy reason, but it was all I felt comfortable offering her.

"Because. . . you're into women?"

"What?" I choked.

Sarah threw her hands up. "Hey, no judgment. I tried it once in college—too much drama for me. But if that's what you're into, I respect it." She was being sincere, and I didn't know whether to laugh or be insulted.

"I'm not a lesbian," I said, raising an eyebrow. "I just. . . I don't know. I guess I haven't found the one worth hurting myself over."

She stared at me for a long while before saying, "Hmm, that's too bad. You being gay would have made you more interesting. Turns out, you're just as boring as the rest of us."

"Sorry to disappoint you," I replied.

If only she knew. . .

"You know, it's not so bad," Sarah commented, pulling out a small compact mirror from her apron and reapplying the bright red lipstick she had stashed alongside it.

"What isn't?" I asked, unsure of where this was going.

"Being in love."

Part of me wanted to ask her why she thought I didn't know what love felt like, and another part of me felt sad that she assumed it in the first place.

It wasn't my fault. *It wasn't my choice.*

It's what had to be done. And because of this, I'd become so shut in, so closed off to the idea of sharing my life with another person, that other people looked at me and only saw a lonely, aromantic woman.

"Are you in love with Tom?" I questioned, eager to take the spotlight off me.

Sarah laughed. "God no," she said, wiping her hands on her jeans like she was trying to wipe the thought away. "I was married once." The look on my face must have said it all because she quickly followed up with, "I know, I know, but it's true. God, it feels like a lifetime ago, I guess it was. He was the only man I ever loved—the only man I. . ." she stopped, shook her head, then said, "You know what, nevermind."

Except I *did mind.* "What happened?" I pressed, curiosity getting the best of me.

Sarah shrugged. "We were young and dumb. Over time, we wanted different things. He wanted kids and a grand house with a white picket fence. I didn't. Something about being stuck in the suburbs with a family seemed like a prison sentence to me. I wanted color and excitement. I wanted passion. Eventually, we grew apart until we finally split.

"A year or so later, he remarried some uppity woman he worked with, and she was able to give him what I couldn't." There was hurt in her eyes, hurt and regret, and harbored affection for a man she wasn't willing to love more than herself.

"Do you two still talk?" I asked.

"Nope," she said, tilting her head to stare at the ash smear left behind from her cigarette. "But I check up on him occasionally to see how he's doing."

"And?"

"And what? We both got what we wanted. In the end, everyone's happy." Something told me that wasn't true, but I didn't push it.

Sarah smiled halfheartedly. "I'm just saying, everything in life is temporary. Even this moment, right here, right now—it's fleeting and fast, and before you know it, you blink, and life moves on. So, enjoy it. You waste more time talking yourself out of things than you do experiencing the moments that matter. Next thing you know, you're fifty and waiting tables at a shithole diner in the middle of nowhere. Don't let yourself get stuck."

She was still staring at the dusty smudge when the back door creaked open, and Tom's bald head peeked out.

"There's a waste container in the galley that needs to go to Ron's," he said, eyeballing me.

"Why do I have to go?" I complained, even though it was obvious.

Tom looked between us, his eyes glazing over Sarah. "Because I need her here to swab the deck," he insisted.

Yeah, his deck, I thought silently.

Sarah rolled her eyes. "For Christ's sake, Tom, there's nobody around. You can stop with the pirate lingo."

He glared at her but didn't argue before slamming the door behind him.

Sarah stood, straightening her wig. "Insufferable ass," she muttered.

"You're the one fucking him," I reminded her.

She tossed a smile over her shoulder. "Yeah, but I'm not the one on chum duty."

Fair enough.

Dragging several pounds of rotting fish through the streets of Saltridge was not ideal. Still, it got me out of the building for a while and away from whatever Tom and Sarah were doing now that I was gone.

Once a week, we donated our scraps to the local bait and tackle, where Ron used them for chum or bait.

By the time I reached the crossing, a pool of sweat seeped through my shirt. It wasn't a far walk from Captain's, but in this heat, it felt like an eternity. Huffing against the hot summer sun, I reached the edge of the wharf and saw what looked like a crowd gathered against the side of the embankment, peering down at the beach below.

I set the bucket down and wiped my brow. Curious, I shuffled over and noticed the sheriff's truck parked behind a yellow barricade. Standing on my tiptoes, I couldn't see much over the bobbing heads of everyone else, trying to catch a glimpse of what was happening.

"What's going on?" I asked a woman standing next to me. Her glistening forehead told me she'd been standing here for a while.

Up ahead, a van labeled "Coroner" veered off the main road and down the embankment.

My heart sank.

"A body washed up on shore," she said, her eyes fixed on where the van disappeared.

"A body?" I echoed in disbelief.

She nodded. "This morning. Everyone's saying it's a tourist but nobody knows for sure."

I thanked her and walked through the crowd, toward the officer standing near the front, who was doing his best to keep everyone back.

He was a younger guy with a clean-shaven face that made him appear younger than he probably was. He didn't acknowledge me, but I could see his eyes trailing me behind his oversized aviators as I positioned myself before him.

"What happened?"

His squad car blocked the view below, a purposeful tactic to keep prying eyes like mine at bay.

"Ma'am, I need you to take a step back."

I glanced down at the foot of distance between us, deliberately making a show of inching back a few steps. "Better?"

He didn't answer, only continued staring into the crowd behind me. He wasn't wearing the traditional Saltridge police uniform of blue and yellow, but green and white—colors reserved for state officers only.

Behind him, I caught words drifting through the open windows of his patrol car. Words like *victim* and *deceased* crackled through the radio as if they held no real weight.

"Did someone die?" I tried again.

The officer pulled his sunglasses onto the bridge of his nose. "Please stay behind the yellow line."

I looked at my feet, then back at him. The only yellow line I saw was the giant trail of police tape edging along the wharf, where it eventually tapered off a few yards past the pier.

Behind me, people whispered, and I snatched small sentences as they let them go.

"Torn to pieces," claimed a young girl.

"Shredded to ribbons," another man said.

Fed up, I walked away, realizing I'd gather more information from the crowd of busy bodies, than from the actual police. So instead, I trailed alongside the barrier taped along the embankment.

A haunting curiosity settled over me—an unnatural buzz that sent me into a numb, almost thrilled state. Moving away from the officer and mob of onlookers, I managed to slip unnoticed behind the caution tape.

From there, I slid down the hillside, ducking behind one of the giant wooden pillars holding up the pier. The sand here was sodden, and it left behind wet footprints that disappeared just as fast as I created them.

Above me, light gleamed through the cracks of the boardwalk, and I crouched behind the wood column, sticking to the shadows. High tide was several hours away, but evidence of its nightly encroachment left discolored lines on the algae-stained sinew.

Up ahead, a flurry of movement gathered at the edge of the shore. Police and forensic investigators, along with Sherriff Thompson, darted across the beach, taking photos and jotting down notes on little paper pads.

My eyes canvased the scene—settling over the body lying lifeless in the sand. They were covered by a blanket, shielded from curious eyes, and I felt a subtle twinge of remorse in my gut. I was barely breathing as they unfolded the gurney to load up the deceased. My grip on the pillar tightened, and my fingernails bit into the wooden post.

I couldn't tear my eyes away as the coroner laid out a black nylon bag while two others lifted the body and carefully placed it inside the folds. When they did this, the sheet fell away, revealing the victim's identity—or what was left of him anyway.

On instinct, I tried to scream, but it came out a choked, dry cough. I covered my mouth as I staggered backward against the wet sand. The water's edge was only a few feet away, and I threw my arms out to avoid falling in.

There were deep gashes all over his body, giant lacerations that tore away at his skin in a grueling, brutal attempt to rip him apart. My stomach churned as I caught sight of a rib bone protruding through a flap of skin that was ripped open. His eyes were gone—plucked from their sockets like they were scooped out with a spoon, and my heart collapsed inside my chest.

Mitch.

His mouth was stretched unnaturally wide where blades of seaweed jutted out from between his perfect white teeth. His gleaming hair, highlighted against the sun, was wet and full of sand.

I stood in frozen horror as they zipped the bag up, covering what was left of him before loading him into the back of the coroner's van and driving away.

A few officers lingered, talking amongst themselves, but I wasn't listening—I was too busy staring at the blood-soaked sand. Soon, the tide would roll in, washing it away, and nothing would be left. They'd reopen the beach, probably tomorrow, and by then, the scarlet stain would have disappeared.

The churning in my gut made its way into my throat, and I turned away to vomit.

He deserved it—the darkness in me roared.

Maybe he did.

Mitch was a shit bag, there was no denying that, but the thought of holding empathy for a man who didn't deserve it made me feel even worse. I vomited again until there was nothing left but a burning in my throat.

Wiping my mouth, I spit out the bile filming over my tongue. I needed to leave. I needed to be somewhere where I could think, where I could be alone.

When everyone left, including the group, gathered on the wharf, I decided it was safe enough to venture out. Heading toward the embankment, I stopped short before the edge of the sloping hillside.

Standing at the top, with his hands in his pockets—was Alex, and he was staring right at me.

Chapter Twenty-Three
Alex

"WHERE DID YOU GET THESE?" Alex roared. He held Jenkins against the wall, his arm pressed to his throat. With his free hand, he held up the envelope, shaking it angrily between them.

"I. . . told. . . you. . . I had. . . proof," Jenkins choked out desperately.

But Alex didn't let up. During the drive over here, all he could see was red. Anger burned inside him. Anger and confusion and hurt and guilt—an explosive combination for a man who'd been ignoring his feelings these last few months, now suddenly being forced to face them.

He didn't wait for Jenkins to welcome him in. And he didn't shy away from the lightless crystal that bore down on him now, pulsing in sync with the rapid thunder of his beating heart.

"Proof of what?" Alex spat. He was in James's face now—so close he could taste the smell of his rotten breath. "Proof that you've been stalking me—that you're a lunatic—that everyone was right about you?"

Jenkins winced as if what Alex had said, hurt him. "Please. . . let me. . . explain."

Alex loosened his grip slightly, and Jenkins let out a shaky breath that rattled loosely in his chest.

When he didn't say anything, Alex moved in again, but Jenkins threw his hands up and cried, "Your brother!" Alex froze. "I stole them from your brother right after he went—"

"Missing?" Alex cut in—his voice shattering like broken glass.

Jenkins nodded with his hands still raised in desperation. "I tried to warn him. I tried to tell him, but he wouldn't listen to me, not right away. Then he—"

"Enough!" Alex snapped, regaining his grip on the old man. "You've got one more chance to tell me the truth."

The distress on James's face quickly shifted into a mocking grin. "Or what? You'll arrest me? Ransack my apartment? Go ahead, *detective*. Hell, I'll even help you tear it apart. Everything I have to lose has already been stolen from me. So go ahead, take whatever's left. You'd be doing me a favor."

Alex looked at the disheveled apartment—at the trash and despair. Then he looked at Jenkins, who was doing his best to remain stoic, but the subtle fear in his good eye gave him away.

Releasing him, Alex took a step back. "I'm sorry," he relented, and he meant it. How could he have allowed things to get this far? To ride on the verge of assaulting a man who he believed was insane when it was Alex who'd gone crazy.

"Desperation brings out the worst in a man," Jenkins said, rubbing his throat. "You're not the first person to show up here looking for answers—you certainly won't be the last."

Shame rose in Alex's cheeks. It took several seconds before he could bring himself to look at Jenkins as he held the envelope towards him, but Jenkins didn't take it.

"You say you want the truth, and I believe you. But I also believe part of you isn't ready to face it either. It's only fair to assume that for me to be honest with you, you must be honest with yourself."

The tables turned so quickly that Alex quickly found himself scrambling for steady ground. Jenkins might not have had him by the throat, but the weight of his words pressed down on him, and Alex thought he'd fold from the pressure.

"Please," he begged.

Jenkins looked him over in pity, then sighed. "Wait here."

Confused, Alex hung back as he disappeared down the hall, only to return empty-handed. He gave the old man a quizzical look as Jenkins passed him, leading him through the front door.

Alex hesitated. "Where are we going?"

Jenkins grinned. "It would be easier if I showed you."

———.———

"Your brother owned the building," Jenkins said, sliding a small silver key from his pocket. "He purchased it some years ago with the intention of fixing it up. It's too bad he never got the chance."

While James fiddled with the lock, Alex did his best not to glance at Maeve's door across the hall. When the bolt finally clicked and gave way, he held his breath in anticipation.

Light from the hallway spilled into the dark apartment, and with a trembling hand, Jenkins slid his fingers inside until he found the light switch. When he flipped it up, nothing happened.

"Like I said, it's too bad he never got to see it through. The whole building needs to be rewired."

With the door open, Alex paused.

"Well, what are you waiting for?" Jenkins asked, smiling.

His yellow teeth were like popcorn kernels stuck between the gums of his delighted grin, as if he'd been waiting his entire life for this moment.

The first thing Alex noticed when they stepped inside was how clean everything was. There wasn't much to indicate someone lived here—*had lived here*, if it weren't for the subtle things he knew were unmistakably personal.

Like the signed Red Sox jersey carefully mounted on the wall or the array of delicately carved wooden curios neatly aligned on the mantel beneath the television—much like the anchor he'd found weeks prior. Alex knelt before it and saw that one was missing.

Jenkins clicked on the small bronze lamp on the end table next to the sofa, and this time, dusty light flooded the room.

"Looks like you'll need to pick up a few lightbulbs," he said as Alex maneuvered into the kitchen.

On the floor, near the fridge, was an empty food bowl. The name "Pickles" was stamped alongside the ceramic dish. "Did he have a dog or a cat?"

"Cat, I believe. I don't know what happened to it, my best guess is that it took off and found itself a new home shortly after. . ." He didn't finish the rest.

Alex took in the claw marks etched into the arms of the sofa. "How do I know you're telling me the truth?"

"You don't." Jenkins pointed to an array of framed photos on a shelf across from him. "But take a look."

Alex studied each frame carefully. There were ones of his parents on various occasions and a few that featured Alex amongst the array of assorted memories. Then there were the more obvious ones, the ones where you could tell someone had been erased, replaced by empty landscapes instead.

Jenkins's voice was low. "Shortly after they took him, I came down here and grabbed what I could. I figured, or at least *I hoped,* you'd come sniffing around one of these days. I'd learned my lesson the last time I tried to convince someone their loved one was. . . well, you know." He rubbed a hand over his jaw, contemplating. "This time, I didn't want to leave any room for doubt."

If someone had told Alex a year ago that both his parents would wind up dead and he had a brother he couldn't remember, he would have laughed in their face. He would have said they were crazy.

Now, as he stood there with the uncomfortable weight of it all pressing down on him, suddenly he felt like the crazy one.

"What happened that night?" Alex asked, pointing to the angry scar on Jenkins's face. The black rock shifted unnervingly underneath his brow as James studied him.

"Believe it or not, Alex, you and I aren't so different from each other. I may not have experienced some of the wicked things you've seen, but I've endured my fair share of misfortune."

Alex pictured James's apartment. It seemed the old man was still burdened by his hardships.

"I was orphaned young. My parents were awful people—my father was a drunk, and my mother lost her mind shortly after I was born. I spent most of my adolescence sleeping in someone else's bed, in someone else's home, and when I became an adult, I had two choices—live out on the streets or become a soldier."

Alex thought back to what he'd learned about James before they met. "So you decided to join the Navy," he said.

"Seems, I'm not the only one who knows how to use the internet," Jenkins smiled. "I've never been much of a fighter, scrawny as I am, but the ocean has always fascinated me. It's endless and magnificent. I find it compelling how something so beautiful can be so deadly," he admitted.

"And Max?"

A faraway look spilled into his good eye as memories of his friend resurfaced. "Max was the first friend I ever made—the only friend I ever made." He laughed, "We hated each other at first, but being stuck at sea for months at a time changes you, and we were forced to share a berth. It took a while, but eventually, we forged a brotherhood.

Brother. The word rang in Alex's ears as Jenkins continued.

"When we got out, I settled here, and Max made his own way in the world. Everything was good until it wasn't. Some years later, his life fell apart, and I offered him a place to stay until he got back on his feet. That's when everything went to shit."

Alex thought about his parents, his mind wandering off to the day they died and where he was instead of with them.

"You blame yourself," he realized. Alex knew a thing or two about that and suddenly he saw Jenkins differently now.

"Of course I do," Jenkins snapped. "How can I not? If it wasn't for me, he'd still be here."

"You don't know that," Alex argued—understating how ironic it sounded coming from him.

Jenkins swallowed. "It doesn't matter," he said, clearing his throat. "What's done is done. Max is dead, and he's not coming back."

Silence befell them. Alex knew better than to push a man who coveted grief for as long as Jenkins had. He wasn't even in his first year yet, and any mention of how he was faring ignited a fire in his veins.

Jenkins had a lifetime on him.

"So, what now?" Alex finally asked when it was clear that James wasn't going to offer him more. There'd be plenty more time for Jenkins to confess his story later, now that Alex would be lingering a while longer.

"Well, for starters, there's a nasty leak in the roof. The gutters need a good deep clean, and I'm sure you saw that the porch out front could use a little TLC."

"—I meant about the apartment," Alex interrupted.

"Ahh, yes. Well, that's entirely up to you," Jenkins said, laying the key flat on the counter between them. "Stay here, go home, I don't care. It's your apartment now."

"What about the rest of the building?"

"What about it?"

"What's going to happen to it, now that he's gone?" Alex asked, unable to bring himself to admit that *gone* meant *dead*. He'd courted death enough already—he didn't need to give it any more attention.

Jenkins stared down his crooked nose at him. "I suppose if you don't want to shoulder the burden of your brothers' affairs, then it'll go into foreclosure until someone else comes along and purchases the property." There was an implication there, but Alex ignored it anyway.

Instead, he asked, "What was his name?" Jenkins had yet to speak it, and Alex had yet to ask. Something about learning the identity of his brother, made things seem more personal—*more real.*

Without missing a beat, James admitted somberly, "His name was Andrew."

CHAPTER TWENTY-FOUR
Alex

IT WASN'T POSSIBLE, NONE of it was possible, yet there was this internal feeling, this overwhelming sense of acceptance that *this was* the truth, the one Alex had been searching for.

It was like part of him he didn't know was missing, had finally found its way back home. Everything he thought he knew about his life—he was questioning now.

Stumbling out of the building, he tripped over his own two feet, trying to shield his eyes from the blinding sun. The world was closing in on him, crushing him from all sides as he lurched forward.

Inhaling a deep breath, Alex steadied himself against the porch. His body shook with convulsing tremors rolling like waves over his shoulders.

"Are you alright?" A voice sounded quietly behind him.

He turned his head to see an elderly woman cautiously staring at him. "Yeah—yeah, I'm fine, thanks." He didn't realize anyone was out here.

"You don't look alright to me," she replied. She was leaning against the opposite side of the porch, and her silver braided hair was pressed tight against her nightshade skin.

"I just needed some fresh air, that's all." Alex rubbed his hand over the back of his neck.

The old woman stared at him, her mouth set in a hard line, as if she were deciding something. "You look familiar. Have we met before?"

Alex stiffened. Knowing what he knew now, or at least what he'd been told, he gathered she knew Andrew from when he'd lived here before. He still didn't know what his brother looked like, which was weird.

Alex shook his head. "I'm afraid not, no. I'm Alex." He offered, extending his hand out, and she took it after a moment of hesitation.

Her hand was barely flesh-covered bone as he took it into his. He tried not to stare but he couldn't help it as he noticed the angry bruise slithering over her knuckles and up her dainty fingers.

"My name is Mercy," she greeted him as she pulled away. "Mercy O'Dell."

"How long have you lived here?" Alex asked, assuming she was a tenant.

He could tell she was wary of him, and he wondered if it was because he was a stranger standing on the porch of her home or because he looked identical to someone she'd long forgotten.

Mercy looked at the crumbling building and sighed. "A long, long time."

"Do you like it?" He asked awkwardly.

She gave him a tentative smile. "Why? Are you planning on moving in?"

"Sort of," he laughed, pulling out the key he'd shoved into his pocket.

Mercy's jaw tightened. It was a subtle gesture, hardly noticeable to anyone who wasn't paying attention—but Alex was.

"I suppose that makes us neighbors," she said, any hint of alarm now gone.

"I suppose it does," he replied.

There was tension now, not the kind due to awkwardness—but of something else. Something Alex couldn't quite put his finger on.

"Do you know who used to live here. . . before?" He asked, nodding towards the vacant window darkened behind Mercy's shoulder. He wanted to test the waters a bit, see what she knew—or didn't, for that matter.

Mercy shook her head. "I'm sorry, I don't. It's been so long, and as you can imagine, my mind isn't as sharp as it used to be." She laughed hoarsely, though the amusement didn't quite reach the opal-shaded hue outlining her coffee-stained eyes. "Many people have been in and out over the years. It's hard to keep track of who comes and goes."

Alex watched her slide along the railing to where her walker stood, perched against the side of the building. Sweat beaded on the bridge of her nose as Mercy strained against her frail body. The heat was climbing, and the humidity in the air was becoming increasingly more apparent.

He'd taken note of her clothes earlier—a large robe stitched in a variety of red colors. It pooled over the wooden planks as she dragged her feet along, and he wondered why she'd chosen to wear something so thick and heavy in hot weather like this.

Alex held the door open for her, and Mercy thanked him. She moved slowly, one inch at a time, into the open threshold, and it dawned on him then that she must live across from Jenkins.

"Would you like some help getting upstairs?" He offered her his arm, but she shrugged him away.

"I appreciate it, but I'll manage." By the time she cleared the first step, she was already out of breath, with the entire flight still left to go.

Alex opened his mouth to argue but quickly shut it despite himself. If she was hell-bent on doing it alone, he'd let her. It was hard to tell if it was sheer stupidity or stubbornness that willed her, but either way, he'd remain at the foot of the stairs until she reached the top. The last thing he needed on his conscience was the preventable death of an elderly woman. A stubborn elderly woman, but an elderly one nonetheless.

Mercy didn't say anything as she climbed, and she didn't dare glance back down at him either. All the while, Alex tried not to glance at the closed door on his right, the one leading to Andrew's apartment. He still couldn't wrap his mind around it, around any of it. Especially when it came to the sirens—that part, he didn't believe. He probably never would—not without seeing one, at least.

Once she made it to the top of the stairs safely, Alex finally took his eyes off Mercy. He was alone now, with his thoughts and the memory of his brother's ghost lingering alongside him.

———•———

He'd barely managed to sneak past the modest ranch-style home when Wendy came flying out the back door.

"Oh, Alex, thank God you're alright," she sobbed. Her light blue eyes were red-rimmed and puffy.

"What's wrong?" He asked, his voice sharp. "Is everything alright? Where's Frank?"

Wendy nodded. "Franks, fine, it's you I was worried about. I was afraid you were dead."

"What? Why on earth would you think that?"

Her soft arms shook as she tried to collect herself. "You didn't hear?" She asked between breath-catching sobs. Alex shook his head. "A body washed up on the beach this afternoon."

Behind her, the back door swung open again, and Frank came to stand alongside his wife. "Glad to see you're still standing upright," he laughed, but Alex caught the slight relief in his voice. "I tried to tell Wendy it could have been anyone, but she wasn't having it—she said she needed to see you, just to make sure."

Alex was stunned, unsure of what surprised him more—the news of a dead body being discovered or Wendy's relief when she realized it wasn't him. Even Frank was struggling to hide his easement.

Alex ran a hand through his sun-soaked hair. He barely knew these people—they didn't owe him anything, least of all their concern for his welfare.

"I'm sorry I worried you. I got caught up with some. . . *family business,*" he struggled to admit. "I just came by to grab my things and head out."

"Yeah, about that," Frank said, shifting on his feet. "We, uh, were wondering if perhaps you'd like to stay a bit longer. After all, we enjoy your company, and we'd be more than happy to accommodate you if you would allow us to."

Alex thought about Andrew. He might not remember him, but he felt he owed it to his brother to stay at his place. "I appreciate it, but I've already made other arrangements."

Frank's mouth turned downward. "We understand. Nonetheless, we enjoyed having you here." He stuck his hand out, and Alex took it. "If there's anything you ever need, please give us a call."

Alex smiled, "I've got some loose ends I need to tie up before I head back home. We should get together before I leave and say goodbye the right way."

"I'd like that," said Frank.

By now, Wendy had stopped shaking. "Where will you be staying?" she asked, hoping it was somewhere nearby.

Without thinking, he replied, "With my brother."

———·———

After a long-winded goodbye, Alex drove to the beach. He wanted to see things for himself.

When he reached the wharf, the bystanders were scattering, and he caught the unmistakable sight of the coroner's van as it sped toward the opposite end of town.

A few officers were still milling about, and Alex flagged down a younger deputy stationed at the edge of the boardwalk—flashing his badge as he met the man.

"You're a little late to the party," said the officer.

"Looks like you guys managed to clean up the mess without me," Alex replied as if he belonged there.

The deputy scoffed, a rookie by the looks of him. "The coroner left, but the sergeant is still down there if you want to talk to him."

Alex shook his head. If this guy was too stupid to realize he wasn't part of their department, that meant he was foolish enough to give away information he wasn't supposed to.

"That won't be necessary. I'm just crossing my t's and dotting my i's, if you know what I mean."

The officer nodded. "What's there to know? Some guy walking his dog discovered the body. I didn't get a good look at him, but I heard he was in rough shape," he shuddered. "To be honest, I'm kind of glad I wasn't the first one on scene. Sounds like it was brutal."

"Do you know what happened?" Alex asked, his expression dull. He was doing his best not to show any emotion, but internally, his thoughts were a confused mess of panic churning inside him.

The officer shook his head. "I have no idea. It sounds like whoever it was went for a swim in high tide last night. Honestly, I'll never understand why people do what they do."

Alex chuckled. "I've been doing this job a long time, and I still don't understand it."

After a few minutes of small talk, Alex thanked him, and they parted ways. He lingered on the wharf for a few minutes, allowing the other—more seasoned officers below to head out. They'd be smart enough to ask questions—questions he didn't want to answer.

Once everyone left, he meandered along the embankment. When he reached the edge, he looked out at where the investigators were crawling earlier.

A shark attack, that's what this was—nothing more, nothing less.

It wasn't possible. Even if sirens *did* exist, someone other than Jenkins would've seen one by now.

He took in the waves rolling onto the shore, soaking up the blood-soaked sand. What would he do if all this turned out to be true? What *could he do?*

Out of the corner of his eye, Alex caught the shadow of movement at the bottom of the hill, and his pulse quickened. Nobody should be down there.

A flash of black told him he didn't need to get any closer to recognize the woman at it's base. Even from this distance, her celestial features were sharp enough to distinguish who she was. An instant buzz of excitement flooded through him, replaced by unsettling suspicion.

Wanting to get a better look at a crime scene wasn't a crime.

Alex shook his head. Jenkins was starting to get to him. His wild ideas were like a nasty infection seeping into his pores and making him think crazy things.

Maeve was just an ordinary woman, after all.

Chapter Twenty-Five
Maeve

When I reached the top of the hill, I was breathless and soaked in sweat. My clothes were stuck to my skin as if I'd emerged from the sea below, and I could feel the grittiness of sand in my shoes.

Alex was waiting for me. His hazel eyes were more gold in the intense sunlight as he took in my disheveled features.

"Are you stalking me?" I blurted out.

He made a noise that sounded more like a snort than a laugh, but his lips were turned upwards in a half smile. "No, but I can see why you'd think that."

I coughed, trying to suck in air as I leaned over, and he held out his hand to help.

I shook my head, "I just need a minute." A minute to catch my breath, a minute to process what I'd seen. A minute to figure out how the hell I was going to explain what I was doing down there.

"Did you get a good look?" Alex asked, reading my mind.

I nodded, my face turning green, my stomach twisting into another knot. "I know what it looks like, but I can explain." If I didn't look guilty before, I sure as hell did now.

"If I had a dime for every time I heard that, I'd be a very rich man," he said, letting out a mirthless laugh.

I cinched my brows. "Why is that funny?"

Reaching into his pocket, Alex pulled out a small leather wallet. The gold-plated badge glinted in the light. My face blanched, and my body went rigid.

"Don't worry, I won't arrest you for being nosey. I couldn't even if I wanted to—jurisdictions and all."

"You arrested Mitch," I said. Another wave of nausea rolled over me.

"That was different," he said. Peering over my shoulder, he asked, "Did you know them?"

I took in a deep breath, trembling as I exhaled slowly. "It was Mitch."

I let his name fall between us as he stood there—calm, as if the weight of what I just said had no impact on him the way it did me.

The muscles in Alex's jaw flexed as he studied me. "He deserved it," he finally said.

I shrugged. Maybe he did, but he hadn't seen what I saw.

"Nobody deserves that," I whispered.

If he'd heard me, he didn't say anything. Instead, he casually asked, "Are you headed home? Can I give you a ride?"

I shook my head, causing loose strands of hair to fall in front of my face. I didn't want to know what I looked like. I didn't want to know what I smelled like either.

"Are you sure? I can wait," he tried again.

"I appreciate it, but I'll be ok." Alex frowned, and I did my best to reassure him. "I promise. I'll be fine."

"I believe you," he said, his voice wavering a bit. "At the risk of sounding bold," he paused, fishing out a small card from his wallet and handing it to me. "Here's my number. Call me if you need anything."

"Detective Alex Hayworth," I read out loud, staring at the card in my hands. I glanced up at him. "You don't. . . *look* like a detective."

Alex laughed. "Were you expecting a trench coat and a Sherlock pipe?"

I shook my head. I didn't know what I was expecting. Not this, not any of it. "You look so. . . normal," I said.

"Isn't that the point?"

Touché.

"Listen, about the other night. . ." I started, feeling embarrassed now. "I never got a chance to thank you."

"You don't have anything to thank me for," he replied honestly.

It was a lie, but neither of us wanted to admit what we were really thinking.

What *I was really thinking.*

I shoved his card into my pocket and afforded him a polite smile. "I should get going. I've got to get back to work."

He nodded but didn't say anything, and I wondered if he planned on hanging back to snoop around.

He wouldn't find anything if he did.

With my head up and my back straight, I walked away, eager to convince Alex, who I knew was still watching me, that everything was ok.

But inside, I was screaming, trapped like a prisoner by the creature that finally decided to emerge and whisper.

Who would be next?

———•———

I didn't go back to work. I didn't go to Ron's either. Instead, I wandered back to my apartment, tired and eager to strip myself of my grimy clothes.

My phone shrieked endlessly as an abundance of missed calls and unread text messages poured in from Tom and Sarah,

DAPHNE PARKER

wondering where the hell I was. I didn't care. I'd deal with them later.

Every time I blinked, I saw his face—or what was left of it anyway. A deep and involuntary shudder went through me, and I stumbled against the weight of myself as I struggled to let myself into my apartment.

Once inside, I splashed cold water over my face—desperate to wash away the image of Mitch's mutilated corpse, but it didn't help. All I could see were the carved-out cavities where his gray eyes once were, and my body trembled again.

I should've been grateful—I should've been happy that a man like that finally got what he deserved, but I felt no relief—no gratification for his horrific death. Instead, I felt sick, and I wretched again until my insides were raw, and all that was left was a dry heave.

When I was done, I grasped the edges of the sink—forcing myself to look in the mirror. The vibrant colors that once stained my face were fading into a shade of dull green and blended yellow. Soon, it would be as if nothing had happened at all. Life would go on, people would forget, and everything would go back to normal.

Mostly.

———.———

I was lying on my back, my eyes tracing the swirling patterns on the ceiling, when I heard someone pounding on my front door.

Bang. Bang. Bang.

The vigorous force of it rattled the walls as I rose to my feet and scampered down the hall.

Bang. Bang. Bang.

Panic coursed through me, a sensation of fear that flooded my veins as I snatched a knife from the block on the counter.

Bang. Bang. Bang.

It was a demand—a command to be let in or else. Whoever stood on the other side knew I was home, and they weren't leaving until I answered the door.

Charley pranced into the room, darting beneath the sofa following another loud knock. I scowled at him—*coward.*

There wasn't a peephole, and even if there was, I didn't know if I could muster up enough courage to look through it. What if they had a gun?

"Wh-who is it?" I tried sounding tough, but my voice shook anyway.

Nobody answered, just another round of harsh knocking that sent a small glass vase falling to the floor, shattering into several pieces.

That pissed me off. I didn't even like that vase, but that wasn't the point.

Fuck it.

Unlatching the lock, I held the knife out in front of me. The reflection of my eyes glinted in the silver blade as they shifted from bright coastal blue to a frigid, salty sea. Plastering the nastiest look I could manage onto my face, I flung open the door.

"WHAT?!" I shouted, hoping I sounded more threatening than I looked.

She took a few steps back in surprise, or fear—I wasn't sure. Then she blinked. Her emerald eyes darted between the laughable weapon I was fisting and the twisted look I was giving.

Then, her lips curled into a mischievous grin, and I wilted at the sight of her. "Hello, Maeve."

———·———

"Why didn't you answer me?" I demanded.

My mother shrugged, "I didn't think you'd open the door."

Fair enough. I probably wouldn't have.

I was still angry at her—resentful that she never bothered to check in on me after that night at the Shack. Part of me still blamed her—mostly because she was still alive *to blame.*

"You look awful," she said, pushing past me. I was still considering whether or not I should shut the door with her inside.

"What do you want?" I asked, not bothering to hide the ire budding on my tongue.

It was nice of her to notice the aftermath of her poor choices, but not enough to care. I watched as she ambled into the living room, staring at things—*my things* as if they were coated in filth.

She ran her fingers along the edges of a shelf before turning to me. "Is that any way to talk to your mother?"

I was still holding the knife, and for a moment, I wondered what it would feel like to stick the dull blade between her ribs. Would it go in easily—smooth like butter, or would the flesh between her bones be rigid and unforgiving? I quickly set it down before rash impulse caused me to do something I *might* regret.

"Forgive me if I'm not more enthusiastic about the fact that you just spent the last few minutes trying to bust down my front door."

My mother rolled her eyes. "I don't know why you insist on being so dramatic," she said, falling onto the couch.

Charley skittered out from underneath it, hissing viciously at her. "Why do you keep that wretched thing anyway? Does he even do anything?"

"He's a cat," I said flatly. "What do you want him to do?"

She sighed. "I just think it's weird that you'd rather spend your free time holed up here with that filthy mongrel rather than out in the real world with actual... people."

"Like you?" I challenged. This time, I allowed my resentment to flow free.

She raised her colored brows at me. "You say that like it's a bad thing."

"Because *it is* a bad thing," I argued.

My mother barked out a forced laugh. "Says who? Honestly Maeve, sometimes I can't help but wonder what's worse—that you chose to isolate yourself from reality or that you think you're better than me because of it." Disgust was written all over her face, or maybe that was just her face. It was hard to tell.

"What do you want?" I asked again.

"I heard a body washed up on shore this morning." Her eyes avoided mine as she picked at the arm of my couch. "You wouldn't happen to know anything about that... would you?"

I swallowed hard. "No, I don't," I lied. She didn't need to know why it bothered me.

"Such a tragedy," she claimed, her lush eyes meeting mine, taunting me—*taunting it*.

We stared at each other daringly for several seconds before another knock fluttered on the door.

"Seems I'm the most popular person in Saltridge today," I smirked.

"Oh good, you're home," Mercy said, cradling her walker as she stepped inside. When she saw who was in my living room, she froze. "Hello, Anna."

My mother scowled. "I see you haven't died yet. Pity. I thought your age would have caught up to you by now."

Mercy straightened, her back snapping as her joints popped. "Funny, I was just about to say the same thing to you."

My mother blanched but quickly recovered. "Is there something we can help you with? As you can see, my daughter and I were in the middle of something."

"No, we weren't," I said, stepping toward Mercy. I doubted anything physical would happen between them, but the tension in the room was enough to knock the old woman over.

My mother glanced between us. "I see you two are still as close as ever."

Mercy looked at me and smiled. "We take care of each other."

"Maeve is a grown woman—she can take care of herself," my mother growled.

"You're right, she can But right now, she could use a little support." Mercy's voice was a calm and confident melody, which drove my mother even further into her rage.

"Support? You call that support?" My mother pointed to the stain across my face, and my blood boiled.

Mercy laid a gentle hand on my arm, and I relaxed a little. "Why do you think I'm here?"

"To take her away from me. . . again."

Mercy's eyes narrowed. "You took something from me first."

The temperature in the room shifted, and I caught the fire in my mother's eyes as her temper flared.

"Fine," she said, standing. "I was just leaving anyway."

The two of us stepped aside, but as my mother moved through the threshold, she leveled her eyes on Mercy. "I heard he begged for his life," she whispered—her voice lethal. "I heard he wept for you. Tell me, how does it feel to know that your name was the last thing he tasted before they ripped out his tongue—"

"That's enough," I growled.

The corner of my mother's mouth twisted into a sly grin, but she didn't reply.

When she was gone, Mercy turned to me. "Are you alright?" I nodded, realizing my mouth had gone completely dry. "Good," she said, leading herself the rest of the way inside. "Because we need to talk."

CHAPTER TWENTY-SIX
Alex

ALEX STOOD BEFORE HIS brother's door, fiddling with the key still tucked inside his pocket. He contemplated whether he should venture inside. According to Jenkins, it was his door now—*his apartment*—until it wasn't anymore.

A red sun hung heavy in the sky, as daylight slowly bled into night, and Alex feared that the longer he stood there, lost in his wariness, the more likely he'd be discovered.

He didn't want to stumble across Maeve, once was enough for today. He didn't want to happen upon Mercy either. She was harmless enough—an old lady whose fragile body posed no threat to him—but still, he didn't trust her—he didn't trust anyone.

Alex inserted the key. The jagged ridges alongside the shaft glided effortlessly into the lock as he rotated it slightly. Once inside, darkness greeted him, darkness and silence, and the burdensome realization that, once again, he was utterly alone.

It wasn't like the news of his brother's passing made him sad—not in the way his parent's death had. How do you mourn someone you don't remember? He didn't know Andrew any better than a stranger he might pass on the street.

He wanted to feel something—he *did feel* something, but it wasn't sadness or grief that cloaked him. It was discomfort he felt—like wearing a pair of shoes that didn't quite fit.

He thought about his parents and what they might feel if they were still around. Then he realized that if they had been alive, Andrew would have continued to be a lost memory. He knew it was a cop-out, but it didn't stop the sliver of resentment kindling inside him. Sure, Andrew was gone, but look at the mess he'd left behind.

As if he didn't already have enough on his plate. He'd barely managed to get through the last few months, and now he was forced to deal with his brother's misfortune—a brother he didn't owe anything to as far as he was concerned.

A brother he didn't ask for.

A brother he didn't remember.

Anger simmered in his chest. At least he felt something now—even if it was misplaced.

In the bathroom, Alex rifled through the cabinet in search of something to ease the burn when a small orange bottle fell into the sink. Andrew's name was erased, but the name of the prescription was still there. Ambien. He knew the sedative well because his mom used to take it on nights she couldn't sleep.

Picking it up, he held the bottle in his hand, the red-yellow hue tinging his palm. It was a high dose, enough to knock out a horse—enough to cause hallucinations, especially if abused.

Alex shook the bottle, causing the leftover pills to rattle against each other. Putting them back where he'd found it, a thought slithered into his mind. Why was Andrew taking such a strong sedative? Was he having trouble sleeping because of the sirens? Or did the sirens only exist because of the hallucinations caused by the Ambien?

Combing through the rest of the medicine cabinet, he discovered nothing but the usual items you'd expect to find—Tylenol, toothpaste, a bottle of shaving cream, and a razor.

Alex wiped a hand over his jaw, pulling at the fine hairs jutting out from his chin. Since his arrival in Saltridge, he'd let himself go, and those hairs started creeping up his cheeks. Imagining what he might look like if he let it grow out, he wondered if he and Andrew shared similar features—judging by the rusty blade, it seemed they might have. This warranted other questions, like who was older? Did Andrew favor their mother or their father? Were they close? Or was there sibling rivalry between them?

Looking at himself in the mirror, Alex glazed over the shadow hugging his jawline and the luggage beneath his eyes. He looked like shit, worse than shit—he looked like fucking shit.

He couldn't remember the last time he really slept. His body had become so used to running on fumes that the thought of resting made him feel more depleted, as if sleeping were a chore all on its own.

Alex thought about the bottle of Ambien but quickly shoved it away. The last thing he needed was to envision things that weren't real. Instead, he turned on the faucet, thankful for the flow that sputtered out, and splashed cold water on his face.

The ache he'd felt earlier swelled as he stepped into the bedroom and hovered over the unmade bed. The blue satin sheets were a twisted mess, flung onto the floor as if his brother had been in the midst of a violent nightmare before he was lured from it.

Alex shuddered and turned away.

Beside the unkempt bed was a stack of books, with one only half-read, it's marker sticking out between the dusty pages. Anguish mounted in his chest as the rest of Andrew's life unfolded around him. Legos were carefully pieced together and left to collect dust on the dresser and the walls were adorned with art, with several sketches resembling the style he'd found in the sketchbook he still carried. It seemed Andrew was a dreamer—a stark difference from the man Alex was.

It was getting late, and the subtle weight of exhaustion clung to him, tugging at his eyelids as his limbs became heavy. He glanced at the bed. There was no way in hell he was sleeping between the sheets of a dead man—brother or not. The couch would have to do.

After raiding the closet for an extra blanket, Alex settled onto the living room sofa. His six-foot frame was too large for the worn-out cushions, and his feet dangled over the edge as he struggled to get comfortable. He wouldn't sleep tonight, not with the ghost of Andrew's memory haunting him. He probably wouldn't sleep tomorrow, or the next night either.

Turning onto his back, Alex tried focusing on the low hum of James's television, vibrating through the walls. He wondered how Mercy and Maeve managed to sleep with the constant noise or if they were used to it.

Staring up at the ceiling, he remembered something Jenkins said.

You can't hear them over the noise.

Snatching the remote off the coffee table, Alex turned on the TV, wincing at the staticky white noise flooding through the speakers. Flipping through the channels, he finally settled on an old movie—it's black and white noir casting bleak shadows over the room.

Turning the volume up a few notches, Alex settled back down and closed his eyes. The actors voices, now a booming echo, crept over the dark walls. He might not believe in monsters, but he wasn't going to take any chances either.

CHAPTER TWENTY-SEVEN
Alex

ALEX WAS STARTLED AWAKE by the shrill voice of a woman selling overpriced Tupperware on the television. Morning filtered into the room, and a grey wash light hung heavy in the melancholy air.

He tossed and turned all night, with his body fast asleep but his mind wide awake.

At one point, he could have sworn he saw Maeve standing over him, watching him sleep from behind a fine ebony curtain of long hair. He knew it was a dream because when she touched him, her hands felt like smoke—light and weightless as they drifted in between his legs.

Imaginary or not, Alex felt himself harden against her touch, and he leaned into it, desperate for release, as she stroked him softly.

Her eyes glowed like sapphires against her ivory skin in the dark, and her coral lips curved into a seductive smile. Alex reached for her, eager to pull her on top of him and let her ride him until he burst.

She didn't speak but instead pumped him faster, harder. Alex closed his eyes and thrust his hips upwards in a silent plea. He could feel the tension building, a budding emersion of untethered desire until he finally exploded, causing his body to tremble and his legs to shake.

When he opened his eyes, Maeve was gone, evaporated into thin air like a ghostly apparition—leaving him with his hand fisted around his cock, still aching beneath his fingers. Embarrassment flooded his cheeks as he noticed the mess he'd made—a mess he hadn't been confronted with since adolescence.

Sitting up, Alex uncurled his legs and let his spine crack as he stretched out his back. Each time he turned his head, a dull throb in his neck resonated between his shoulders.

Maybe the couch wasn't such a good idea after all.

His stomach roared, a deep and bellowing groan that would have been more noticeable had it not been for the competing volumes between him and Jenkins place. He clicked off the TV and wandered into the kitchen, only to find the cabinets bare because nobody had been living there.

Eating at Captains was an option, but that would mean he'd have to face Maeve, an uncomfortable situation he wasn't ready to put himself in, especially not after the dreams he'd just been having.

This meant he'd have to go into town, and while he was there, he could pick up some lightbulbs for the front hallway and a few other essentials he was sure to be running low on.

His phone dinged, and Alex freed it from his pocket.

Are you alive? A text from Diego read.

Barely, Alex thought to himself. The irony that this was supposed to be a vacation, yet he had felt more emotionally drained since arriving, was not lost on him.

He contemplated what to say, unsure of what he *should say.*

Diego knew him better than anyone, and if Alex continued skirting around the obvious—eventually his friend would know something was up.

He couldn't lie if he didn't say anything at all.

Steam billowed over the ceiling as Alex stepped into the shower, a welcome relief as it eased the sore muscles in his back. Perhaps he could try sleeping in the bed tonight, but he'd need to pick up new sheets first.

With his arms raised above his head, Alex leaned against the wall. His head was pulsing, a direct result of the mounting stress he'd been carrying around.

What was he supposed to do with this place? He could let it go and allow the bank to take possession. But then what? What would happen to Jenkins? To Mercy? To Maeve. . .

226

Not my pasture, not my bullshit.

Except it *was his* pasture, and it *was his* bullshit now.

It didn't have to be. Not if he just walked away. He had his own problems, and sooner or later, Alex would be forced to face them. He'd have to confront his parents' house and the complications that would arise from offloading their estate. He'd have to face Diego.

He'd have to face himself.

Then there was work and the unsolved cases that were sure to be piling up on his desk faster than he could solve them.

Alex took a deep breath, holding it in for as long as he could—until his lungs burned and his lips quivered. But what if he stayed? What if he switched departments and settled in here? What if he left his old life behind. . .

People did it all the time. There were plenty of cases he'd worked where people disappeared, only to reemerge years later as someone else, free from the chains of their old life.

Why couldn't he be one of those people? Hell, he was practically handed the opportunity. Andrew was his brother after all. Why couldn't he slip into his shoes? It's not like anyone remembered him anyway. Except for Jenkins, and who the hell was going to believe him?

The water started running cold, pricking at his skin like sharp needles until the smoothness of his flesh resembled rugged terrain. Alex stepped onto the cool linoleum and stared at himself in the mirror, analyzing each detail emerging over his wet skin.

He could do it. He could pretend to be his brother and not think twice about it. He could be comfortable here, settle down, and start a life—a good life.

Alex shook his head, whipping his wet hair side to side, causing water droplets to fall lazily at his feet. It was tempting, but it wasn't realistic. Not for men like him.

———·———

An hour later, Alex maneuvered along the winding streets of downtown Saltridge, stopping by the hardware store then Freeman's—the local grocery store. He'd only managed a few steps inside when his phone rang, and an unrecognized number flashed across the screen.

"This is Hayworth," Alex said, shifting his voice with intimidating force.

"Oh good, you're not dead," Diego replied, his words a petulant sting.

"You sound disappointed," Alex shot back.

"A little. It would explain where the hell you've been."

"Why are you calling me from a random number?" He asked, shrugging off Diego's annoyance.

"Because you've been radio silent the last few days, and I was starting to think you were avoiding me," his friend said tightly.

Alex started to object but didn't. Diego wasn't wrong—he had been avoiding him—he'd been avoiding everyone.

"It's been a hell of a week," said Alex, running a hand through his hair, the ends still damp from earlier.

"Did you find what you were looking for?" Diego asked.

It was a simple question—one Alex should have been able to answer easily, except he couldn't. He couldn't tell Diego that the box he'd discovered belonged to his forgotten brother, and he certainly couldn't mention the sirens. If Diego was concerned about his mental health before, he'd sure as hell have a reason to be now.

"Uh yeah," Alex hesitated. "Turns out it was a dead end."

He hated lying to his best friend—it made him sick, but the alternative would be so much worse.

Diego blew into the phone, a sigh of relief, or disappointment—Alex wasn't sure. "Sorry to hear that. But you know how it goes, you win some, you lose some." Alex nodded, realizing the gesture was pointless. "When do you plan on coming home? You do plan on coming home, don't you?"

No. Yes. *Maybe.* All valid responses in Alex's mind. How long could he run before his legs finally gave out? Before his mind finally tired?

He opened his mouth to reply but his attention was stolen by the giant corkboard on the wall before him—the kind littered in business cards and help-wanted ads tacked amongst competing piles.

The papers fluttered every time the doors swung open, creating a draft that revealed whatever was buried underneath.

The photograph was clear, meaning it was newer, having not faded over the years due to being left behind and forgotten. The man's face was a rounded ball of fat, and his greasy brown hair was stacked in a messy heap above his shiny forehead.

Have you seen me?

The sentence jumped out at him, and as Alex stared at the man with wide cheeks stretched over his pudgy jowls in an uncomfortable grin, Alex heard Diego's voice calling to him.

"Alex? Hello? Are you there?" But Diego sounded far away over the sudden roar in his ears.

Ignoring him, Alex yanked the photo off its tack and studied it—wondering if this was nothing more than someone who had simply vanished or if perhaps he was the victim of something more sinister.

"Hey! Hello?" Diego yelled louder this time.

Alex cleared his throat, "Yeah, sorry, I'm here."

"What is with you, man? Is everything ok?" He had a right to ask, a right to be concerned, but Alex didn't have an answer.

"I'll call you back," he said abruptly, hanging up before Diego could argue.

This time, when he called again, Alex forwarded it to voicemail before pulling up the keypad again. He'd deal with him later when he had the chance to explain—*if he ever could explain.*

His hands shook as he dialed the number listed on the paper. He wasn't sure if anyone would answer, so he was prepared to hang up after the fourth and final ring when a small female voice finally bled into the phone.

"Hello?" She said, hardly loud enough for him to hear.

"Hi, yes, sorry to bother you. My name is Alex Hayworth and I'm calling about the missing poster you have hanging up at Freeman's." There was shuffling on the other end, followed by brief silence as he waited for her to say something.

"Oh!" She replied suddenly—almost like she'd *forgotten* about it.

"Is this a bad time?" Alex asked, still staring at the photo in his hands. He traced his fingers over the man's name—over the ink that was starting to slowly fade.

How long would it take until all of it was gone?

"No, it's fine. Sorry, I was just uhm…" she paused. Then her voice came in between light breaths. "Have you seen him?"

Maybe—it was possible. Would he remember if he had?

"I'm sorry, I haven't." It was the truth as far as he was concerned. "But I'd like to help you find him."

Silence.

An unsettling feeling churned in Alex's gut. Maybe it was intuition, or perhaps it was the lack of sleep. Either way, something about the man gnawed at him like a rabid dog, and he couldn't shake it off.

"Would it be possible to meet? Maybe grab a cup of coffee, and you can give me some more information," Alex tried coaxing.

"I don't know," she replied hesitantly.

More shuffling. More light breathing.

"I can meet you on the pier in an hour," he pushed.

"One hour," she repeated, her voice distant. "Yeah, sure, ok."

"Perfect," Alex said, still trying to decide if she wanted his help. "I'll see you then."

He studied the flyer for another minute before folding it in half and shoving it into his pocket. He didn't know who Greg was, but he was going to find out.

Chapter Twenty-Eight
Maeve

"**Why do they call** it Romance Red?" Sarah asked, eyeing her toes while the woman kneeling before her pulled out the polish.

"Because red is the color of romance," I said, closing my eyes and leaning into the leather recliner—allowing the hard roll of the massager to knead small circles into my back.

"Says who?" Sarah snorted. "Whenever I think of red, I think of sexy. If you ask me, I think it should be called Sexy Rouge."

I cracked open an eye and caught the nail tech stifling a laugh. "I guess it's a good thing nobody asked you then."

When Sarah asked me to tag along, I was surprised. She wasn't one to hold a grudge, but I knew she was still upset with me for leaving her to clean up Captains the day Mitch's body was found. We didn't talk about it, and I was relieved when she kept the questions about what I'd seen to a minimum.

"What about Seductive Sin?" She asked, sitting up now.

Giving up, I opened both of my eyes, realizing this relaxing trip wouldn't be as peaceful as I'd hoped.

"Are you marketing to strippers?"

"Hey, that's not a bad idea!" she brightened.

The nail tech rolled her eyes, then whispered something to the woman sitting next to her in a language I didn't understand. They were talking shit about us, and honestly, I didn't blame them. With her black leather skirt and tiny white blouse accented by her voluptuous red wig, Sarah looked like she could *be* a stripper.

As for me, I'd chosen a quieter color—a blue polish tinted by green flecks of glitter that shimmered in the fluorescent light. It was simple and easy—the kind of subtlety I liked.

"You should call that one Sinister Siren."

I stiffened. "Why sinister?"

"Why not?" Sarah shrugged, utterly oblivious to my hard stare. "Aren't sirens supposed to be evil? They're like, the anti-version of a mermaid."

"Relax your foot, please," the young woman in front of me instructed as she scrubbed the dead skin from my heels.

"Sorry," I murmured, not taking my eyes off Sarah. "I don't think that's fair," I told her, trying to ease myself back into the chair. "Maybe they're just misunderstood."

"Misunderstood?" Sarah laughed, cocking her head at me like I was stupid. "And I'm sure the Devil is a really nice guy—he's just had a hard life."

I rolled my eyes. "Don't be ridiculous."

"Me?" She scoffed. "You're the one getting offended."

"I'm not offended." I argued. "I'm just saying, I don't think it's fair to assume something is bad just because it's what everyone is told to believe."

Sarah squinted at me. "She's never going to change."

"Who?" I asked, craning my neck.

"Your mother." The hardness she'd spoken with earlier was gone, replaced by the softness of pity. "That's who you're talking about, isn't it?"

I swallowed, desperate to ease the fire smoldering in my throat. "Yeah, of course."

She sighed. "I hate to say it, but it's your own fault ya know."

"My fault?"

"Come on, Maeve..." she said, dragging out my name as she rounded her lips. "You're not a victim if you keep allowing her behavior to affect you."

"I don't—" I started but stopped. I stared into my lap, ashamed. "It's not that simple."

"I didn't think it was," she said, twisting in her seat to face me. "In fact, I know it isn't."

"You don't know anything," I suddenly snapped, my face red and hot.

"No offense, Maeve, but we've known each other a long time, so I feel like I can confidently tell you that you're too smart to be acting this stupid."

"Just because you say, 'no offense' doesn't make it less offensive," I shot back, yanking my half-painted foot out of the nail tech's hands.

"You're not done yet," she yelled, following me with a bottle of open polish in one hand and a towel in the other.

Ignoring her, I pulled out my wallet and dropped a handful of crisp bills on the counter. It was probably more than I owed, but I didn't care. I wasn't going to sit here and be insulted by someone who claimed to be my friend.

Sarah remained in her seat, not bothering so much as a glance in my direction as I fled.

Snatching a pair of disposable flip-flops off a side rack, the foam eased between my half-painted toes as I swung open the door and stepped outside. Tears stung the backs of my eyes as that thing inside me whispered.

She's right, you know. . .

I knew she meant well. I knew she wanted what was best for me, but Sarah had no idea about the things I'd done, about the things *I could do* if I wasn't careful.

There are some things out there that are worse than monsters. I should know, because I was one.

———·———

My tires screeched against the pavement as I barreled into the parking lot—pissed off, frustrated, and a little hurt. Once inside, I ripped my purse open, rummaging for my keys and trying not to cry as I sifted through old receipts and loose change. Frustrated, I emptied the bag onto the floor.

That's when it hit me—the silence.

Sitting on my knees, I glanced at the stairs where nothing but eerie quiet stared back.

Mr. Jenkins.

Standing, I left the contents of my purse scattered on the floor and took the stairs two at a time.

"Mr. Jenkins?" I shouted, reaching the landing. "Mr. Jenkins, is everything alright?" The door was cracked, and I hesitated. Peering into the darkness, I listened.

"Mr. Jenkins?" I called out again. "Is everything ok?" Nothing. The stillness, coupled with the sound of my own harsh breathing, was intimidating.

I called for Mercy, but she didn't come, and I realized that I would have to go inside. Alone.

What if he just left his door open by mistake? That still didn't explain the quiet. Something was wrong. I could feel it in my gut.

Stepping towards Jenkins's apartment, I stuck my head inside. "Mr. Jenkins, it's Maeve from downstairs. I'm coming in."

It took a moment for my eyes to adjust and I gasped when they did. His recliner was tipped over, lying on its side in a heap of trash left on the floor. It looked like he'd been robbed. In the kitchen, cabinet doors were open, hanging limply by broken hinges. The TV was cracked, explaining the sudden silence. My body was shaking as I maneuvered my way through the chaos.

"M—Mr. Jenkins?" I called again, my voice trembling. "Are you there?"

The door to his bedroom was closed and I debated going forward. What if he was sleeping? What if everything was fine, and I barged in there like a lunatic? What if he wasn't even home at all?

Sweat slicked the back of my neck and over my forehead, pooling at my temple and dripping down the side of my face. It was so hot in here, well over 80 degrees, even with the shades drawn and the air conditioner humming.

I knocked on the door—loud and demanding as I shouted his name one last time. "Mr. Jenkins," my voice echoed. "Mr. Jenkins, it's Maeve. Can I come in?"

Not waiting for a reply, I gripped the knob in my nervous hands, and pushed open the door. But unlike the rest of the apartment, this room was empty.

Stepping inside, I took in the nicotine-stained walls, and the hairs on the back of my neck stood up. There was something eerie about the barren space that didn't sit well with me. The rest of Jenkins's apartment was a disaster, yet this room looked like it had never been touched.

I told myself I should leave. By now, I doubted he was home, and the last thing I needed was to be caught standing in his bedroom if he decided to show up.

Then I stepped in something wet.

"What the fuck?" I whispered, staring down at my feet. They squished against the carpet as I lifted them, and I realized the entire floor was completely soaked.

I hadn't thought to check the bathroom. The entrance was off to the side, hidden by a small inlet where the closet was located. And unless there was a serious leak—the pool of water had to be coming from there. The door was ajar, but when I tried opening it, it wouldn't budge.

Something—*or someone,* was in the way.

"Mr. Jenkins, are you in there?" I knocked. No answer.

Steadying myself, I shoved my shoulders into the door—forcing whatever was blocking it to move just enough so that I could stick my head inside.

"Oh my god," I cried

Jenkins was slumped over the bathtub. His head was facing the wall and his body was pressed against the side. The faucet was off, but the tub was filled to the brim, and water sloshed over the sides and onto the floor, seeping into the bedroom.

What do I do? What do I do? I thought frantically.

What did you do? The darkness in me sneered.

Freeing my phone from my pocket, my fingers grazed the edges of something hard—Alex's card.

"Call me if you need anything," he'd said.

So, I did.

CHAPTER TWENTY-NINE
Alex

THE WOMAN AT THE table shifted uncomfortably. Alex approached her gently, setting down the two cups of coffee he'd ordered when they first arrived.

"Can I get you anything else?" He asked softly.

She shook her head, her short auburn hair falling over her heavy face. Across from her, Alex relaxed into his seat, breathing in the salty air around him.

Draping a lazy arm over his chair, he smiled. "I'm sorry, I don't think I got your name."

"It's Margaret, but everyone calls me Maggie," she said, staring into her lap like a frightened child.

"My sister's name is Margaret," he lied, a tactic he'd used numerous times to relate to someone who might feel uneasy. "She used to go by Maggie but now that she's all grown up, she says it's not as professional."

Maggies eyes fluttered beneath her lashes, but she didn't speak. Based on her timid nature, Alex wondered what her and Greg's relationship was really like.

He'd learned the two were married, and he'd spent enough time handling domestic cases to know an abuse victim when he saw one. Judging by the lack of physical evidence, he was willing to bet this type of abuse was emotional—which could often be just as damaging, if not worse. Shifting uncomfortably in her seat, Alex knew she was tense. And he couldn't help but think that perhaps having her husband go missing was more of a blessing than a tragedy.

"What does she do for a living?" Maggie asked, finally glancing up at him for the first time.

Now they were getting somewhere.

"Who? My sister?" Alex asked, deceit rolling off his tongue with ease. "She's a lawyer, mostly corporate financial stuff. Nothing crazy, but she loves it. I never understood why."

Maggie took the coffee into her hands and gently twirled the sleeve around the cup. "I wanted to be a lawyer once," she said, her brown eyes lighting up before dimming again.

"Oh really?" He replied, hiding his surprise. He had a hard time picturing this meek woman standing in the middle of a courtroom, arguing a case before a judge. "What made you change your mind?"

She sighed, turning her head to stare down the busy pier. "Greg thought it was inappropriate for me to surround myself with criminals. He said nobody would take me seriously and that I would be putting myself in danger."

But what Alex heard was that Greg was an insecure coward threatened by the possibility of his wife becoming more successful than him. Taking a sip of his coffee, he did his best to hide the sorrow he felt for her as he segued into the reason of why they were here in the first place.

"Tell me what happened," he said. "When did you first realize Greg was gone?"

"We'd gotten into a huge fight," she said, mindlessly picking at her cup's lid.

Alex noticed the shriveled skin on her fingertips, next to the too-short nails embedded along the top—another sign of stress, of extreme anxiety resulting from whatever revilement Greg caused her over the years.

"We don't usually fight. My husband is—*was* a reasonable man. He just wanted what was best for me."

Alex nodded, pretending that he understood, but deep down, he was roiling.

"One day, I snuck into his office. I was never allowed in there, but I had this sneaking suspicion—call it a gut feeling, that he was cheating on me. I didn't know what I was looking for, some kind of proof, I guess. If he was hiding something, it would be in there. That's when I found it—a pair of bright pink lingerie that didn't belong to me."

Maggie's lower lip trembled, as a tear slid down her cheek. "There were nights he said he was working late, only to come home smelling like perfume. He told me it was all in my head, and I believed him until I found those lacey panties shoved in the bottom of his desk drawer. Those seemed pretty real to me."

Alex didn't know what to say. He felt sorry for her, but pity is a selfish thing and Maggie certainly didn't need it from him right now.

"Did you confront him?"

She nodded. "Greg denied it at first. He even tried convincing me that they were mine, except they were three sizes too small, and I haven't worn a thong since high school." Maggie gave him a lopsided smile, her face flushed with embarrassment. "Eventually, he fessed up, and for the first time in ten years, I finally found the courage to stand up for myself."

"I'm guessing it didn't go so well," said Alex.

"I told him I wanted a divorce." Maggie straightened, as if the very word gave her confidence. "I didn't realize how bad I wanted it until I said it out loud."

"And this led to a big fight, I assume?"

She shook her head. "I didn't give him the chance. I left. That night, I stayed with my mother. When I came home the next day, he was gone. A few days later I called the bank—afraid he might have drained our account—they informed me of his recent transactions, and that's how I found out he was here."

Alex took out his notebook. "When was the last time you spoke to him?"

"Not since that day I told him I wanted a divorce," she said, her voice aching. "I tried calling him a few days later, but he didn't answer. I thought he just needed some time to process things, but when I tried again a week later, it went straight to voicemail. That's when I realized the money in our account wasn't moving, and I knew something was wrong."

Alex's phone rang, startling them both. Another random number scrolled across the screen. Assuming it was Diego, he ignored it.

"Do you need to get that?" She asked politely.

Alex shook his head. "It's not important. Did you report any of this to the police?"

Maggie reached inside her purse and pulled out a tissue, blotting her tear-stained face. "I tried reporting him missing, but they wouldn't listen."

"You called the Saltridge police?"

"Yes. I figured since this was the last place he'd been, they might be able to help."

Alex's phone rang again and again he ignored it. "And did you tell them any of this? What you just told me?"

Maggie stared down at his phone and then at him before answering. "Y-yes. I thought maybe if they knew the whole story, they'd realize something was wrong. I thought when someone goes missing, every second counts. But they told me Greg was an adult, and judging by my story, he was probably avoiding me."

"They said that to you?" He asked, balling his hand into a fist. Although his encounter with the sheriff wasn't pleasant, he was astonished at the department's blatant lack of empathy.

Maggie nodded. "That's when I decided to come here and look for myself. The flyers were a stupid idea but I don't exactly have a team of detectives at my disposal."

"Well, you've got one now," Alex assured her. "I can't promise anything, but I'll see what I can do. Is there anything else I should know? Any details you might think could be important?" But before Maggie could answer, his phone rang again with the same, unrecognized number. "I'm sorry. Can you excuse me for one second?"

"Take your time," she said, finally pulling the cup she'd been cradling to her lips.

Walking to the edge of the pier, Alex leaned over the railing. "What is so important that you—"

But the honeyed voice that spoke didn't belong to Diego.

"Y-you said to call if I ever needed anything."

Alex deflated.

Maeve's voice was a shaky whisper. "I need your help."

"Where are you?" He asked, throwing a glance over his shoulder.

"I'm at home," she replied quickly. "Well, sort of. I'm in Jenkins's apartment. He... he..." Her voice trailed off, leaving a footprint of fear for him to follow. Below, waves crashed against the rocks, sending a fine mist into the air.

Alex swallowed and wiped his face. "I'm on my way."

CHAPTER THIRTY
Alex

MAEVE WAS SITTING IN the hallway with her back to the wall and her knees drawn to her chest. She was visibly shaking, and Alex realized that whatever she stumbled upon must have been bad.

Really bad.

"What happened?" He asked, kneeling in front of her.

Her jewel-like eyes were raw as she met his gaze. "I don't know," she said, her voice weak. "When I got home, it was quiet. I came up here to check on him, and I noticed the door was open, so I went inside."

Alex glanced up at the darkened doorway.

"At first, I thought, maybe he wasn't home. I thought he might have left the door open by mistake, but that still didn't explain the quiet." Maeve swallowed, her breath quickening. "I got to the bedroom and was about to leave when. . ." Her voice trailed off, and she started shaking again. "I found him in the bathroom. I don't know if he slipped and fell or had a heart attack or what, but he wasn't moving."

"Was he breathing?" Alex asked, rising to his feet.

She shook her head. "I don't know, I didn't look. I'm sorry, I didn't know what to do. I called you as soon as I found him, and I've been sitting out here since."

"You did the right thing," he reassured her. "Why don't you get some air? I'll take care of it."

Maeve stood, brushing her shoulders against his. "Thank you," she said before heading down the stairs.

Alex took a deep breath, trying to prepare himself for what he was about to face, but his mind wandered, lingering on the thought of her touching him just now—of how soft her skin was. He shook his head. Now was not the time to focus on what the rest of her body might feel like pressed against his.

When he entered the bathroom, Alex noticed that Jenkins was leaning over the tub—not in it. He couldn't see his face because it was facing away from him, and his head rested against the rim where his body was draped over the ledge.

Then he noticed the lack of color in James's hands and feet—particularly the absence of blue and purple shades one would typically find on a dead body once the blood stopped circulating and started pooling. This meant he died recently, within the last four hours, if he were to wager a guess.

The water in the tub was tinted pink. Alex didn't see any evidence of trauma or any other traces of blood throughout the room. Still, he wouldn't know until the body was moved and he could get a clearer picture of Jenkins's face.

Maeve speculated a slip and fall or perhaps a heart attack. But judging by the position of the body, Jenkins was standing outside of the tub when he'd fallen. It was possible that when he'd gotten out, he'd slipped and hit his head, but that didn't explain the water overflowing or why the faucet was turned off.

This wasn't an accident.

He didn't have much time. Without any jurisdiction here, Alex needed to call the police, and based on how they seemed to handle things around here, he didn't exactly trust their competence.

He couldn't do anything about the body—not without tampering with evidence, but there wasn't anything wrong with looking around. He wouldn't touch anything. Years of skilled detective work taught him that the best asset one could have was your eyes. And so, he scanned the room, focusing on the finer details one might miss if they didn't know what they were looking for.

Toiletries like the old mans toothbrush and razor had fallen to the floor. Various prescription bottles and a bar of soap he assumed had once been on the counter now lingered between the toilet and the sink.

The door was intact, meaning he must have been in the bathroom when he was attacked or placed in there afterward, but there was no evidence of drag marks. If that were the case, whoever did this had enough strength to lift and carry him into the bathroom before placing him where he was now.

But why the water? Maybe the intent was to drown him. Maybe whoever did this wanted him weak, so forcing him underwater might have been easier.

There was a struggle, he knew that the moment he'd stepped into the apartment, but that didn't necessarily indicate an attack. Alex had witnessed James's lifestyle—the man housed chaos like a lover, and so perhaps the "struggle" he'd seen was no more than Jenkins's daily life.

Then there was the alternative. The theory he didn't want to entertain but was forced to regardless.

Suicide.

Maybe this was an elaborate setup to make it look like an attack. Perhaps Jenkins destroyed his own apartment, filled up the bathtub before shutting off the faucet, and forced his own head underwater until his lungs gave out and his body stilled.

There had to be *something,* a reason for someone to come here and attack an old man seemingly out of the blue. He doubted James's reputation would have warranted such violence, but Alex had seen people kill over far less.

Dissatisfied with the amount of evidence left behind and no real theory—not a plausible one anyway, Alex surmised he'd seen all there was to see, and now he'd have to involve the Saltridge police. Punching in the number, he was about to call it in when he heard a soft and throaty groan bubble over the water.

When someone dies, gases build up inside their body, and after a while, those gases leak out, causing soft moans and subtle sighs that can often be mistaken for breathing. Alex knew this, but he still held his own breath, desperate for a sign of life.

Another moan, louder this time, followed by a short burst of raspy breathing.

Jenkins was alive. The son of a bitch was still alive.

Alex slipped against the wet floor, catching himself quickly as he hovered over Jenkins.

"James, James, are you alright?"

Jenkins moaned but didn't move—his body still limp against the tub.

Alex leaned over him, careful of his head, as he slid his hands underneath James's arms and lifted him off the tub. Jenkins groaned again, lulling his head to the side as Alex freed his body from the edge.

"Don't move. I've got you," he strained, dragging Jenkins from behind and walking backward into the adjoining room.

After laying him on the floor, Alex turned to face him. It was the first time he'd gotten a good look at his face and what he saw made his toes curl, and his legs shake.

Three distinct claw marks trailed viciously from the top of his forehead down over his good eye, settling just below his stubbled chin. The flesh around it was marred, ripped open wholly, and flayed at the sides where flaps of skin hung open loosely, revealing an angry swirl of red tissue underneath.

Blood caked his mouth, with fresh drops forming around the open lacerations. His other eye, the black one, was gone—plucked out entirely, leaving nothing more than a vacant cavity behind.

Alex's face stretched in horror. "What the hell happened to you?"

Jenkins did his best to offer a sardonic grin. "An eye for an eye," he croaked—each word an exhausting feat.

James's lips were severely dry, and the vermillion cracked and flaked away. A bright red ring circled the border of his mouth where the blood vessels had been broken, an effect only achieved by sucking on the skin.

Alex needed to call the police—he knew James could still be saved. But what would he say—*what could he say* about the condition he'd found him in?

And then there was Maeve, waiting downstairs, frightened and confused. What would he tell her? Would she even believe him if he told her the truth?

What was the truth?

James's breathing was shallow as his body loosened. He was fading—*fast,* and Alex needed to get him out of here before it was too late.

Because once Jenkins was gone, so was his memory—and Alex wasn't ready to forget him yet.

CHAPTER THIRTY-ONE
Maeve

I'VE NEVER SAVED A life before. Technically, I didn't save Jenkins either, but as the paramedics loaded him into the back of the ambulance, I felt a sense of assurance wash over me.

A sense of *relief*.

"Is he going to be ok?" I asked Alex, hopeful.

The front porch groaned beneath his feet. "I hope so," he said, but the confidence wasn't there.

"I'm sure he'll be fine," assured Mercy, who'd shown up when first responders did.

I had no idea where she'd been, and I didn't ask. When she trailed in behind the glow of emergency lights, demanding to know what was happening, I was just thankful she was ok.

"That man is as tough as they come. It'll take more than a little scratch to put him down," she said.

Alex's back stiffened. "It wasn't *a little scratch*," he chided. "Half his face was ripped open."

Mercy sucked in a breath, stealing a glance in my direction.

Alex bristled. "I'm going to talk to the sheriff and make sure they don't need anything else from me."

"Am I . . . in trouble?" I asked Mercy once he was gone.

Her eyes were still hard on Alex. "Is he going to be a problem?" She asked, her voice low and cautious.

I knew what she meant, but I lied to her anyway. "No," I shook my head, ignoring the sour aftertaste of deception on my tongue.

Her chestnut eyes were dark as she set them on me. "You said that the last time."

I closed my eyes briefly, letting the cool air cascade over my skin. "What am I supposed to do, act like he doesn't exist?"

"That's *exactly* what you're supposed to do."

"Yeah? And how well did that work out for you?" I wished I could suck the words back in. I wished I could rewind the moment, especially when the lines around Mercy's mouth tightened.

She came to stand beside me, bringing with her the overpowering aroma of patchouli and citrus. "Do I need to remind you of what happens when you become too involved?"

"I'm not—"

"You are," she threw back. "I can see it on your face. I can smell it on your skin. You're treading shallow waters Maeve, and if you're not careful. . ."

"I know," I said, pressing myself against the brick and tilting my head to stare at the sky. "But what if this time it's different?"

"It's not," Mercy said pointedly.

I turned away, eager to keep whatever hurt I felt from spilling across my face.

"I know it's hard, and I know it's unfair, but unless you want to end up like your mother—or worse, *like me*," she glanced down at her legs, hidden beneath a lengthy skirt pouring over her feet. "Then I suggest you reel it in."

"I'm not my mother," I spit, insulted she would even suggest such a thing.

She sighed, gently laying her hand across my arm. "No, you're not. Why do you think I'm trying so hard to protect you? To keep you from making the same mistakes I did, the same ones she continues to make."

I yanked my arm away. "I never asked you to protect me. I'm not your daughter. It's not your job to make sure I do the right thing."

Mercy wilted—her dark skin suddenly ashen. "Alright," she whispered. "Well, I guess that settles that then." The bottom of her walker scraped against the rough wood as she turned and headed for the door.

"Mercy, wait," I pleaded, the acidic turmoil of regret hot in my mouth. "I'm sorry, I didn't mean that."

"No, you were right," she insisted. "You're not my daughter, and I have no right to tell you how to live your life."

I opened my mouth to argue, but Alex's voice curled over my shoulder. "Is everything ok?"

How long was he standing there? How much did he hear?

Mercy disappeared, the door shutting behind her, and I turned to face him, his earthen eyes tugging on the arctic blue of mine.

"No," I said, my voice hurt and full of regret. It was the first truth I'd spoken all night. "How are you holding up?"

Alex rocked back on his heels, puffing out his cheeks as he blew out a deep breath. "Not great," he admitted, and I knew he was being honest, too.

The night was still, giving way to the reticent quiet now that Jenkins was gone.

"Do you want to go somewhere?" He finally asked when the silence became too loud.

I bit into my lower lip, debating. "Where do you want to go?"

He shrugged. "You tell me, you're the local."

I should have said no. I should have walked away and said goodnight, but I didn't. Instead, I ignored the ominous entity chilling my skin and speaking in riddles amongst the wind.

"I think I know a place."

We crossed the parking lot together, and I followed Alex to his truck, enveloped like a shadow lurking in the dark. As we pulled away, I looked back at Jenkins's somber apartment window and swallowed.

I've never saved a life before, but I have taken many.

CHAPTER THIRTY-TWO
Alex

THE NIGHT WAS A dark and petulant void carved out like a crater between the endless sea and sky. In the distance, seagulls called out to each other, hovering strangely over the top of a lighthouse—the same lighthouse Alex had seen pictured several weeks earlier—except now, its condition had deteriorated.

"What happened to it?" He asked, referring to its crumbling structure. It was unreachable from here, perched on top of algae-covered stones in the middle of the ocean.

Maeve followed his gaze. "I don't know. It's been like that for as long as I can remember."

What remained of its spiral staircase was still visible through a giant hole in the masonry. Its copper dome, now the color of seaweed, housed darkness instead of filtered light.

"The city condemned it years ago. There used to be a bridge there, but it's been destroyed by the swells. When the tide isn't in, you can walk along the rocks connecting it to the shore, but I wouldn't recommend it—people have been known to fall in."

He didn't need to ask her what happened to those whose fate was decided by the hungry water. If the current didn't drag them out to sea, the jagged rocks hugging the tiny island were sharp enough to tear flesh from bone.

It was the first time they'd spoken since they'd left the apartment. Alex tried forming words a few times, but they died in his throat—afraid he might say the wrong thing. Now they were sitting dangerously close to each other. And Alex could feel the heat of her skin barred between them as their legs dangled carelessly over the edge of a stone-slated crag.

The ocean roared, blanketing the rock pools below as the tide swept in. Occasionally, a rogue wave crashed violently against the uneven rocks, sending over a misty breeze that dampened his skin.

From his pocket, Alex freed a leather-bound flask he'd pilfered from the back seat of his truck. He kept it there in case of emergencies—when the overwhelming reminders of all his failures whispered dangerous thoughts into his ear.

The aroma of vanilla and oaky caramel fluttered through the top as he unscrewed the gasket. Pressing his lips to the bottle, Alex tilted his head back, forcing the amber liquid down his throat. When he finished, he handed the flask to Maeve, who hesitated briefly before conceding.

Alex watched as she brought the flask's mouth to her lips, her throat bobbing as she coaxed the syrup over her tongue. After inhaling what he thought was an impressive sip, Maeve dragged her hand over her mouth and smiled.

To their left, the lights of Saltridge filtered through the moonless night, casting a favorable glow over her silvery skin. Staring at her, Alex found himself in a state of reverie, unable to pull away.

"What are you doing here?" She asked, her voice suddenly breaking the reticence between them.

Alex cinched his brows. "I thought you wanted to come here?"

Maeve shook her head. "No, I don't mean here. . . I mean, *here* as in Saltridge." She pivoted to face him, catching the breeze off her shoulder as it blew off the water—tying them together in a scent of seagrass.

It was a valid question—one he'd been asking himself since he arrived weeks ago—one he still didn't have an answer for now.

Before he could speak, her voice cut in again. "I'm not trying to be rude—it's just that people only come here for one thing."

"And what's that?"

Maeve leaned forward like she was confessing a secret, her dark hair spilling over her face like a curtain of night. "To disappear."

The word was a rock in Alex's throat. "What do you mean?"

Her face was a stone. "Outside, the world is busy—fast and ever-changing. Here, everything is the same—easy and quiet. When people come here, it's because they're trying to escape something." Maeve raised her chin. "You reek of secrets," she said clearly. "So, what are you running from?"

Myself, Alex thought but didn't say. He stole another sip of whiskey—however, this time, it tasted sour.

"Do you ever feel like there are two versions of you?" He asked, leaning back on his hands—the wet rock, smooth beneath his palms. He wasn't looking for an answer—he was seeking validation. She shifted uneasily, and Alex cleared his throat. "I'm sorry, I know that probably didn't make any sense—"

"It made perfect sense," Maeve whispered, placing her hand over his and Alex felt a rush of heat surge through him.

Maybe it was the whiskey, but for a second, he contemplated kissing her. He *should* have kissed her. He should have leaned over and pressed his lips to hers, but he didn't. Instead, he hugged the ledge, forcing her to pull away.

Always the coward, never the fool.

"Did you grow up here?" Alex asked, eager to change the subject. He couldn't remember the last time he'd felt this useless around a woman.

Maeve nodded. "I've never been anywhere else."

"Never?" he asked, surprised.

"Never," she echoed.

"Do you ever think about leaving?"

She shrugged. "I don't think I could ever leave," she admitted before affording herself another sip from the flask, now almost empty. "But I think about it all the time. I dream about where I'd live, what I'd do, who I'd meet, and where I'd go. I hear Paris is nice, and Italy too. God, what it must be like to have the freedom you do—to come and go whenever you please."

Alex lifted his chin. "What's stopping you?"

"Everything and nothing at all," she sighed. Another sip. Another glaze over her eyes. "I couldn't imagine leaving Mercy, and then there's my mother. . ."

"I'm sure they'd understand," he offered.

"They wouldn't." Her voice was sharp—permanent. She recognized it and eased back. "It's complicated."

"What about your father?" Alex asked without thinking.

"My father died before I was born."

He winced, thankful he'd at least had the opportunity to know his. "I'm so sorry."

"For what?" she laughed, a rogue hiccup bubbling over her lips. "I didn't know him. It's not like there's anything to be sorry for." Her voice was smokey from the liquor, and he could tell by the way her words melted together that she was

WHAT LIES BENEATH THE TIDE

starting to feel the effects more intimately now. Pivoting, she asked, "What about you? What's your life like?"

Now it was his turn to suck down a swallow. "Full of tragedy," he whispered somberly.

"That must be. . . lonely," said Maeve.

Alex drew in a long breath. "It can be, but I don't mind it," he lied. "When you don't have anyone else to worry about, you can only disappoint yourself."

"What about when things are good? Who do you share those moments with?"

No one, he thought. "I have friends," Alex insisted—though truthfully, he only had one. A gust of salty air curled over them, and Maeve hugged herself against the breeze.

"What about your parents?" She asked innocently. "Are you close with them?"

Her question scraped over his skin like a razor, and it left him feeling raw. "My parents are dead," he replied.

Maeve's eyes rounded, the shadow of her lashes darkening them. "I'm so—"

"Don't say it," he lashed out without thinking, but he couldn't bring himself to apologize. "People keep saying that. They're dead, not lost. I didn't *lose* anything—they were taken from me." The words came out hotter than he intended, but they burned all the same.

She met him with silence. Then, "What were they like?"

Jesus Christ. There wasn't enough whiskey in the world for this conversation. There sure as hell wasn't enough in the flask.

Alex stared out at the endless horizon. "My mom loved to bake. She couldn't cook to save her life, but I would have been well fed if it were feasible to live off cupcakes and pies." He thought about his mother's favorite apron, which was so well worn that it sprouted multiple holes and patchwork over the hem. It was lying at the bottom of a box now.

"She always had flour in her hair, even when she wasn't baking. My dad and I were convinced she got up before dawn and doused herself in it so we wouldn't know it was turning grey."

Maeve laughed, and the sound of it wounded him. "And your dad?"

"My dad was a mechanic. The first thing he did when he came home from work every night, was pull my mother into him. And when she finally pulled away, the flour in her hair clung to the oil and grease staining his shirt."

Alex had forgotten those memories, the reminiscence of his father's grease-stained hands or the way his mother's cookies melted over his tongue.

"How did they die?" Maeve asked abruptly.

"Excuse me?"

"How did they die?" She repeated.

He'd never been asked that before. Mostly because everyone that knew him, knew what happened, but also because he wasn't used to someone being so direct.

Alex raked a hand through his dark hair, damp from the spindrift. "Car accident," he winced.

Maeve's face revealed nothing—as if what he'd just said was a mundane thought.

"If it was an accident," she finally said. "Then why do you feel so guilty?"

"I don't—" but he stopped, clenching and unclenching his fists as he straddled the line between denial and acceptance.

Maeve studied him. "You do, and now you're angry," she announced. "Why?"

"Because. . ." He bit out through clenched teeth. "I should have been there." The admission broke something in him as he shouted into the wind. "Because I was *supposed* to be there."

The night his parents died was the anniversary of his mother's remission. They planned this every year, and every year, Alex dreaded it. Not because he wasn't proud of her for beating cancer but because it somehow always turned into a guilt trip. He'd planned on being there, told them he would be—but deep down, he didn't want to go. Then, when Diego called, he jumped on the opportunity. What was one missed dinner going to cost him?

Everything.

He didn't want to sit there and listen to his parents guilt him into marriage. He didn't want to sit there and listen to his mother complain about how he was robbing her of the opportunity to be a grandmother. He couldn't bear the thought of his father's face—rigid with disappointment. So, instead, he went out with a woman he couldn't give two shits about to relieve himself of the only people in the world who gave two shits about him.

And now they were gone.

"If you *were* there, you'd be dead too," Maeve said, pulling him back to her.

Her comment was a blow to the chest—catching him off guard, and he struggled to find steady ground. In the distance, thunder roared, and Alex found himself suddenly praying for rain.

"After they died, I found all this stuff I didn't recognize. I've never been one to believe in signs, but I was desperate, determined to hang on to anything I could just so I could get through one more fucking day," he admitted. "Turns out it belonged to my brother."

Maeve shifted next to him. "What's he like?"

Lightning cut across the sky, illuminating the dark horizon before retreating into the night.

"I don't know," he said—his voice was worn, like the sound of rustling leaves against wet cement. "I don't remember him."

CHAPTER THIRTY-THREE
Maeve

THE SKY OPENED UP, and rain pelted my skin, soaking my hair and my clothes as we rushed inside.

We'd barely spoken. Alex's face remained a hard line, but I could see his thoughts tumbling freely as he sorted out whatever conclusions he'd come to on top of Beckerman's Landing. His dark hair stuck to his forehead, with wet strands brushing delicately over his lashes.

The sweetness of whiskey lingered on my tongue, and for a moment, I wished for more. My tolerance for alcohol was never strong, and so by the third or fourth shot, my head swirled, and my face flushed. It was why I'd felt compelled to say the things I did—and why I had chosen not to say the things I didn't.

Guiding me by the arm, Alex's touch was light but electric as he walked me to my door, where I stood, fumbling with my keys like a waiting fool.

"Do you want to come inside?" I asked, ignoring the hum beneath my skin.

The muscles in his jaw flexed as he thought it over. He was soaked to the bone, his white shirt sticking to the muscles forged along his chest, outlining the curves and sharp lines beneath it.

"I don't think that's a good idea," he said—an answer I was expecting but was disappointed to hear.

Probably he was right.

Alex leaned down and planted a soft kiss against my cheek. He smelled like the earth—of cedar and rain and fresh sky, like an echo of the thunderstorm raging outside.

Turning my head slightly, I forced his lips to meet mine. It was brief, less than a second, but in that fleeting moment I inhaled him, my inhibitions lost in a sea of terse desire.

His hands moved quickly, forcing me away. "Goodnight, Maeve."

"Goodnight," I whispered, my lips still excited from the feel of him—a familiar and intoxicating sensation—*one I've tasted before.*

Inside, Charley howled, screaming as the wind battered against the windows. It had been a long time since Saltridge had seen a storm this fierce, and I couldn't help but question its coincidence.

The ocean is capable of many things. It is a living, breathing entity blessed with unrelenting power. It can swallow entire cities, forge new landscapes, and drown civilizations without mercy.

Stealing myself into dry clothes, I draped myself over the sofa, staring out the window as the storm gained momentum. Tipsy, my mind wandered to Alex, of how broken and beaten down he was. He reminded me so much of myself in ways I never thought relatable to anyone.

And yet, we couldn't be more different.

It's moments like these where I longed for a different life. I wondered what it must be like to feel fully human—capable of giving myself to someone without the threat of repercussion.

Over the years, I've worked assiduously to keep my distance, never allowing myself the chance to feel something as humanizing as love—and over the years, it's slowly stolen away my benevolence.

I thought of Mercy and how she's survived all these years—and I do mean *survive*. Because what she's been forced to endure alternatively has been far from a life worth living.

Every day she swallows it, that thing inside her, while the rest of her dissolves into the very foam she's made of—until eventually, there will be nothing left at all.

The Lorelei in me stirred, lulled to sleep earlier by the liquor I'd poisoned it with. Sometimes it worked. Tonight, I wasn't so sure.

It's why my mother does it—to drown it out, to silence it. But part of me believes she enjoys the thrill. Controlling someone's fate is a powerful thing, and she gets drunk off it.

Stretching my legs, I stared aimlessly out the window and watched as nature engaged in war. Beside me, the light flickered before dimming and shining again as the electricity wavered.

My skin was still warm from the alcohol, and my head was heavy and full of fog. I let it consume me.

You're treading dangerous waters, Maeve.

I knew this, but I couldn't help it. The quietude was easy, and for a moment, I wanted to enjoy the peace. For a moment, I wanted to dwell in the luxury of not having to experience the whispers or sinister sneers edged along my inner thoughts.

I constantly felt like I was drowning, struggling to hang onto the life raft that is my humanity while the rest of me is slowly dragged under. And I wasn't sure how much longer I could keep my head above water.

Lightning tore across the sky, illuminating the tree line and sending a short-lived glow into my apartment. My eyes darkened, shifting from a clear sky—to charcoal grey.

Three seconds later, the lights went out.

———.———

"The powers out," Alex stated, his six-foot frame filling my doorway.

"It is," I replied, unsure of why we were being so obvious.

"Mind if I take a look at your fuse box?"

I nodded, leading him towards the utility closet in the kitchen. I tried not to take in his grey sweatpants and the thin black t-shirt, hugging his body in all the right places. I've come to realize that Alex prefers an elementary style—one that compliments his virility.

"Whole damn building needs to be rewired," he muttered to himself, flipping several switches back and forth inside the panel. When I didn't say anything, he turned to me. "Got a flashlight?"

I told him that I did, and after trying—and failing—to generate power, Alex finally threw in the towel. Inside I was teetering, reacquainting myself with the dark.

He handed me back the flashlight, but I refused it.

"I think I have candles somewhere around here," I assured him, knowing they wouldn't be enough.

Alex hesitated, his whiskey-soaked eyes dragging over me. Contemplating.

"Stay?" I asked, though it was more of a command than a request. The muscles in his body twitched as he fought to resist but couldn't.

They never do.

One word. That's all it took to convince Alex that he needed me.

Two steps. The space with which he crossed to close the distance between us.

Three seconds. The amount of time it took for his mouth to find mine.

———.———

There is intimacy in pain. One that is both gentle and profound.

Before his clothes were off, I knew Alex was prepared to offer all of himself to me. I could tell by the way his teeth scraped against mine fervently as he opened my mouth up to his.

My fingers threaded into his hair, pulling him into me. He tasted like whiskey and mint and rain as he lifted me up and forced me against the wall, his thick arms flexing, holding me steady.

With his hands in my hair, he tilted my head slightly and slowly caressed my neck with his mouth, trailing down my collarbone and over my breasts.

I draped my hands over his neck as he eagerly took one of my nipples into his mouth.

Instantly, I released a breathy moan as he suckled, trading one out for the other, moving diligently across my chest—his tongue flickering in soft strokes, nurturing them one by one.

When he was done, he gripped me from behind and strode over to the kitchen table, lying me gracefully on my back.

I didn't wait. With nothing but a silent request, I shimmied out of my clothes. Alex's gaze lingered on me—his eyes hungry now that I was fully exposed.

"Do you want to taste me?" I asked intimately. Inside, I was aching. The heat between my legs flushed as my wetness pooled on the table.

His answer was a wicked grin, and with his hands on my legs, he slowly spread them apart, dipping his head down until the heat of his mouth was on me. I sucked in a breath.

"Fuck," I moaned as he tenderly kissed the bundle of nerves swelling between my legs.

He was gentle—his touch forgiving as he dragged his tongue lazily over me before working a finger, then two inside.

"More," I whispered greedily. It was a hungry plea, a cry of desperation as I held his head steady between my legs.

The stubble on his jaw was drenched as he drowned himself in ecstasy. He couldn't breathe. I could tell by the way he was struggling, but I wasn't done yet. I wanted more. *I needed more,* and so I forced myself into his mouth, rocking back and forth mercilessly as he feasted on me.

His tongue plunged greedily in and out, and I screamed. "Just like that, fuck yes, just like that. . ."

I love it when they devour me first.

It's only fair after all. . .

When I finally decided I'd had enough, I pulled him away and brought his lips to mine, the nectar of my juices still sweet on his lips.

"My turn," I grinned, sinking between his legs.

Alex leaned back, welcoming me. Freeing his cock, I settled onto my knees, taking all of him into my mouth. Slowly, I pulled him into the back of my throat, and my eyes locked tightly on his as he thrust himself upwards—faster, harder, one stroke after another until I was all but choking.

Alex groaned, hardening inside my mouth as I stroked him softly with my tongue.

"Fuuuuck," he cried, and I sucked harder.

His knuckles went white against the arms of the chair as he gripped them, and the heels of his feet lifted as he rose against me. If I kept this up, he would implode, and I was desperate to feel him—all of him, inside me.

Wiping my mouth, I rose to face him. He was still gripped between my fingers, throbbing and eager for release. Understanding what I wanted, he reached for me, and together, we disappeared into the bedroom.

In here, the darkness was rich, draped over the walls like a curtain of the night swallowing the outline of his body as we moved onto the bed. My fingers traced over his broad shoulders as he mounted me, leaving behind a trail of goosebumps over his skin.

"Do you want me?" I asked—my voice euphonious and honeyed.

There were stars in his eyes. Constellations etched along the inside of his irises as he drank me in—mesmerized, *enchanted*.

Alex nodded mindlessly. "Yes," he breathed against me.

I wrapped my hands around his neck, pulling him closer. "Then I'm yours," I whispered.

In one swift motion, he buried himself in me. Pushing against his thrusts, I released a desperate, unbounded cry that echoed between us.

"Oh god," I screamed. But there was no god here. Just Alex, and me and my internal darkness.

In this form, I am enchanting—irresistible, lovely, and alluring. But in the water, we are wicked things—hideous and grisly. I am what nightmares are made of and what the devil himself fears.

It is why our voices sound like silk beneath the waves. We are a lie, *an illusion*. And why, when forced to live on land, we craft ourselves into something else. Something brilliant, something *desired*. If men were forced to see us for what we truly are, they would not be willing—and a soul is much harder to steal when you have to force it free.

With him hard inside me, Alex released a desperate, filthy moan—his hips rolling against mine as we rocked back and forth. The sound of our hearts beating was a metronomic rhythm, and I wrapped my legs around his waist, eager to feel every inch of him as he slid his cock inside me. But just when I thought he was on the verge of erupting, Alex slowed down.

"What's wrong?" I moaned through panted breaths.

His answer was a low groan emanating from the back of his throat. "I—I—" He stumbled.

I loved this part. The part where they think this could be something more—that *their love* for me was eternal when, naturally, it's the allurement—the sound of my voice.

The way I look.

"Fuck," Alex roared, he splayed his hands over mine, forcing them above my head—pinning my wrists. "I want to feel every inch of you," he growled into my mouth. "*I need you.*" His once soft strokes were hungrier now.

"Don't stop," I begged, and he didn't.

He went faster, harder until the top of my head rocked against the headboard. Steadily, Alex coaxed his way deep inside me, and I could feel myself tightening. My legs were trembling, still wrapped around his waist until I couldn't hold on any longer. He must have realized I was close because, once again, he slowed, pulling his cock to the tip. For a while, he lingered there, teasing me—taunting me.

I hated being teased. I hated being taunted.

"Please—fuck—me," I choked out, the words rotating in my mouth.

He didn't make me wait. Eagerly, he slammed into me, knocking the air from my lungs and I let out a sweet little cry. It was enough to shatter him. And together, we fractured in tandem.

All at once, Alex exploded into a roar of cataclysmic elation. A rush of heat flooded into my legs, coating the two of us as I shattered like glass against him.

When our bodies stopped shaking, and Alex fell beside me, I leaned over and placed my mouth over his. It wasn't a kiss but a mark—a hearken for the sea that he was next and that it must come to claim him.

Outside, the storm subsided, and the gentle patter of rain pelted the window. Above me, the lights flickered on, and the smoke in my eyes finally cleared.

I rolled onto my back, my entire body aching, abetted with the evidence of what we'd just done, slick between my legs. . . and yet, inside I felt hollow. Not because he didn't feel good, not because I didn't enjoy the heat of his breath against my skin or in my hair, but because of what I did—what it did.

What we did.

Together, we have condemned him—and soon, he would die.

CHAPTER THIRTY-FOUR
Alex

ALEX COULDN'T BREATHE. ABOVE him, water glistened, rolling against the sky as the ocean's overbearing weight pressed down on him.

Terror filled his lungs, terror and salty sea water as he opened his mouth to scream, but nothing came out. His throat was empty. Kicking his legs, he tried breaking the surface, but when he looked down, he realized his feet were caught in the hands of something he couldn't see but only hear. It hummed and purred—a sweet refrain beckoning him into oblivion.

He noticed her hair first, an icy sheet of black swirling around her like ink as the blue of her eyes cut through the water—deadpan on him.

"Maeve!" He tried, but she ignored him.

He was running out of time, running out of air—the pressure in his chest surmounting as he struggled—deciding whether he should save her, or *save himself.*

Alex eyed the surface, then Maeve—only to find that her fair-skinned complexion had turned a sickly shade of green. Her lips stretched into a vast, gaping slit curled over sharp, pointed teeth.

Terrified, Alex forced himself to swim harder but in the end, it was a fruitless endeavor.

She was fast—too fast. And in an instant, she was on him, her spindly fingers wrapped around his throat, forcing her lethal face to his. He opened his mouth to scream, to cry, to beg, but there was nothing.

Maeve smiled, or at least what he interpreted as a smile, before dragging her mouth over his and sucking out his soul.

———.———

Flinging his eyes open, Alex discovered a pair of yellow orbs staring back at him. The room was dark, shaded by drawn curtains where a sliver of buttery light leaked in. Pulling himself onto his elbows, he rubbed the sleep from his eyes and stared down at the bundle of fur resting comfortably on his bare chest.

Where the hell was he? And why was he naked?

Bits and pieces of last night cut into his thoughts. Jenkins. The tide pools. The thunderstorm—*Maeve*. How much did he have to drink. . . Not much, so then why did it feel like he drank his weight in whiskey?

Alex dragged his tongue over the inside of his teeth. The inside of his mouth tasted bitter, and he shook away images of Maeve on the table with her legs spread out before him.

Shit.

He heard movement—dishes clanging against each other and rushing water sputtering through the sink. This was her apartment, *her bed*, and she was out there waiting.

Alex shot a look towards the window, wondering if he could sneak out into the daylight unnoticed. But he was butt-ass naked, and he couldn't remember where he left his clothes. It was one thing to perform the walk of shame—it was another to do it in your birthday suit. Besides, Maeve wasn't just some random woman he'd picked up at a bar. She deserved better than that.

Swinging his legs over the side of the bed, Alex wrapped a thin sheet over his waist. The last thing he wanted was for her to stumble in here and catch him naked and vulnerable—even if she'd seen it all the night before.

Creeping along the edges of the bed, Alex searched desperately for his clothes. Brief flashes of him on top of her cut into his thoughts—vivid images of him fucking her so hard it shifted the entire bed. The memory sent a flood of heat between his legs, and he could feel himself stiffening again. He needed to find his pants—fast, before he couldn't conceal himself any longer.

Coming up empty, Alex was beginning to worry he might have taken them off somewhere else, and then what would he do? Present himself to her, naked and half hard? Another rush of blood shot into his legs as he thought of Maeve's fingers stroking him gently. Her mouth, hot over his. . .

He needed to get out of here—*now.*

Flattening himself against the floor, he peered under the bed, searching for something—anything that might belong to him. What caught his attention instead sent an electric shiver down his spine. Reaching for it, Alex extended his arm, freeing it from between the wall and frame.

With it now heavy in his hand, he balked at it, its gold links folding together as he shifted it gently in his palm. The front glass was cracked, its tiny hands frozen along the dial. It was covered in dust, accentuated by cat hair that was left behind in clusters all over the floor, but still, its gilded chain was unmistakable. The last time Alex had seen it, he was struggling against the man who wore it.

Now that man was dead.

There was a sick feeling in his gut, and as he beheld Mitch's watch in his hands, he wondered how the hell it had ended up here.

"—Alex."

He whirled around, cupping the watch behind his back and attempting to cover himself from Maeve's arctic stare.

"Oh. . . uhm, I'm so sorry. I thought I heard you moving around, and I just wanted to uhm. . . you know what, I'll just meet you out here when you're ready," she stammered, her cheeks red.

"Hey, Maeve?" He called after her, and she stopped. Her hands hovered over her eyes as if she hadn't just feasted on him—*or him her.*

"Where are my clothes?"

"Right, sorry," she said, speeding off only to return with his shirt and a pair of pants seconds later.

Once he was dressed, he found Maeve in the kitchen, perched at the very table he devoured her on.

"Hey," he said, running a hand over the back of his neck.

"Hey," she repeated, her voice weak. Her hair was a wild mess of tangles resting gently against her face.

"Powers back on," he noticed—feeling stupid now.

She nodded. "Came on last night."

He wondered if she felt as bad as he did—if perhaps this was unintended for her as well. Maybe she wasn't looking to pursue things any further. Maybe she felt just as embarrassed as him and was searching for the right words to say—to let him down easy.

Alex swallowed hard, sinking into the chair across from her. Might as well rip the band-aid off now. "Look, I'm sorry. I didn't mean for this to happen."

"Oh," Maeve murmured, realizing now where this was going.

Alex buckled, and a rip of guilt tore through his belly. For a second, he thought about Lucy and the night they'd spent together. How he'd fled from her bed in the middle of the night and never called, and how she confronted him days later, calling him out for what he was—a coward.

Now here he was again, doing the same thing to a woman who wasn't Lucy, who'd suffered enough pain and upheaval since his arrival in Saltridge and who he'd taken advantage of anyway—despite the somewhat lingering feelings he'd managed to develop for her in the short time he'd been here.

With a heavy sigh, Alex shoved himself away from the table as he searched for something to say—anything that would make this moment easier.

"Maeve I—" but he stopped, realizing that it didn't matter what he said, whatever words spilled out of him would be soaked in a lie, and he was so tired of running from the truth. "I'm a fucking mess," he finally admitted, dropping his head into his hands. "I've been a mess for a long time, and I thought maybe coming here would fix me but it hasn't. It's only made things worse."

Alex leaned forward, his hazel eyes radiating like burnt gold in the sun-streaked apartment. "I like you, I really do, and I think you're great. Fuck I mean, last night was. . ."

"It's ok, Alex, you don't have to explain yourself."

"No, but I do. I do because I don't want you to think I'm just some selfish prick who came here on a whim only to sleep with you the night before I planned on leaving," he said.

"You're leaving?" She asked, her words suddenly sharp.

He could feel the heat of her eyes on him, and like the dastardly man he was, he couldn't bring himself to meet them.

"It's time," he admitted soberly. "I came here looking for answers, and I found them. Now I need to go home. I need to go back to work. I need to piece myself back together and move on. This isn't my life, Maeve."

When she didn't say anything, Alex looked up and winced. The ocean in her eyes had faded into a dull, lifeless stare.

"Please say something," he begged.

Maeve chewed on her bottom lip. "What do you want me to say?"

Tell me you understand. Tell me I'm not making a huge mistake, he thought. But instead, he shrugged, defeated.

Crossing her arms over her chest, Maeve leaned back in her chair and sighed. "You don't owe me anything, Alex. Last night was fun, but it shouldn't have happened."

His head snapped up, surprised. "So, you understand?"

"I understand."

An awkward silence fell over them, prompting him to take his leave. This is what he wanted, after all. A clean break. An easy out, and she was more than willing to give it to him.

Ambling towards the door, a dark ball of fur darted between his legs, causing Alex to trip.

"Charley!" Maeve hissed, shooing him away. "I'm sorry, I don't know what's gotten into him. He's usually not this friendly."

"It's ok," Alex said, bending down and scratching Charley behind the ears. "I'm not much of a cat person, but my brother had a—" he stopped and stared at the cat whose mewling turned territorial. "How long have you had him?" He asked abruptly.

On the outside, she looked calm and collected—normal even, but Alex could hear the way her breath rattled against her tongue, her chin trembling just slightly as she scrutinized him.

"I don't know. It's been a few years, I think. Why?"

Alex cocked his head. Suddenly, the weight of Mitch's watch felt heavy in his pocket.

"No reason," he lied. "Listen, I don't want to drag this out any further than we already have, so I think it's best if I just go."

Maeve nodded. "Yeah, of course."

Neither of them made a move to hug or kiss goodbye. Fine by him.

Once inside Andrew's apartment, Alex pulled the watch from his pocket. It was hot in his hand, like a warning from the grave.

He thought about the day Mitch's body washed up on shore and how he'd caught Maeve snooping around near the water. At the time, he assumed she was just another nosey bystander, eager to glimpse morbidity, but what if she wasn't? What if she wasn't snooping around at all, but fleeing—desperate to get away before someone saw her. . .

Someone like Alex.

He thought of Jenkins, and the fear splashed across her face. He thought about how her body shook and how her voice trembled as she struggled to recount what happened. He thought about last night and the way it felt more like a dream than a physical moment.

In a handful of heavy strides, Alex crossed the room. He hadn't touched that cursed box since he'd arrived some weeks ago, and he planned to rid himself of it entirely once this was all over. But now there was something he needed from it.

Carefully, he freed the latch and raised the lid. The emanation of old wood greeted him as he peered down at the leather-bound notebook, its worn cover somehow less sinister now that he knew what lurked there.

When he reached the page he was looking for, Alex tried rationalizing it. He tried telling himself that it could have been anyone—or no one at all. Except there was nothing but naked truth here now.

Naked truth, and a blend of frosted blue through a black shade of onyx hair. Through the muddled blend of ink and paper—his fingers traced over the hard lines of her sharp cheekbones.

Once he thought these to be nothing more than the drawings of a madman, someone with a twisted mind and talented hand. Now, with a frightening chill settling into his bones, he recognized them for what they were. . . a warning.

CHAPTER THIRTY-FIVE
Alex

HE WAS GOING TO die. Alex knew that. He knew that just as well as he knew the sky outside was blue and that if you touched a hot stove, you would get burned.

He could feel it in his gut—*in his bones.*

And now that he knew he was going to die, he felt anger towards the universe for saddling him with nothing more than shitty instant coffee. Shitty *and stale* instant coffee because God only knew how long it had been sitting in Andrew's cupboards.

Putting the pieces together, Alex felt chagrin over his own ignorance. His whole fucking job was to notice the small details and yet, somehow, he missed the greatest one of all.

Maeve.

Alex didn't know jack shit about mythology or mystical creatures such as mermaids and sirens, but they weren't supposed to walk on land—that much he did know.

So how was this possible?

Forcing himself to consume another ounce of coffee—if you could even call it that—Alex spent the next several hours researching everything he could about the seductive sea maidens—which turned out not to be very seductive at all.

In Greek mythology, sirens were illustrated as half-human, half-bird-like creatures with honeyed voices and colossal wingspans. He tried picturing Maeve with her stunning black hair lengthened against equally ravenous feathers.

It wasn't until the Roman Empire that sirens were depicted as half-human-half-fish beings with exquisite voices tasked with the gruesome job of luring sailors and men to their watery deaths.

Alex shuddered.

He'd been toying with Mitch's watch all day, mindlessly curling and uncurling it between his fingers as he tried to figure out how to save himself.

If he could save himself.

So far, that didn't seem like an option.

When would she come for him? When would he hear it sing? He had no clue how this worked and desperately wished for Jenkins's company, but that wasn't an option either.

Jenkins.

Had Maeve? *No. . .*

Alex knew genuine fear when he saw it—he'd seen it many times, and when he found Maeve frightened in the hallway, she was just as shaken as he was.

How many were there? Two? Three? Hundreds? Jenkins said they called to you in the night, but what if Alex couldn't be summoned?

He could leave. He *should leave.* He should take off right now and drive until his eyes were heavy and his body begged for sleep. If he were far away enough, whatever song the ocean sang would fall on deaf ears as he put distance between them.

Alex bolted.

Fuck this place. Fuck this town, and fuck everyone in it. It was every man for himself now—literally. With his bag packed and his truck engine idling, Alex climbed into the cab and shut the door. He hesitated.

Andrew's cat—*damnit.*

It would be fine. It was fat and fully furred and happy—wasn't it?

"Shit!" Alex yelled, banging his hand against the wheel. Damn his morality. It was a cat, for Christ's sake—why should he care about this one?

Because it belonged to his brother, and even though he couldn't remember him, Alex had the good sense to know that Andrew would have gone back for him.

Giving the parking lot a precursory scan, he was relieved to find that Maeve's car was missing from its spot. But for how long? The clock on his dashboard read half past one, which meant if Maeve stayed for the early dinner rush—assuming she was at work—he'd still have plenty of time to get on the road and disappear.

With his truck still running, Alex quickly swung the door open and scrambled back inside.

He was never the best at picking locks but luckily for him, this was an old building, and a credit card was all he needed to jimmy the latch from its frame.

His hands were slick with sweat, making what should have been an easy job more difficult. Without James's TV camouflaging the sound of his movements, it wouldn't have taken much to alert anyone that he was prowling around.

How adept was a siren's hearing anyway? He didn't know. It didn't matter. All it would take was for Mercy to stick her head out and see him, prying the lock on Maeve's door, or worse—for Maeve herself to catch him.

Finally, the latch freed, and Alex stepped inside.

The afternoon sun painted a heavenly glow of shimmering light over the silent apartment. It looked just as it had this morning—*normal*. Not that he expected there to be a difference, or maybe he did now that he realized what Maeve was.

"Charley," Alex shouted in a whisper. But Charley didn't come.

The irony of the situation wasn't eluding. How many laws had he broken now? Three, at least, since he'd arrived some weeks ago. His department would have a field day if they ever found out.

Pray to God he'd be alive so they *could* find out.

Alex moved further into the living room, glancing under the couch and beneath the coffee table before trying again.

"Charley!" He hissed. Again, nothing.

He rolled his eyes, remembering the name stamped along his food dish in Andrew's apartment.

"Pickles. . ." He said, feeling stupid.

This time, the grey-tufted cat came scampering down the hall as if he were merely waiting to be addressed properly. At the sight of Alex's face, the feline looked relieved—if cats could show such emotion. He curled between Alex's legs, purring affectionately as Alex knelt beside him.

"You know who I am, don't you?"

Pickles cocked his head as if to say, *duh.* And Alex felt a rip of sorrow bleat into his chest. This cat had something Alex didn't—memories. Where Alex was forced to fill in the blanks of what Andrew may or may not have looked like, Pickles remembered.

God—if there was one—was an asshole.

Rising to his full height, Alex heaved a heavy sigh—there would be plenty of time for lamenting on the drive home. Right now, they needed to get the hell out of here before it was too late.

Reaching for the cat, he reared back quickly as Pickles started hissing violently at him—mewling and howling a throaty warning before bolting down the hall, followed by a loud and sudden crash.

Great, Alex thought, chasing after him as if he had nothing better to do but play a game of cat and mouse.

Hovering near Maeve's bedroom, the hair on his arms rose as he slid his eyes between the crack in the door. The sheets on the bed were fresh, and a brand-new comforter was draped elegantly over the mattress.

The cloud in his mind was still thick, murky, and full of smoke and he wondered if this was what it felt like to be drugged, the images hazy, yet sharp. Like the way a TV flickers in and out of signal or how a car window frosts over in the winter. You can still see bits and pieces through the glass, but they're harder to catch, so you do your best with whatever fragments you manage to steal and piece everything together from there.

Alex thought about his face between her legs, his tongue plunging in and out of her while she moaned in hungry delight. She tasted *so fucking good,* and he remembered her fingers in his hair and the way she smelled like lavender and citrus and sea as he explored her body with grace.

Then there was the way she felt, the way her body wrapped itself so effortlessly around his. Last night, he got the chance to experience pure, unrelenting ecstasy.

Now he felt dirty and used. Even worse—*he fucking loved it.*

At one point, Alex might have thought he loved her. He didn't—he knew that now, but as his cock throbbed mercilessly inside her, he damn sure felt like it was possible. Now he was awake and alert—vigilant to his senses, and he recognized it for what it was.

Pure and simple rapture. She tricked him, mind, soul, and body—and like an idiot, he fell for it.

How many men had she lured in here prior, including his brother?

That part made him uneasy. Even if he couldn't remember Andrew, the thought of knowing he'd sheathed his cock inside the same woman made him want to assert a vow of celibacy.

The nightstand next to the bed was tipped over, with its contents spilled recklessly across the floor. Alex assumed it had fallen when the cat barreled into the room, who was now trembling and whining under the bed.

"What the hell is wrong with you?" He asked, eyeing the mess Pickles left behind.

Quickly, Alex raked up a handful of loose bobby pins, a fine-point Sharpie missing its cap, and about three or four un-opened cherry-flavored chapsticks. Once he managed to clean up the mess, he lifted the table back onto its tapered legs and rapidly threw everything back inside.

Including Mitch's watch.

He didn't intend to leave it, but now that he was here, he felt it appropriate. The damn thing was cursed, and he didn't need to tempt fate any more than he already had.

With the weight of the watch now free from his hands, figuratively and literally, he shut the drawer—or at least he tried to anyway as it only allowed him to close it partially.

"You've got to be fucking kidding me," he groaned, giving it another nudge with a bit more force. It seemed to do the trick, only to pop back open seconds later.

Something was stuck behind it.

Alex yanked on the drawer, removing it from its tracks and peering into the empty slot. Sure enough, something was blocking it. Whatever it was must have fallen behind the top of the drawer when Pickles knocked it over. Sticking his hands inside, Alex removed the rounded object.

His heart sank in unrelenting horror as he stared at the stygian crystal orb, still warm in his hand.

An eye for an eye.

———.———

Alex wretched—his stomach sour as he hurled onto the floor.

He couldn't breathe. His chest was tight at the memory of Jenkins's body slumped over the bathtub, his face ripped open by something desperate.

Something inhuman.

"Is he going to be ok?" Maeve had asked him somberly. Her words sounded less hopeful and more disappointed now that he knew she'd been the one to rip him open.

And all this time, Jenkins knew. He knew, and he didn't say a fucking word when Alex probed him. Shock turned to rage. It was almost like the old man *wanted* Alex to end up here, marked for death and desperate.

He needed to leave. Now. He needed to put as much distance between him and this place as possible. If he left, if he got far enough away from the ocean, from Maeve, from this fucking nightmare—he'd be free.

Scooping up Charley—err, Pickles, or whatever his name was or used to be, Alex pivoted on his heels and fled. The cat whined in his arms, digging his claws into Alex's flesh as he cried like a battered thing.

Alex had half a mind to leave him behind, but he froze as he stepped into the living room. Pickles hissed violently at the woman standing between him and his freedom—a woman he'd never seen before.

"Well. . . well. . . well," she purred, her red lips curling into a menacing grin. "Seems the furry mongrel is useful after all."

CHAPTER THIRTY-SIX
Maeve

I HEARD IT WHEN the moon shadowed daylight. It was soft at first, barely a faint whisper as Sarah droned on about Tom's sudden desire to marry her—even though she'd insisted that what they were doing was just fun.

Then it got louder—more violent, and I knew the ocean had come to claim its due.

"—And then I slashed his throat with a knife."

"What?" I asked, whirling around to face her.

Sarah smirked. "I knew you weren't listening."

"Yes, I was." *Liar*

She rolled her eyes. "Where have you been lately?"

Trapped, I thought, but didn't say. "It's complicated."

Sarah brushed a strand of dark purple hair away from her eyes before focusing them intently on me. "It's that guy, isn't it?"

My spine went rigid. Inside, that entity was screaming—begging to be set free so that it might bear witness to its nefarious deed. *I won't go into the water,* I scowled at it. *I won't.*

Once I stepped into the water, Maeve would cease to exist, and all that would remain was the Lorelei within me.

I kept a list of their names tucked between my mattress—*Tyler, Seth, Matthew, Sean. . . Andrew.*

And now Alex.

It wasn't for victory but for punishment—a reminder that no matter how hard I tried to hold onto my humanity, I'd never fully deserve it.

The song outside raised itself several octaves. Sarah couldn't hear the lyrics hidden in the wind, but she could see the inevitable shift in the weather outside.

"Maeve—"

"What?" I asked, unaware of how sharp my voice was.

"What's wrong?" She asked—sensing my fear.

He's going to die, I wanted to tell her. *He's going to die, and it's all my fault.* I wanted to grab her by the shoulders and scream it in her face as if what was so obvious to me, should be obvious to her, but I didn't. Instead, I rushed for the door, the violent wind nearly ripping it off its hinges as I stepped into the early twilight.

"Where are you going?" Sarah's voice was a shout against the screaming in my ears.

But I ignored her.

Outside, waves crashed forcefully against the rocky seawall meant to protect the diner—however, this time, it failed. A rush of water flooded the parking lot, and I could hear Sarah curse in bewilderment.

To my relief, I made it into my car as a rogue wave crashed into the parking lot, flooding the pavement and forcing Sarah to lock herself inside before another one followed close behind.

Shoving the key into the ignition, I thanked whatever god might be watching as the engine cranked over with ease.

When I got home, Alex's truck was in the parking lot, and I felt a sigh filter through my lungs. It was brief because when I noticed the driver-side door was open, and the engine was idling—that same breath of relief quickly evaporated.

I barely parked before I swung open my door, its rusted hinges creaking menacingly into the windswept air. Rushing inside, I fisted my hands against Alex's door.

"Alex!" I screamed—my voice filled with terror. "Alex, it's Maeve, open up!"

". . . He's not here."

Her words were sharp against my back like tiny little knives edged between my shoulders. I pivoted to face my mother, whose sea-glass eyes were narrowed on me.

"How did you get into my apartment?" I asked slowly. Unease and turmoil simmered in my stomach, and I took a hesitant step forward.

She grinned, her fingers trailing deftly over the chipped paint on the door. "Your boyfriend let me in."

Time stood still, and I became very aware of my heart beating rapidly in my chest.

"What did you do?" I bit out, each syllable was a bullet meant to strike her down.

My mother laughed impishly. "*What did I do?* Oh Maeve, as much as I wish to take credit for your splendor, you and I both know that for once, I'm not the guilty party here."

I risked a glance up at Mercy's door. Where the hell was she? We hadn't spoken since I'd snapped at her the night before. Regret leaked into my veins.

My mother followed my gaze. "Oh," she quipped. "That's rich."

Don't give her what she wants. Don't fall into her trap, I told myself. But my face betrayed me, and hate spilled into my eyes—unrelenting hate as I glanced between my mother and where Mercy failed to appear.

"She couldn't even save her own lover—what makes you think she can help save yours?"

I didn't reply. Not because she was right, but because there was no satisfaction in it.

My mother took a tentative step towards me. Then another, until she was all but mere inches away. Her willowy fingers brushed lightly over my skin as she toyed with a strand of my hair, and I cringed. Her touch felt like acid, burning away at my cheek as her entity greeted mine.

"What does that make now? Eight? Nine?" Her eyes were alight with fire, and I realized she wasn't asking me—she was asking *it*, toying with it as if they were engaged in competition.

"I have to say, I'm rather impressed. I mean, brothers? Even I'm not that vile. Still. . ." She paused—her face blanched with sheer pride as if I'd done something glorious. "It fills me with such joy to know that you and I are not so different after all."

Her back slammed against the wall as I shoved her away from me with great force. "I am nothing like you," I spat.

I expected her to lunge for me. I'll be honest, I wanted her to, but she didn't.

Instead, she laughed wickedly. "Are you sure about that?"

I reared on her—my eyes filled with lethal venom. "I will *never* be like you."

Turning, I marched towards the door, but the sound of her laughter crawled up my back as her voice crept over my shoulder. "He's marked Maeve. He's marked, and there's nothing you can do to save him."

Ignoring her, I stepped back into the tempestuous night. I might not be able to save Alex's soul, but I could sure as hell, save mine.

CHAPTER THIRTY-SEVEN
Alex

ALEX WAS CHASING A memory. He knew that—even as he stumbled along carelessly with the wind ripping through his jeans and tearing away at his shirt.

Like teeth, it was a biting force, compelling him along as his feet slipped against the uneven surface of the rocks. Ahead, the lighthouse was a ghost, hovering in the shadows like a harbinger of death.

And next to it stood his brother.

He was taller than Alex expected, with hair several shades lighter than his and eyes much greener—like their mothers. He resembled her almost perfectly whereas Alex always favored his father.

Internally, he knew it wasn't really Andrew. Andrew was dead—his body nothing more than a pile of bones buried deep within the silted sand at the bottom of the ocean. Still, he couldn't persuade his body of it as he followed along aimlessly.

The melody of the waves crashing against each other was a soothing aria meant to drive him into eternity.

The rocky bridge between the shore and the lighthouse was a narrow one. His feet slipped several times over the sodden rocks, and Alex wondered how much time he had left before the tide finally swept in, covering them like they never existed at all.

Above him, the sky was clear—the silhouette of stars gleamed against the iridescent sky as day slowly gave way to night. Yet, the wind bent like a raging storm curated off the voracious swells slamming into the lighthouse before him.

Deja Vu greeted him kindly. He'd been here before when he thought his dreams were nothing more than nightmares. Except in those nightmares, he always woke up.

He was very much awake now.

I'm going to die, he thought. *I'm going to die, and no one will remember me.*

Is this how his brother felt? Is this what he saw the night he left his bed—the night he walked himself into the sea? Speaking of Andrew, his long-lost sibling waited patiently for him, his face still, his body unmoving. A harsh swell curled over Alex as he clung to the slippery surface—desperate for reprieve.

Help me, he wanted to shout, but Andrew had vanished, and in his place stood the temptress herself.

Choler rose in his cheeks as he searched Maeve's face—searching for the leviathan he knew lurked there. But he saw nothing. Instead, her argent skin shimmered in the early twilight. Her coral lips were like supple roses laden with dew as she called out his name.

"Alex. . ."

She was the most exquisite creature he'd ever seen. Not a monster at all, but a magnificent woman with hair the color of darkened sky and eyes so pure he could see his soul in them.

One step. Then another.

Sunlight was fading rapidly over the tips of the precipice, and soon obscurity would root itself between them. Maeve called to him again, except this time it sounded much sweeter.

"Alex. . ."

He gazed longingly at her—at her breasts peeking through the white billowing gown she'd donned, now sheer from the spindrift. His eyes traced over every curve, every line in her body as he fought against the heavy wind—his own body soaked and shivering.

Last step.

To feel the weight of the small island beneath his feet was great, but it was a respite he couldn't dwell in. He had to get to Maeve. From where she stood, her mouth formed words he couldn't hear, carried off by the violent roaring in his ears.

He *needed her.* It wasn't desire or ravenous yearning that compelled him forward, but the way his lungs needed air to breathe or how the sun could only exist alongside the essence of the moon.

Turning her back on him, Alex called to her, but his voice came out a garbled mess of syllables and words.

He tried again—his voice lost.

Tossing her hair over her shoulder, Maeve craned her neck and smiled.

"Come with me," she sang euphoniously. *"Come with me and you will see..."*

Wherever she went, Alex would follow. He was tired—so tired, but he was desperate to feel something and nothing at all.

"Just you and me and the sea," she promised. *"Beneath the tide, we'll both be free."*

No more guilt. No more self-loathing. No more regret, or grief, or tribulations eating away at him until there was nothing left but bare bone.

Nothing left but this husk of a man he'd become.

He watched as Maeve slowly backed into the ocean—her white gown disappearing beneath the surface as her hair bled into the water.

"Alex!"

His name was a whisper in the wind, a harmonious echo.

"ALEX!" It rang again, this time louder—clearer.

On his knees, he gazed into the water, unable to see Maeve beneath the murky surface, but he knew she was there, waiting for him. He could hear his name on her tongue.

"ALEX STOP!"

This time, it cut him open from behind—the sound of it sharp and dire, like it had been ripped from her throat. Alex jerked around to see Maeve straddling the stony bridge behind him.

That wasn't possible because Maeve was—

A burning sensation tore through his limb, crawling up his fingers as something sharp gripped him with such force that it almost ripped his arm off completely.

Maeve was gone, and in her place swam a hideous, monstrous being with eyes the color of malice.

Alex let out a brief scream. It was the only breath he'd managed to inhale.

The last one he'd ever taste.

CHAPTER THIRTY-EIGHT
Maeve

OF ALL THE MEN I've condemned—I've never watched them die.

Still, as I clamored over the slippery rocks leading up toward the lighthouse, I was doing my best to convince myself that Alex wasn't dead.

Not yet. If he were, I'd know it.

I wasn't sure whose scream pierced the gale first, mine—or his. One minute, I could see him kneeling before the ocean like a sacrifice, and the next, he was gone.

Humans are silly creatures—easily manipulated and never aware. Such easy prey. . . the siren in me sneered.

"FUCK YOU," I cursed out loud—my eyes still trained on where Alex was pulled in.

The heavy sun all but disappeared behind the scarp, tinting the sky a sinful red—the color of blood. A tear ripped through my belly, coercing another unsolicited monologue from the creature lurking beneath my flesh.

I am the one who needs to be fed. I am the one whose hunger is never satiated. It doesn't matter how many of them I take or how many souls I claim, it will never be enough.

Ignoring it, I continued forward, knowing the tide would soon sweep in and carry any remaining thing out to sea.

Including me—*and wouldn't that bitch just love that.*

A few more steps—a few more steps, and then what? I fell, my hands scraping over the jagged rocks, ripping them open and I couldn't bring myself any further.

Another ache in my bones, another rip in my belly.

From here, the swells whispered cruelly to each other. And still, it wasn't enough to drag me from where I refused to pursue him any further. Not because I didn't want to but because I simply couldn't.

If I jumped in, whatever was left of my humanity would be stripped from me, and *that thing*—the siren whose embedded nature I was born with—would be set free. I would never feel the land beneath my feet again.

The very air I breathe would cease to exist—replaced by bitter salt in waves I'd no longer be able to live without. All traces of my humanness would disappear—and that grueling monstrous thing would finally prowl these waters.

The way it was supposed to be.

I sat back on my heels, tears streaming down my face—my heart crumpling like paper inside my chest.

Then I heard it.

Feet running up behind me, the sound of water splashing beneath thick shoes. Turning my head, I caught the blur of a man racing towards me.

Not just any man—Jenkins.

He was clad in a pale blue hospital gown—waving wildly in the wind as he barreled towards me. From here, I could see his face—hardened in the dimming light. Against his forehead, running down his cheek were three long bandages—a gruesome reminder of where I—*where it,* tore him open.

For a moment I was convinced he wasn't real, but as he bounded closer to me, his heavy footsteps echoing over the roar of the violent sea—I quickly realized Jenkins was very much alive.

And now he's come to seek his vengeance.

I rolled out of the way, forcing my back into the shivering rock of the plateau. Jenkins stopped—his good eye finding mine. "A life for a life," he sneered before lunging himself off the rocks and into the hungry water.

———·———

One. . . Two. . . Three minutes passed, and still, there was nothing.

I glanced at the spot where Jenkins disappeared, searching for something—a sign of life, anything that would have made his sacrifice worth it.

Four. . . Five. . . Six. Still nothing.

All those years ago, Jenkins failed to save Max, and now he'd given himself for Alex. I held my breath, the blood in my veins—a rushing course of burning need to not go in after them.

Seven. . . Eight. . . Nine. . .

There's no way he'd survive this long. The ocean was violent, the elements wicked, and even from here, I could feel the frigidity of the water coursing through the air.

I turned my back on the watery grave. For years, I've stupidly convinced myself that I was different. That I wasn't like them. That I was better.

Turns out I was worse.

A sputtering sound echoed over the water, and I pivoted—my eyes wide as I watched Alex drag himself to the surface. His dark hair was nearly black, covering his face and curling over his ears as I ran to him. Shoving my hands beneath his arms, I dragged him the rest of the way over. Once he was clear, Alex rolled onto his side and vomited.

"Oh my god," I gaped at him, my hands coveting his shoulders—afraid to let go. "Are you alright?"

Alex coughed, his chest rattling in his throat. "Don't fucking touch me," he seethed—his voice raw and caustic.

He tried standing, but his legs were weak, and he fell clumsily onto his hands. His knuckles were sliced open, and on his back, a pool of blood soaked through what was left of his torn shirt.

"You're hurt," I choked out—my eyes scanning the rest of him as he finally stumbled to his feet.

Alex's hands went to his back, and he winced before stumbling past me.

"Where are you going?" I shouted at him. The tide was rising over the rocks—blanketing them in hungry sea water—cutting off his escape.

"It's a short swim," he bristled, his marred flesh facing me.

"Are you out of your fucking mind?" I shouted, balking at him. "The current will drag you away long before you reach the shore." At this, he stopped. "Soon, this entire island will be underwater, and us with it if we don't get to higher ground now."

He glanced up at the lighthouse—its outline, a shadow in the rapidly approaching night and I knew what he was thinking.

"Please. . ." I begged, the word a faint tether. "I promise I won't hurt you."

The muscles in his back shifted, and thick blood poured from his wounds. We had only mere minutes before the tide was fully upon us—until the very land beneath our feet was gone. Alex crossed back to where I was waiting, leveling a look of hatred so pure that the heat of it burned my skin.

"Too late," he whispered.

———.———

There was no electricity. Inside, the lighthouse was a hazardous mess of fallen stone and pitch-black ambiance. Every so often, a giant swell knocked into the side of the foundation, causing the crumbling lighthouse to sway and shift, and crumble some more.

We made it into the living quarters. Above us sat the service room and gallery—both were missing structural walls on several sides.

Neither of us spoke.

Across the room, Alex hugged the brick interior—adding several feet of space between us. There wasn't much in the way of furnishings. The previous Lightkeeper cleaned house long ago. The only items left scattered about the cold, dingy room were an empty table, an old chair, and an antique desk with two of its four drawers missing, along with a broken oil lamp.

Even the fireplace sat bored and lifeless.

I nearly cried when I discovered a half-used pack of matches, holding it up like a lifeline between me and salvation.

"What are you doing?" Alex asked, his voice breaking the quiet.

"What does it look like I'm doing?" I replied, working to strike a match. When the tip finally sparked, I tossed it onto the wooden drawer, igniting it instantly.

The glow of the flames danced wickedly over Alex's face. His eyes were wide and bloodshot, singed by the briny ocean water. A thin film of white bleached his lips as he shivered violently underneath his wet clothes.

"Here," I said, tossing a pair of trousers and a jacket left hanging in a nearby closet. "You're freezing—"

"I'm fine."

"You're not," I said, my nerves tiring. He had every right to be pissed at me. He had every right to hate me, but pride is a selfish thing—known to get men killed, and in this case, Alex would be dead by morning.

Kneeling beside him, I stretched out my hands, reaching for his back, but Alex shoved me away.

"I said don't fucking touch me." His words were full of venom, and they sliced through me like a newly forged blade.

I sighed, falling back on my heels. "You're bleeding all over the floor. At least let me see how bad it is."

He didn't budge.

"Fine," I said, standing. Lifting my arms above my head, I shrugged out of my shirt. With my teeth, I ripped the seam beneath the collar, tearing away the fabric until all that was left were lengthy strands. "If you won't let me help you, at least help yourself."

Wind from the break above us tunneled through the room, biting into my now bare skin, but it didn't bother me. Sirens were built to handle the cold, but I edged closer to the fire anyway.

It was going to be a long night.

Behind me, Alex's breath was shaky. A low moan slipped into the quiet more than once as he maneuvered out of his wet clothes and into the dry ones. Outside, the ocean was angry and violent.

A life for a life, it screamed.

For a while, things between us were quiet. Even without words, I could feel Alex's eyes hard on my back—the fire in them raging hotter than the one before us.

When the embers turned red, I withdrew the remaining drawer from the desk and tossed it onto the ash of the old one.

It sizzled and sparked and cracked, sending a brilliant glow over the two of us.

"Why?" It took a moment for Alex's voice to register but when it did, I turned my head to face him.

He was shivering, though less now that he was wearing dry clothes. The coat hugged his chest, and I could see the fabric of my shirt bound tightly against him. The pants were left unbuttoned, too taut to fasten, so the v-lines of his abdominal muscles were left exposed.

I swallowed, returning my gaze to the hungry flames. "I didn't choose to be what I am any more than you chose to be what you are," I stated simply.

"Bullshit," he sneered.

"What do you want me to say?" I returned.

"I want you to look me in the eyes and tell me you didn't fucking lie to me this whole time." There was pain in his voice. Pain and anger, and shame and hurt all rolled into one, and the swing of it hit me hard in the chest.

I rounded on him. "I didn't lie!" I insisted, although withholding the truth was just as much a falsehood as any.

Alex leaned forward, tossing something at me. It rolled freely over the uneven floor, settling ominously in front of the fire.

An eye for an eye.

The siren in me screamed, thrashing and slamming itself against my bones like prison bars.

I sucked in a sharp breath. "Where did you get that?"

"Where did *you get it?*" He spit back at me.

I turned away.

"You tried to kill James." It was an accusation, not a question.

I closed my eyes, determined to erase the memory of Jenkins's body struggling beneath the weight of mine.

"You killed Mitch." Alex continued, his voice sharp and brutal.

"Stop it," I begged as images of Jenkins slowly bled into visions of Mitch.

"You murdered my brother. . ."

"Enough!" I yelled. The truth can be unbearable when slated against you.

". . . And you damned me."

I stood violently. The heat of the flames curled over my shoulder like a cape, and for a moment, I felt like the devil.

"You don't know a fucking thing about me," I seethed, my face so close to his I could see the fine pores in his skin.

Alex looked up at me stoically. "I know you're a monster."

I should have expected this, but for some reason, it still caught me by surprise. The bottom of my lip trembled, and my voice spilled out a soft and broken thing. "What if I don't want to be?"

CHAPTER THIRTY-NINE
Maeve

IT IS A COMMON misconception that a great ruler presides over the sea. Several cultures have many names for their gods but the truth is that the ocean is its own deity.

It is also a cruel one—ruthless and unforgiving.

Alex flinched against the flayed wounds marring his back. Blood soaked through the makeshift bandages, but there was nothing left to spare for more, and I wasn't going to strip myself bare, not even for a wounded man.

The light of the fire echoed in his eyes like a warrior, and if it weren't for the obvious malice between us, I would have found it enticing.

Outside, the wind died down, and the ocean rested. No songs or tempting enchantments lured off the swells, but the tide remained steady, and with the torrent came unrelenting danger lurking below the surface.

Sirens work alone—every woman for herself, but once a soul's been claimed, they'll often linger in droves until the water has receded and they're driven back into the depths from which they emerged.

"How come you don't look—"

"Like one of them?" I finished for him. "Who says I don't?"

The sudden intake of breath between his teeth was enough to tell me he wasn't expecting that.

Better to be feared than hated.

The conversation between us, like the fire burning before us, sparked and flared and died and smoldered. Whenever Alex lashed out, his accusations ignited a rapid fire of emotion. Like the flames licking away at the brick inside the hearth, his words left a charred, blackened smoke over my skin.

I did my best to stoke them, to ease both him and the monster swelling inside me, but like the embers, they seethed, leaving behind a blistering raw truth.

"How many?" Alex asked, the debility in his voice wavering from exhaustion and pain.

"Several," I said, recounting their names in my head.

Tyler, Seth, Matthew, Sean, Andrew, Jenkins. . .

Sometimes, if I was lucky, part of me would fade away—and I wouldn't be forced to witness it's horrible wickedness. It was a small mercy, in the moment. But eventually the aftermath would come flooding back, and the haunting memory of their blood staining my hands would return.

Tyler, Seth, Matthew, Sean, Andrew, Jenkins...

I always wanted to forget—a luxury others had that I was jealous of.

I wished for it most of all now.

"What happened to Mitch?" He tried again.

For the first time, I faltered, and he noticed. "What about him?"

Alex pursed his lips. "Jenkins said when a siren steals a soul, it steals their memory. It's been over a week, and I still remember him."

"Some men don't have souls," I whispered soberly. "And besides, I didn't mark Mitch. He took what he wanted because, like most men, he felt entitled to something that wasn't his."

I might be what I am, but in my experience, humans are equally sinister—if not worse. Mitch was left behind to serve as a warning—an example. A *consequence*.

Alex didn't argue. Instead, he asked, "Jenkins suspected you, didn't he?"

I nodded silently.

"And you killed him for it."

"I didn't kill him," I argued. Technically Jenkins killed himself—*sacrificed* himself. And even then, my intentions were

never to kill him. But he wanted to kill me. And what was I
going to do. . . *let him?*

"And Andrew?" Alex urged his brother's name—a tor-
mented ghost between us.

Brothers, even I'm not that vile. My mother's words echoed
in my ears, and suddenly, I felt like puking. *You and I aren't so
different after all.*

Maybe she was right.

———.———

Heartache and grief made my eyes heavy, but I couldn't sleep.
Not with Alex's gaze searing holes into my back.

"If you have something to say, say it," I said, tired of dancing
around each other.

He opened his mouth, then closed it. For what it's worth, I
didn't mean for this to happen. I didn't want this to happen.

I stood, trying not to notice how he flinched as I stalked
over to him, kneeling to stoke the fire—the charred remains,
nothing more than glowing embers now.

"I thought sirens lived in the water," he said, eyeing me
warily.

"They do," I replied. Taking my chances, I folded my legs and planted myself beside him. Alex wrapped his arms around himself. We were running out of things to burn, and daylight was still hours away.

"How many are there?" He asked, shivering.

"In the water? Thousands. There are many oceans and plenty of seas, but on land, there's only us three."

Alex raised his brows. "Us?"

I nodded. "My mother, whom you've already met—" The mention of her burned like a hot iron to my chest. I swallowed. ". . . And Mercy."

I assumed he already knew this, considering he'd figured everything else out on his own. But when his eyes widened, I realized the mention of Mercy's name surprised him.

"They're landlocked," I continued. "Sentenced to live the remainder of their life on land for crimes they've committed against the sea."

"What kind of crimes?" Alex asked. I couldn't tell if he was simply trying to pass the time, trying to make the best out of a shitty situation, or if he genuinely wanted to know.

Humans are curious things.

I rubbed my hands over my legs, over the birthmark staining them. It ached now, being so close to the ocean. "My mother stole something from it, and Mercy. . ." I winced, still reeling from our fallout. "Mercy fell in love."

To fall in love was a cardinal sin—a transgression punishable by death. Mercy not only broke that rule, she encouraged it—abandoning who she was to live alongside the man she loved.

The night I was born, the ocean wreaked havoc. The sky split open, and the wind cleaved rocks from trenches. An endless rain flooded the streets of Saltridge—and the lighthouse, once a thriving beacon, succumbed to its violence.

Of course, I don't remember it, but it's been told to me enough times—*thrown in my face* enough times—to recite the details accurately. When my mother came for Mercy's great love, she begged my mother to spare him.

"What's one soul over a hundred more?" Mercy pleaded.

My mother stroked her belly, her fingers moving delicately over the spot where I was tucked away. "Personally, I think he's worth nothing. But—It's either you or him."

A life for a life.

"That's a lie, and you know it," Mercy argued—her brown skin glowing in the moonlight. "The moment I step back in the water, you'll kill me, and then you'll kill him."

My mother glanced between Mercy and her lover, still teetering the rocks near the lighthouse. "Choose," she demanded.

"Please," Mercy beseeched. "Spare him, and I promise to send a thousand others in his place."

My mother narrowed her eyes. "Move," she commanded dangerously. "Or I'll take both of you with me, and his death will be for nothing."

"I will not," Mercy challenged, her voice lost over the screaming wind.

My mother smiled wickedly. "Suit yourself."

"What was his name?" Alex's voice cut into my thoughts.

"Who?" I asked, my mind slipping between then and now.

"The man Mercy fell in love with."

Names hold great power. They are a beacon—a tether to individual identity. They are how you are known coming into the world and how you are known when leaving it. It's why they are the very first thing we strip away when claiming a soul.

I chewed on my lower lip, contemplating before releasing his identity. "His name, was Max Wiley."

CHAPTER FORTY
Alex

THE SOFT ALLURE OF the fire crackling beside him should have been enough to ease Alex's mind. But the searing pain in his back served as a reminder that even if he'd managed to free himself from the monster in the water—one still sat across from him now.

It was easy to hate something ugly, and by all accounts, he *wanted* to hate her—he certainly feared her now that he knew what she was.

Maeve's voice fluttered between them. "We walk on land to hunt when the tide is out, but we must return before it comes back in—if we don't, we're landlocked," she said. "When Mercy failed to return to the sea that night, it tasked my mother with finding her."

Alex could see it in her eyes—flickering like a shadow behind a flame. It didn't have a form or a shape, just a presence, an essence lingering within her.

I bet you taste the same... it spoke to him in tongues.

A gust of wind blew into the open crevice above, and Alex tensed to keep from shaking. His bones felt like ice.

"Will you please let me look?" Maeve's eyes fell on his back.

He wanted to argue. The last thing he wanted was for her to touch him, but he was weary, and fuck if it didn't hurt. Against his better judgment, he gave her a silent nod. With her help, he shrugged off the jacket, flinching and seething between his teeth.

As Maeve unwinded the strips of fabric from his chest, Alex tried not to meet her heavy gaze. Her touch felt different now, lighter and more delicate than the night before, revealing the stark difference between *who she was* and *what she was.*

He didn't know how to explain it. Last night, her touch was primal, now it felt more fragile—more human. Shifting uncomfortably, another searing wave of pain rippled over his shoulders as Maeve pressed her fingers to his back.

"You said your father died before you were born," he bit through clenched teeth. "Was he like you? Or was he. . . like me?"

"Human?" Maeve asked, inspecting his injuries. "Sirens are strictly female—we can't reproduce on our own. So yes, to answer your question, he is—*was,* like you."

Alex's eyes leered over her abdomen—horror blanching his face. "You're not. . . there's not. . . is there?"

Maeve laughed nervously. "No—if there were, you'd be dead."

Speaking of which, "What happens now that Jenkins is gone?" He asked, straightening as she rewound the bandages over his chest. Instead of pulling his arms through the jacket, she draped it over his shoulders, blanketing him.

"I don't know," she whispered. "I suppose you're free. If Jenkins sacrificed himself for you, and if a life has been claimed in exchange for another, the mark I—" Maeve winced. "The mark *it* gave you no longer exists."

Alex ran his tongue over his lips as if he could still feel it there, and a flood of relief swelled in the pit of his stomach. The moment the tide receded, Alex would leave, and hell if he ever went near the ocean again.

"What happens to you?" He asked, slumping his body against the brick once Maeve pulled away.

"Life goes on the way it always has," she admitted.

Alex understood what that meant. It might not have been him tonight, but it would be someone else—another man lured in by her beauty, by the creature lurking behind her eyes.

Only that man wouldn't be so lucky.

He opened his mouth to say something but thought better of it. What could he say? Tomorrow, before the sun rose, he'd be gone along with whatever frightening memories were sure to plague him. No amount of therapy in the world could undo what had been done.

Neither of them knew what time it was, late—early—somewhere in between, judging by the moon's position in the sky. Alex sighed, his body succumbing to fatigue. He fought to keep his eyes open, fearful of what might happen once he was vulnerable to sleep, but he couldn't force them open any longer. His mind drifted along the cusps of repose, and his body gave in and between him and Maeve, things were quiet.

Almost quiet.

CHAPTER FORTY-ONE
Maeve

THE OCEAN'S HUNGER WAS satiated—for now. Eventually, that hunger would return, and when it did, the haunting sound of it would echo in my ears like a continuous strum of quavers and minims.

I shivered.

Overnight, I didn't dream—I barely slept, and underneath my flesh, my siren was quiet.

Too quiet.

The silence thrummed over me like fingers tracing over my skin—a final note in a crashing symphony against the fluttering ambiance of waves rolling into one another. There were no more alluring rhythms—no melodic tunes or enchanting ballads chorded among them.

For once, I spared a life instead of taking one. And oh, how angry it would be once it woke.

Every day, I tethered myself to my humanity. Every day, I fought the urge to give in to the evil lurking inside me. And every day, it was a little harder to resist.

I was tired—*so fucking tired.*

My body ached in ways one could never imagine. The constant pain of hunger in my belly was raw and hollow, and over time, it weakened me.

How many more men would have to die until I'm finally set free?

Looking at Alex, who was fast asleep—his chest rising and falling carefully with each breath, I thought of my mother. It's taken years—decades, but in this moment, I finally understood her.

Alex's back would heal, scar, and fade, but as long as I continued fighting who—*what* I was, I would carry a constant open wound inside me.

And I would never, truly be free.

For several minutes after Alex fell asleep, I watched him. My eyes traced over the slight curve of his nose, dancing beneath the length of his fine lashes.

I've never known love. Not the way Mercy did, and I envied her for it. To give up everything you are for something so powerful was a sacrifice I'd never have the privilege of experiencing.

In the end, I may drown a thousand men, but the solitude that follows carries a much greater punishment.

It is a curse we are born with and one we will die bearing.

At some point, I must have fallen asleep. Morning light spilled into the wide gap of the masonry—veiling my eyes as I opened them. Sitting up, I jolted, rattled awake by the screeching sound of the siren's cries—fierce and unwavering.

Across from me, the fire smoldered, sending light wisps of smoke over its dusty ashes. Panicked, I rubbed the sleep from my eyes and peered across the room, seeking Alex, but he was gone.

———.———

Taking the broken steps one, two. . . three at a time, my legs were shaking, and my hands slipped over the algae slicked brick, weathered by the sea. When I reached the bottom, I jumped over the ladened rocks, edged along the foundation, and peered out into the blazing summer sun.

The tide receded some hours ago, pulling itself back into the ocean until it would eventually rise again. Behind me, it whispered, its song shimmering over my skin as I frantically searched for Alex—relief washing over me when I finally spotted him perched between the stony shelf of the jetty and the shore.

When he heard me approaching, he turned to me. "I can hear it," he said. "It's soft and soothing, and when it says my name, I don't feel any pain."

I stared wildly into the horizon, my eyes shifting over the shore.

"Cover your ears," I instructed, unsure if that would make a difference. He did as I asked, and together, we straddled the stones.

"I thought you said James's sacrifice—"

"I know what I said!" I snapped, feeling horrible, but I was panicked, frightened, and confused.

There were several yards between us and the shore, and I could feel the siren slithering between my veins—curling itself inside my chest as my heart thundered rapidly.

To think the ocean would give him up so easily. . .

I shook it away, focusing on the land ahead of us—on safety. All around us, the ocean roared—sending rogue waves splashing into the side of the jetty. More than once, we fell, our bodies crashing into each other as we clung to each other desperately.

Oh how the tide had turned. Hours ago, he refused to let me touch him. Now, his life depended on it.

When we finally reached the other side, Alex collapsed, his blood soaking the sand from where the bandages gave way—the trauma on his back, ripped freshly open.

"What do we do now?" He asked, his breath heaving against the pain. If Jenkins's life didn't spare Alex's, his reparation was for nothing.

"I don't know," I said, trying to catch my own breath.

But I knew someone who did.

———.———

Mercy was draped over a loveseat in her living room. I knew the moment I opened the door that something was wrong—I knew because I could smell it. The harsh stench of rotting fish permeated the air. Next to me, Alex gagged—the pungency of it, all-encompassing.

"Mercy!" I cried, dashing over to her. She tried sitting up, but the open sores dotting her flesh prevented her from moving. "What happened?"

Mercy sighed, "Nothing happened. I'm dying, that's all."

"No. . ." I whimpered, threading my fingers into hers. I knew this was coming, and I ignored it anyway.

The fuliginous markings that once crawled up her arms were now open, weeping caverns. Beneath them, I could see her bones, brittle and frail like the rest of her.

"What do I do? What do I do?" I cried out wildly—desperate to put her back together.

Mercy gave me a limp smile. "There's nothing you can do. Such is the cycle of life, and by all accounts, I've lived a good one."

Behind us, Alex cleared his throat, and Mercy's gaze drifted over my shoulder. "You're alive," she stated, more relieved than surprised.

"Barely," Alex whispered.

I could tell he was afraid—watchful of how her skin peeled and flaked away—revealing black scales decaying over her long legs. What was left of her flesh bubbled up, creating pockets of spongy fluid that opened and dissolved into foam.

"So it's true," he wavered. "You're really a—"

"Siren? Lorelei? Monster? Demon? Or perhaps devil?" Mercy's voice cracked when she spoke. "I've heard it all, Alex. Your words won't offend me any more than they once did the first time they were slung at me. Tell me, what makes you and I any different?"

Alex canvased her body. "Well, for starters," he pointed to her legs—to the rotting flesh marring her body.

Mercy waved a dismissive hand. "Semantics," she argued simply. "It's not what's on the outside that makes us human. It's what's on the inside that matters."

"You've killed people," Alex argued—his frame still hovering hesitantly near the door.

"I have, and so have you. In fact, mankind has killed more of its own—and plenty of others—since the dawn of time. What makes you less evil than me? Than her?" Mercy's eyes cut to mine. "Empathy, compassion, mercy, and love. . . Those are what make you worthy of life."

"And what about Max's life?" He dared her.

The mention of her lover's name was a heavy weight slammed against her. I could hear the sharp intake of breath as Mercy winced.

"I begged for his life," she defended. "But it wasn't enough. The ocean sought penance for my transgressions and has sought to punish me every day since." Mercy dragged a bony hand over her legs, lifting the hem of her dress, displaying herself more freely. "*This*—this is nothing. Physical pain is temporary, and I've suffered with it long enough. But heartache? Hurt? Loss? That is an illness—one that is much harder to recover from."

Alex opened his mouth to argue, but Mercy held up a hand. "I loved Max fiercely. And when I refused to give him up, the sea came for him anyway. So please, spare me whatever harshness coats your tongue. I've suffered enough already."

The muscles in his jaw flexed. "Jenkins didn't blame himself because he couldn't save Max from his fate—he blamed himself because of you."

"Maybe," Mercy whispered. "But James sealed his fate a long time ago. The night Max died, Jenkins went in after him."

Alex's head snapped up. "Jenkins's eye. . ."

Mercy smiled. "An eye for an eye," she winked.

If he was shocked, he didn't show it. His face was gaunt, camouflaged by the pain searing in his back, and I knew if we didn't figure something out soon, he would meet Jenkins's fate. He would join his brother.

Turning to me, he grunted against the ache as he said, "You told me your mother stole something from it. What did she steal?"

I glanced between him and Mercy, who nodded encouragingly. That night, she'd lost her home, her identity—her greatest love. My mother was merely the Charon tasked to ferry her home.

But Mercy didn't see it that way.

She wanted my mother to suffer the way she suffered. She wanted my mother to feel pain the way she felt it—unrelenting. And so, she ripped me from her belly, on top of the very stones her paramour was stolen from.

A life for a life.

"What did she steal?" Alex asked again.

This time, I met his heavy stare head-on and whispered, "Me."

———.———

No siren has ever been born out of the water. At first, my existence outside of it was uncertain. Mercy thought I would die—she certainly hoped so in the moment.

But when I inhaled my first breath—crisp air instead of acidic sea, the life I was destined to live beneath the swells became unclear.

"I don't know what will happen once I step into the water," I admitted. "I could turn into a hideous thing and lose whatever shred of humanity I have left, or I could die." Torn apart by the very monster I was harboring beneath my flesh. My eyes embraced his. "You're not the only one who's been condemned."

"Yet here we are." Alex's words came out brittle. If he was a broken man before, he was shattered now.

Beside me, Mercy coughed. "I don't regret it, you know. Not a single moment. Not then, not now, not Max, and especially not you."

Her thin fingers tugged weakly on mine, and I let out a choked sob. "I'm sorry, I'm so sorry" I whelped into her lap. "I didn't mean what I said the other night. I didn't mean any of it."

Mercy brushed the hair out of my face and held my chin in her palms. "Now is not the time for apologies. And besides, it's me who should be begging for your forgiveness."

Hate is a worthless emotion. One might think I should hate Mercy O'Dell for what she did to me, but I don't. *I can't.*

Mercy atoned for her misgivings. More than once. More than a thousand times, stepping in and guiding me when my own mother couldn't—when my own mother *wouldn't.*

I was unhinged. Inside, I was breaking apart, my heart shattering and splintering—embedding itself into my flesh.

"There must be something I can do." I offered. "Maybe if we—"

"Stop," she interrupted, her brown eyes hard on mine. "For starters, I don't want my last memory of you to be weeping over my body." I wiped the back of my hand over my eyes. "Good. Now, I want you to listen." Her breath was hot on my face as she spoke. "I have lived a long and wonderful life. I've known love and experienced things most people never have the privilege of appreciating."

I fought hard against trembling lips as I struggled to keep a brave face.

"Even though my desires were stolen from me, and I was never granted the gift of having children, I was given something better. I was gifted the opportunity to know you. To watch you grow up, to witness the woman you've become. Max might have been my greatest love, but *you* were my greatest redemption."

A flood of untethered emotion spilled out of me and over my face. I could no longer contain the inevitable break inside my chest that cleaved my heart in half. My eyes swelled up, my breath coming out in choked sobs as I broke down on the floor in front of her.

But the tragedy unfolding before me was short lived.

Behind me, Alex groaned, and I turned my head just in time to see him fall to the floor.

"Alex," I breathed, torn between him and Mercy.

Outside, the wind groaned, rattling the windows angrily, and in it were the taunting words of a warning.

Mercy looked at me. "You are not your mother. You are good, and kind and brave," she whispered softly.

Alex groaned again.

"It will take him," she said. "And judging by how weak he is, I doubt he has much time."

Frigid fear fell over me. "How do I fix this?"

Mercy, Alex—everything.

"It's not that simple Maeve—"

"Just tell me what I have to do, and I'll do it!" I wailed.

Quiet. Unrelenting, vociferous silence and then her voice—no, its voice. . . bleated inside me.

Get in the water.

———.———

Love is the greatest sacrifice one can make. I've spent my entire life hating *what I was*, that I didn't bother falling in love with *who I was.*

And it's because I didn't love myself, that I let others have power over me. Including my mother.

Including this thing.

Now, as I stood here with the ocean lapping at my feet—I finally understood what it meant to be set free.

I hated my mother because of what she was, I hated her for what she wanted me to be.

I hated myself.

Monsters don't feel things—they just do. Watching Mercy dissolve back into the very foam she was crafted from, broke something in me, repaired something in me—*revived something in me.*

A life for a life.

345

It wouldn't bring them back—the ones I already fated, but it would save Alex.

It would save me.

I offered to bring Mercy with me, but she refused. "I don't want to die where his life ended," she insisted. "I want to die where he lived."

Fair enough.

Panic and anxiety mounted in my throat as the ocean screamed before me.

One step. Then another.

The sun veiled itself over the shimmering horizon, casting over the rippling water as it called out, and I could feel the ocean's entity cradling me.

At the sight of it, the siren in me swelled—a sensation I'd never experienced before—a sense of overwhelming calm and peace. And for a brief moment, I felt a tiny bit of satisfaction knowing I was giving it what it wanted.

And all it wanted was to go home.

In a way—it was a caged thing, just like me.

This was it.

Stealing a final glance over my shoulder—at Saltridge, I smiled.

"Let's go home," I whispered to it.

Then I turned my back, inhaled a final breath, and walked myself into the sea.

CHAPTER FORTY-TWO
Alex

Five Years Later

IT WAS A VIOLENT surrender.

Though Alex couldn't make out the details in the dark, the menacing shadow of the siren bore down on him. Its black haunting eyes—unblinking and full of ire.

He tried to free himself by removing his boots, but the creature's spindly claws tightened, leaving crescent-like wounds carved into his flesh.

This was it. He was going to die.

His lungs strained—his chest caving as the small amount of air he'd mustered slowly evaporated.

What a horrible way to die. Alone and forgotten.

Her hair was like spilled blood—dark, crimson, and full of coral tethered between thick strands. Her face—a vicious thing, with a gaping hole for a mouth and two open slits for a nose.

She looked like a corpse. Like death incarnate.

In one swift motion, the siren whipped her tale, the size of a passenger van, around Alex's waist, knocking the rest of whatever breath he'd managed to preserve right out of his chest.

How long until he passed out and water filled his lungs? It was a willowy thing, yet massive and robust. Its scales were a glistening array of green and blue and deep purple, iridescent in the ever-changing fluidity of the sea.

The water was violent, slicing through Alex's flesh like mordant steel. If this monster didn't kill him, the ocean certainly would.

What would happen once he was gone? Who would forget him first?

His vision darkened. Death was a cloaked assassin, and despite the burning salt, Alex wanted to greet it with his eyes open.

Except death never came.

Instead, a wall of bubbles sheeted in front of him. The siren bleated—her shriek like the sound of a thousand dying men.

Something—*someone,* was attacking it.

His face was hollow, his body a bit thinner, but Alex knew who it was.

Jenkins.

His bony hands were fisted tightly in the siren's hair, yanking her backward and another shrill scream poured out of its loose mouth. Alex caught James's eye, wild and full of rage.

Go, it screamed at him.

Alex didn't falter as he swam mercilessly toward the surface, the light rippling above him like a blessed mirage.

Almost there. . .

Maeve's head peaked out from over the jetty, panicked and full of fear.

Alex froze.

Behind him, the siren bucked like a wild bull beneath Jenkins. Somehow, the old man saddled himself around its back, tugging on its neck like a horse's reins. If Alex went back for him, they'd both die. If he didn't, one of them would surely die.

Morality is a bitch when it comes to self-preservation.

Breaching the shallows for air, Alex didn't bother glancing at Maeve, who'd shouted his name in terror, before he plunged himself back beneath the waves.

By now, the creature managed to shake Jenkins off, his body tumbling freely through the water as it reared away from them. Alex snatched James's hand, pulling him forward. His face said it all, but Alex ignored it. They could argue once they were safe.

The distance between the surface and them was great, but with the two of them working in tandem, they should be able to reach—searing pain tore through Alex's back. The Lorelei cut right through him and James—ripping his flesh open and flaying him alive.

The two of them tumbled through the water blindly. Alex felt for Jenkins's hand, which was no longer tethered to his. He swiveled, and the frigid climate bit into his limbs, his face, and the open lacerations across his back, but that didn't stop him from going back.

Frantically, Alex searched the space where Jenkins once paddled beside him, but he was gone.

———·———

"Alex! ALEX!" His wife's voice consumed him.

Alex shot up, his breath short and ragged in his chest as he strained to see her face in the dark.

"I'm right here," Maggie whispered. "I'm right here, it's ok. It was just a nightmare."

Except it wasn't.

He couldn't tell her that though, just like he couldn't tell her how they *really met*—the first time, all those years ago.

Her blue eyes softened over his. "It wasn't real," she promised, pulling his hand into hers. "I'm real. *This* is real," she said—stroking his hand over her swollen belly. Alex nodded, leaning into her, into their unborn child.

From the hallway echoed tiny feet—pattering softly against the hardwood floors.

Maggie crossed the room, scooping their tiny son into her arms. "Did Daddy wake you up?" She teased, tucking him into the bed alongside them.

Andrew nodded.

"I'm sorry," Alex whispered. He thought he had it under control. He thought he had managed to free himself from the memories of that place. Turns out Saltridge was harder to escape than he thought.

"Why don't you two get some sleep? I'm going to shake this off downstairs."

"Are you sure?" Maggie whispered.

Glancing at the toddler, now fast asleep with his thumb tucked inside his mouth, Alex whispered, "I'm sure."

Early twilight bled through the kitchen windows, casting a favorable glow over the green pastel cabinets. Maggie refused to paint them, and he didn't argue.

Across from him, the fridge was covered in finger-paintings and family photographs—new memories replacing old ones. And in the middle of it all was a picture of Frank and Wendy

DAPHNE PARKER

cradling his son in their arms. It was taken the last time they visited—a year earlier.

Alex had sold them the apartment building, convincing them to take on more long-term rentals than the uncertain ones housed in their backyard. Now, with new tenants—and an overdue remodel, the once derelict building housed new life instead of forgotten ones.

After brewing a pot of coffee, Alex shuffled past the living room—still cluttered from their own remodel. Maggie might not have wanted to rid the kitchen of his mother's cabinets, but she was more than willing to tear out the blue and yellow wallpaper and replace it with something more modern.

He glanced down at a sleeping Charley—*err, Pickles*—curled up in the middle of his father's chair. It was his spot now, his chair, and the old cat, now lazy and unbothered, didn't so much as stir as Alex tiptoed by. Sections of his dark grey fur had gone white over the years, showcasing his age. Alex didn't even like the cat—not really, but Pickles was the only thing left tethering him to his brother, and soon, he'd lose him, too.

The thought ached him, knowing that once the cat was gone, he'd be the only one left to remember Andrew ever existed at all. Slowly, that ache turned into a haunting realization.

. .

Alex had *become* Jenkins—burdened with the knowledge of what lies beneath the tide. He might not have lost a limb or an eye, but the weight of that truth plagued him. *How long until it ate him alive?*

Meandering back upstairs, Alex's phone vibrated—pulling him from his thoughts.

You up? A text from Diego glared back at him.

Since leaving the department to open "Hayworth and Son," an auto body shop he invested in with the money from the building sale, Alex and Diego found whatever time they could to catch up.

The last time they'd seen each other was when Alex stood alongside him at his wedding a few weeks ago. Now Diego and his new wife were heading out on their honeymoon—to a surprise destination Alex had gifted them.

Another text dinged into the quiet. *Getting ready to board. Just wanted to say thanks again man.*

Anything for you, you know I've got you brother, Alex typed back before shining his phone's backlight towards the ceiling as he quietly unfolded the attic stairs above him.

They were well-oiled—Alex had made sure of that, and Maggie didn't ask. Sometimes, he wondered if she ever ventured up there—just to see what he was hiding. He was thankful she'd forgotten things—especially Greg and what he had done to her. But sometimes trauma lingers—he understood that better than anyone.

Most of the boxes were gone—save for a few he'd left behind. But it wasn't old tax documents or elementary crafts he was searching for. Hovering over the floor, he stuck his fingers between the boards and shimmied the broken one loose.

Its iron bands glared back at him under the light of his phone as he heaved the chest out from where it rested. Even after all these years, it haunted him, and in the warm attic, his skin prickled as he opened it.

Pushing aside the baseball cards, the wooden anchor, and the journal—Alex found what he was looking for—a black rounded marble etched in obsidian and shrouded in darkness.

He didn't touch it, just stared at it for a moment as he drew in a long, shuttering breath.

An eye for an eye.

AFTERWORD

Mercy's story isn't over. . . *yet.*

ACKNOWLEDGEMENTS

First and foremost, I am deeply indebted to my husband, who has not only tolerated but embraced my erratic behavior during the book's production. This journey has been filled with stress and uncertainty, and without his unwavering support and unconditional love, I would have faltered countless times. My love—you have been my steady ship on a raging sea, and I am eternally grateful for your presence in my life.

Amidst life's uncertainties, there are two things I am certain of—being an author and being a mother. My children, with their boundless imagination and unwavering love, have been my guiding light and my greatest source of inspiration. Their belief in me and their constant reminders of the power of dreams have fueled my journey. I am forever grateful for their role in shaping my path.

To my friends and family who have stood by me through all of my trials and tribulations, I love you. Your unwavering support has brought me here, and I could not thank you enough.

To Courtney Pidd, whose personality helped me shape Sarah's (even though you're not a harlot), thank you for twenty years of friendship. You just *get me,* ya know?

To Timothy Hardoin, a single line on a dedication page isn't enough to express my gratitude and love for you. Without you, I wouldn't be here. When the world gave up on me, you stood by my side. You are one of the greatest people I have ever known, and it is an honor to be your friend. I hope you know I don't take that privilege lightly. *"This is why we're friends."*

I'd like to thank Mike Tvrdik of the Douglas County Sheriff's Department in Alexandria, Minnesota, for his time and knowledge, which were used to make this book. I'd also like to extend my gratitude to Gydeon Burgess for his mechanical input.

Finally (but certainly not last), I'd like to thank my readers for giving my book a chance. It is difficult to put yourself out into the great big world for others to strip you bare and marvel at your insecurities. It takes a lot of courage and strength, and you guys have been so wonderful and encouraging. Thank you for the boundless support—and for keeping me employed.

About the Author

When not lost in the labyrinth of her own creations, you can find Daphne exploring alternate dimensions (also known as the local coffee shop) or engaged in intense debates with her children on why they can't have cake for breakfast—ok, why they *sometimes* can't have cake for breakfast.

A Michigan native, Daphne currently resides in Minnesota alongside her husband and their tiny minions. The Black Hat Society, previously released and currently pulled for republishing, was Daphne's first publication.

Please visit her on her website or on social media for more information on upcoming releases and updates.